Charles Reade

The Wandering Heir

A matter-of-fact romance

Charles Reade

The Wandering Heir
A matter-of-fact romance

ISBN/EAN: 9783337196806

Printed in Europe, USA, Canada, Australia, Japan

Cover: Foto ©Andreas Hilbeck / pixelio.de

More available books at **www.hansebooks.com**

"'Uncle, dear, please you read that.'"—*Page* 213.

THE

WANDERING HEIR

A MATTER-OF-FACT ROMANCE

By CHARLES READE, D.C.L.

A NEW EDITION

WITH ELEVEN ILLUSTRATIONS BY HELEN PATERSON, S. L. FILDES,
CHARLES GREEN AND HENRY WOODS

London
CHATTO AND WINDUS, PICCADILLY

.

I Dedicate

THIS NARRATIVE TO MY FRIEND

M. E. BRADDON,

AS A SLIGHT MARK OF RESPECT FOR HER PRIVATE VIRTUES

AND PUBLIC TALENTS.

THE WANDERING HEIR.

CHAPTER I.

ONE raw windy day, in the spring of 1726, there
was a strange buzzing by the side of a public road
in the very heart of old Ireland. It came from a
great many boys, seated by the roadside, plying
their books and slates, with here and there a
neighbourly prod, followed by invectives, whispered—for the pedagogue was marching up and
down the line with a keen eye, and an immensely
long black ruler well known to the backs and
limbs of the scholars, except three or four, whose
fathers asked him to dine on poultry, or butcher's
meat, whenever those rarities were at the fire.
The school-room stood opposite, and still belched
through its one window the peat-smoke that
had driven out the hive. There was a chimney;
but so constructed, that, on a windy day, the

B

smoke pooh-poohed it, and sought the sky by vents more congenial to the habits of the nation.

The boys were mostly farmers' sons, in long freize coats, breeches loose at the knee, clouted shoes tied with strips of raw neat-skin, and slovenly caubeens; but there was a sprinkling of broad-cloth, plain three-cornered hats, and shoe-buckles; there were also five or six barefooted urchins, not the worst scholars there; for this strange anomalous people, with many traits of the pure savage, had been leaders in mediæval litera-ture, had founded the University of Paris, and had still a noble reverence for learning; the humblest would struggle to pay a sharp boy's schooling, and so qualify him for business, perhaps for the priesthood itself, pinnacle of an Irish peasant's ambition.

Aloof from this motley line stood a single, timid figure; a boy with delicate skin, and exquisite golden hair; his face, pale and anxious. He wore a straight-cut coat, scarlet once, but now a rusty red, no hat, shoes with steel buckles—and holes. This decayed little gentleman peered anxiously round a corner of the building, and, as soon as ever the school broke up with horrid yells, ran and hid himself.

Too late! one quick young eye had seen him;

and, while the rest dispersed,—two or three galloping off on rough ponies, neck or nought, in a style to set their unfortunate mothers screaming to the saints—a little party of five, eager for diversion on the spot where they had suffered study, chased the golden-haired boy, with an appalling whoop. Fear gave him wings; but numbers prevailed; they caught him, and plagued him sore; jibed him, poked him, pinched him, got him by the head and legs, and flogged a tree with him, and, in the exuberance of their gay hearts, pumped on his head till he gasped, and cried for mercy—in vain.

"That is foul play—five to one," said a cheerful voice—*crick*, *crack*, *crick*, *crack*, *crack*—and in a moment Master Matthews, one of the superior scholars, made all five heads ring with a light shillelah, but not a grain of malice; only he was a promising young cudgel player, and must be diverted as well as the younger ones. The obstreperous mirth turned, with ludicrous swiftness, to yells of dismay.

But the warlike spirit of the O'Tooles and the O'Shaughnessys soon revived; battle was quickly arrayed with traditionary skill; here a crescent of five, armed with stones, there Master Matthews, with a tree at his back, the lid of a slop-pail for shield, and a shillelah for sword, grinding his teeth, and looking dangerous, the fair-headed boy clasping his hands apart. Mr. Hoolaghan and his servant man ran out staring.

"Och, ye disperadoes! ye murtherin' villins; what is this at all?" cried Mr. Hoolaghan.

Then each side set to work to talk him over. "Masther avick," whined the army, " he broke our heads, and kilt us with his murtherin' shillelah, the maraudin' villin, intirely."

"Masther, dear, they were five to one, torminting the life out of this little boccawn. Why didn't ye catch up a flint and crack their skulls like nuts at Hallowe'en?"

"Och! hear to the fungaleering ruffin!" And five hands were lifted high in a moment, each armed with a pebble.

Then the pedagogue grew warm, and gave them what he called his "tall English." "The first that rises a hand I'll poolverize um. Lay down your bellicose weapons, ye insurrectionary thaves, or Norah shall perforate ye—bring the spit out, wench—and transfix ye to the primises, while I flagellate ye by dozens, till the blood pours down yer heels; lay down yer sprig of homicide, and stand on it this minit, ye vagabone, or I'll baste you with the kitchen poker, till your back is coorant jelly and your head is a mashed turnup."

Mrs. Malaprop observed in the next generation, that "there is nothing so conciliating to young people as a little severity," and so it proved even in this: the weapons were laid down; and then Matthew Hoolaghan, changing at once to the most affectionate and dulcet tones, said, "Now, honeys, we'll discoorse the matter, not like the barbarian voolgar, that can only ratiocinate with a bludgeon, but like good Chrischins and rale piripatetic philosophers that I have insensed in polite larning, multiplication, and all the humanities, glory be to God. Spake first, ye omadhaun, ye causa titirrima belly; and revale your crime."

"Masther, sir," said the victim, "I never done no crime. They do be always torminting me. I never offinded them. Spake the truth now; did iver I offind you?"

"Sowl, ye did then. Masther, dear, look at um: he's got a Protestant face."

"Oh, fie! my father is a good Catholic; isn't he then, sir?"

The pedagogue took fright at this turn. "Och, murther! murther!" he shrieked, "ye conthrairy divils, would ye import the apple o' discord, an' set my two parishes cracking skulls, and starving me? Would ye conflagrate the Timple of the Muses with ojum theologicum? The first that divairges to

controvarsial polimics in this acadimy, I'll go to
my brother the priest, and have him exkimmini-
cated alive. Face! it is a likely face enough, I'm
thinkin' "

"It's the purtiest in the school, ony way," said
Norah—the argument having now come within her
scope—"and a dale the clanest." Whereupon,
one of these ready imps reminded her it was the
oftenest pumped on.

Said another, "He shouldn't pretind to be a
lord's son then, the little glorigoteen."

"But I am a lord's son," said the boy, stoutly.
Then there was a roar of derision. But the boy
persisted that he was Lord Altham's son, and half
the county of Wexford belonged to his father. Both
sides appealed to the master; but he only said
"Hum!" So Norah put in her word, and said
the boy had been brought there by a great lord,
in a coach and six; and the lord had kissed him
tenderly, and called him his darling Jemmy, in
her sight and hearing.

Mr. Hoolaghan admitted all that, but said, "If
he was my lord's *real* son, would my lord leave
his board, lodging, and schooling, unpaid, these
fourteen months?"

"Divil a one of him!" replied an urchin, with
the modest promptitude of his tribe.

Jemmy was himself struck by this argument. "Alas! then," said he, "I fear he must be dead. He was always good to me before. I was never away from him in all my life, till now. Norah, when we were at Kinna, I had a little horse, and boots, and rode with him a-hunting. I went to a day-school then, and mine was the only laced hat in the school. I brought it here."

"Thrue for you, ma bouchal," said Norah, "and by the same token 'twas that thief o' the warld, Tim Doolan, that stripped it, and gave the lace to his cross-eyed wench, bloody end to the pair of 'em."

"Oh! masther!" cried James, all of a sudden, clasping his hands, "you that knows everything, tell me, is my father dead? The only friend I have. Ochoon! Ochoon!"

"Nay, nay," said Hoolaghan, touched by this cry of despair, "Jemmy avick, if Lord Altham is your father, ye needn't cry and wring your hands; for he is alive, bad cess to him : my cousin seen him in Dublin a se'nnight ago, spinding money like wather, and divil a tin-penny he paid me this fourteen months."

"Masther, sir," said Jemmy, firmly, "how far is it to Dublin, av ye plase?"

"A hundred miles and more."

" Then I'll go to him there, sir."

There was an ironical shout.

" Give me one good male to start on, and I'll go ; for I'm a lost boy here ; and I'm ashamed to be in this place, an' him not paying for me, like the rest."

Now this sudden resolution was quite agreeable to Hoolaghan. Norah took the boy into the kitchen to feed him for the journey. The cubs began to feel rather sorry, for they were thoughtless, not bad-hearted; they scraped together fourpence for his journey. Norah gave him an old hat, and kisses, and a word of feminine advice. " Ma bouchal," said she, " wheniver you are in trouble, spake to the women ; they will be *your* best friends; but keep clear of your own colour— not intirely — only brown women, and yellow women, is more prifirabler, by raison you are fair, like an angel herself."

The boys set him on his road a mile; then stopped, and blessed him, and asked his forgiveness, being, to tell the truth, now quaking in the shoes of superstition, lest he should put " the hard word " on them at parting, and him " a piece of an orphan," as the biggest remarked. But his nature was too gentle for that : he forgave them, and blessed them, and they all kissed him, and he kissed them, and they went their way. But

Matthews would go another mile with him. At parting, he said, "Tell me God's truth. Are ye that lord's son?"

"Indeed, then, I am, sir."

"I wish I had known before. Let me look at thee well. I wonder whether I shall ever meet thee again, purty Jemmy."

"Indeed and I hope so, sir; for you are all the friend I iver found in this place."

"Jemmy, it seems hard, to make friends one afternoon, and then to part for ever," said the elder boy, philosophizing.

Jemmy's heart was swelling already; and, at this, the lonely boy began to cry piteously. Then Matthews blubbered right out; and so they cried together, and kissed one another many times, and James Annesley began his wanderings.

He walked on till dusk, and saw a small farm: he went by Norah's advice; made up straight to the farmer's wife, and asked her leave to sleep on the premises. She looked at him full before she answered; gave him some potatoes and buttermilk, and let him sleep in a little barn. He walked on the next day, and fared much the same; but, by the third day, he got footsore, and could only limp along; but he persevered: he sometimes got a lift in a cart, and sometimes, when a farmer's wife, or daughter, on horseback, overtook him, he would appeal to her, especially if she was dark; and, true it was, the dark women, of whom were plenty in Ireland, would generally take him up and give him a ride before, or behind, as might be most convenient.

Still creeping on, he got into a county where the people had faces unlike those he had left behind, and both men and women wore long frieze cloaks, and the women linen head-dresses, and sometimes a handkerchief over that: and he limped into a village where was a sort of fair; but he had no money left to spend, and he sat down on the shaft of a cart, disconsolate, and, seeing others so merry, began to weep with fatigue, hunger, and sorrow. By-and-by a man saw him, and asked him what ailed him: and he told his sad case. "Nay, then, sir," said the man, "you must come to The O'Brien." He took him to a little old man, exceedingly shabby, on a little white horse; he doffed his caubeen, and said, "An it plase your honour's worship, this is a gintleman's son in throuble; he's hunting his own father—glory be to God."

"Who is your father, friend?" asked The O'Brien.

"An please your worship, he is my Lord Altham."

"'Who is your father, friend?' asked The O'Brien."—*Page* 10.

The O'Brien made a wry face. "That is not Oirish," said he. "Some mushroom lord; may be one of William's men."

"Nay, sir, he is a good Catholic. Glory be to Hiven."

By this time there was a bit of a crowd collected to hear; but the dialogue was interrupted by a simple fellow who had lost his wife. He burst in wildly, crying, "Arrah, people, people, did ye see Mary Sullivan, a tall woman, a tall yellow woman, not very yellow intirely, with a white pipe in her cheek?" They roared at him; but he just rushed on, repeating that strange formula. The fair rang with it. But the little old scarecrow, descended from Ireland's kings, smiled superior, and took Jemmy home on his saddle bow. Caubeens were lifted in the village, wherever this decayed noble passed. He told the boy the whole county belonged to him and his ancestors, and he should sup and sleep where he liked. Finally, he showed him a large mansion, and a cabin, not far apart; let him know that these houses were his; only various families had lived in the mansion for the last few centuries. "Now, sir," said he, "will you slape in my large house, where other people live this five hundred years, by my lave, or in my small house where I live—at present—for my

convaynience?" Says Jemmy, " Sir, the small
house, if it please you; by reason I desire your
company, as well as your house." The mighty
scarecrow was pleased with this answer, and took
him to his mud cabin. He sent his one servant, a
bare-legged girl, to demand a rasher from a neighbouring farmer. No doubt she said The O'Brien
had company; for eggs and perch were sent
directly, as well as a large piece of bacon. The
two personages supped together, and slept on a
heap of straw.

In the morning, one peasant brought buttermilk, and another trout, and another oatmeal, and
another a vehicle, the body of which was a square
box, suspended on a trap: and The O'Brien's
guest was taken five miles on his road, and his
blessing sought by his conductor, a simple peasant,
who discoursed on the grandeur of The O'Brien,
and boasted that neither he nor his race had ever
done a hand's turn of work—and would never be
allowed to—in the country. James limped out of
that county into another, and met with no adventure, till he came to Dunnyshallan, and was
turned into a dice-box. The young men of the
village had cut a gigantic backgammon board on
the green, very neat; it occupied the sixth part of
an acre; and they had black and white flag-stones

to play with. Their dice-box was always a boy;
and, catching sight of James, one sang out,
"Hurrooh! here's a strange gossoon. *We'll have
luck all round.*"

So James was seated on high, with his back to
the players, and ordered, on pain of death, to sing
out sixes, fours, quatre-ace, and all the combina-
tions *ad libitum.* He complied, to avoid worse;
and then it was he learned the literature of curses;
in which this one small island was so fertile and
ingenious, that all the blasphemy in the rest of
Europe was poor and monotonous by comparison.
The infinite maledictions would doubtless have
instructed and amused him, had they been levelled
at another; but, being fired at him whenever he
called a number that did not suit the player, and
uttered with every appearance of fury, they
frightened him, and he began to tremble and
snivel.

"Now thin, ye vagabone, give me a good
number, or may St. Anthony's sow trample out
your intrails."

"Oh! oh! oh! Sixes."

"Sixes! ye conthrary villin! Is it sixes I'm
asking? The divil go a buck-hunting with ye
up and down (the hunting ground was distinctly
specified).

"Oh! oh! oh!"

"Never heed the bally-ragging ruffin. Cry for me now, honey."

"Och! I'm afraid. Deuce-ace."

"Och, ye're a broth of a boy. May ye live till the skirts of your coat knock your brains out! Now cry for Barney."

"Oh! I am afraid to spake. The Virgin be good to me. Deuce-ace."

"Och, ye thafe o' the world. May you die with a caper in your heel, and give the crows a puddin' "

And so on till dark, when a losing player threatened to murder the dice: a winner objected: the two quarrelled: shillelahs crossed; a ring was made; and there was much subtle play, and the whistling cudgels parried, or met with a clash, and bent over each other; till at last Jemmy's friend parried an excessive blow, and, rising nimbly, delivered such a crasher on the other's skull, that it literally shot him to the ground like a bullet, and he rolled over, by the impetus, after he landed.

Then Jemmy screamed with dismay; but the more experienced laughed at his notion of what the true old Irish skull would bear, and the victor took him home to supper and bed, *i.e.* stirabout and straw.

He came to a fall in a river, eight feet high, and saw salmon glittering prismatic in the sun, like rainbows, as they leaped; but they struck the descending column a foot too low, struggled in it a moment, then came down as stupid as tin fish: and here he saw a sight he might have travelled creation and never seen elsewhere—a corpse-like man lying flat in a coffin, and towed gingerly up to the fall by his bare-armed wife straddling on a rock; the man caught the salmon on the ground, one after the other, by the belly, with a cart rope and three barbed hooks that would have landed a whale. 'Twas his own coffin, ordered by his uneasy wife, with true Hibernian judgment, the moment he was expected to die. But the salmon came up from the sea, and began to leap like mad. Pat put off dying directly, and took to poaching. We are creatures of habit, and salmon-slaughtering was his custom at that time of year, not dying.

The woman being dark—partly with dirt—James asked her for a fish supper. She boiled him half a salmon, and threw the rest to the pig; but she told James that in the big towns there were fools who would give 4s. a hundred-weight for the trash. Within fifteen miles of the capital he witnessed two abductions, one real, one sham; both commonish customs. The imitation was the lineal descendant

of the real, and the men halloed and galloped so
much alike in both pageants, and the two brides
screamed so much alike, that he never knew for
certain which was the pseudo-Sabine, which the
real,—and never will. His feet were bleeding;
his clothes only just hung together; his little heart
was faint; when at last he mounted a hill, and
looked down on Dublin, which, by its buildings, its
size, and its blue-slated roofs, far transcended all
that he had ever imagined of a mortal city. The
town did not then overflow into pretty villas. Mud
cabins prevailed up to the city gates, and from
them this weary, wondering child plunged into
streets and mansions. At the very first street
he stopped, and asked a decent man where Lord
Altham lived. The decent man met this question
by another: "How was he to know?" The same
answer was returned in the next street, and the next;
and this poor little mite of humanity wandered up
and down in vain. Then a great and new fear
fell on him: this Dublin was not a town like Ross;
it was another world; a world of stone and slate,
and hard hearts, not like the simple country
folk. He might as well grope for his father in
all Ireland as in this wilderness of labyrinths of
stone. Snubbed, sneered at, rejected on all sides,
he cried his sick heart and his hungry stomach

to sleep in a church porch; and so he passed his first night in the capital.

Day after day the same, till at last he found a dark woman, a gentleman's cook, who listened to his tale, and gave him some broken victuals. She was an Englishwoman; her name was Martha. One day Jemmy came for his dinner, as usual, but was disappointed. Kathleen, the kitchen-maid, informed him, with a marked elevation of the nose, that "madam" had gone out for the day, and locked up the safe, like a mane, miserly Sassenach as she was, bad cess to her and all her dhirty breed; but she'd be back again by five. Hungry Jemmy attended faithfully at five, in spite of the rain, and great was his surprise and awe when two chairmen brought up a chair, and there emerged from it— a duchess? No; but a fair imitation thereof; Mrs. Martha, with her income on her back, and two little black patches on her cheeks. She smiled at his adoration, paid the chairmen loftily, who retired with expressions of adulation, and sly satirical looks at each other, and she took James by the hand, and led him to her sanctum. "Sir," said she, instead of "child," or "my dear," as heretofore, "I have been visiting my friends; and, from one to another, I have found ye my Lord Altham; as luck would have it, a countrywoman

of mine, one Elizabeth Grainger, she lives in
the house: but she tells me she shall give her
notice." — " Oh, madam! dear good madam!"
began Jemmy—" Nay, sir," said she, " but you
must hear me out. I'm afear'd you will not be
so welcome as you ought to be. You are a sensible
little gentleman as e'er I saw; so I'll e'en tell
you the truth; Mrs. Betty did let me know my
lord is in ill hands; this dame Gregory and her
daughter have got him; the old woman goes about
her own house like a servant; but miss, she is
mistress, and games with the quality, and spends
money like dirt: they are betrothed to each other,
and his wife laying sick in the town, on her way
back to England. Poor soul, she rues the day
she ever saw this hole of a country, I'll go bail.
They look for her to die—for their convenience.
Well, if I was her, I'd spite 'em; I'd play the
woman, and outlive the brute and the hussy both,
saving your presence."

"Oh, madam, an' if it please you, where does
my father live?"

"'Tis in Frapper Lane, the corner house. What,
will you be going, and no supper? Nay, then,
God speed you. Give me a kiss, sweetheart. So.
Your breath is honey. Sir," said she, curtseying
to him, all of a sudden, "I do wish you well.

When you come into your estate, sir, prithee remember Martha Knatchbull, that took your part when fortune frowned."

"Ay, that I will, good, kind lady," said James, still overpowered by her glorious costume; and so he shuffled off, limping fast, and, in the hunger of his longing heart, forgot his hungry belly for a time.

To give the reader some idea of the house he was going to, I will sketch the domestic perform-ances from nine p.m. on the previous evening. Lord Altham and friends had a drinking bout, at the end of which he was assisted to bed, and his friends sent home in chairs. But the ladies did not drink; they gamed their lives away. Mistress Anne Gregory received Lady Dace and Mistress Carmichael, and other ladies gloriously dressed, and, at first starting, most polite and ceremonious: they drank tea, and soon warmed into scandal—each accusing some other lady of her own especial vice—till at last they got upon politics. Inflamed by this topic, they soon boiled over: voices rose over voices; not a single tongue was mute a moment; and such was the Babel, that, at last, the fat, lazy lap-dog wriggled himself erect, and looked furiously at the disturbers of his peace. Then a Neptune arose to still the raging

voices; in other words, Mrs. Betty set out the
card tables. Down they sat, and soon their eyes
were gleaming, and their flesh trembling with
excitement. Mistress Anne Gregory held bad
cards; she had to pawn ring after ring—for these
ladies, being well acquainted with each other, never
played on parole—and she kept bemoaning her
bad luck. "Betty, I knew how 'twould be. The
parson called to-day.—This odious chair, why will
you stick me in it? Stand further, girl. I always
lose when you look on." Mrs. Betty tossed her
head, and went behind another lady. Miss Gregory
still lost, and had to pawn her snuff-box to Lady
Dace. She consoled herself by an insinuation.
"My lady, you touched your wedding ring; that
was a sign to your partner here."

"Nay, madam, 'twas but a sign my finger
itched. But, if you go to that, you spoke a word
began with H. Then she knew you had the king
of hearts."

"That is like miss, here," said another matron;
"she rubs her chair when she hath matadore in
hand."

"Set a thief to catch a thief, madam," was
miss's ingenious and polished reply.

"Hey-dey!" cries one. "Here's spadillo got
a mark on the back; a child might know it in the

dark. Mistress Pigot, I wish you'd be pleased to pare your nails."

In short, they said things to each other all night, the slightest of which, among men, would have filled the Phœnix Park next morning with drawn swords; but it went for little here; they were all cheats, and knew it, and knew the others knew it; and didn't care. It was four o'clock before they broke up, huddled on their cloaks and hoods, and their chairs took them home with cold feet and aching heads.

At twelve next day Miss Gregory was prematurely disturbed by her lap-dog, barking like a demon for his breakfast. She stretched, gaped, unglued her eyes, and rang for Betty. No answer. She rang again, and beat the wall viciously with her slipper. Betty came in yawning.

"Here, child. Let in some light. Nay, not so much; wouldst blind me?—I'm dead of the vapours. Get me a dram of citron-water. So.— Now bring me a looking-glass. I will lie abed. Alack! I look frightfully to-day. If ever I touch a card again! Didst ever see such luck as mine? Four matadores, and lose codille!"

"Nay, madam," said Mrs. Betty, who was infected with the tastes of her betters, "with submission, you played bad cards."

"Hoity toity, wench," cried the lady, "was ever such assurance? What is the world coming to?" And she packed her off contemptuously, to get her tea and cream.

Betty turned pale with wrath, but retired.

Once outside the door, she said, "I'll be even with the jade. I'm as good as she."

Miss Gregory was at her glass when Betty returned with the tea. "Madam," said she, with a sly sneer, "the goldsmith waits below, to know if you will redeem the silver cup."

"There, give him that for interest."

"And my Lady Dace has sent her maid."

"That is for her winnings. Never was such a dun. Here, take these ten pistoles my lord left for the wine merchant. They are all light, thank Heaven!"

At two, being half dressed, and the room tidied, but not a window opened, she received the visit of a fop. He paid her hyperbolical compliments, at which you should have seen Mrs. Betty's lip curl, and was consulted as to where she should put her patches; but was driven out, like chaff before the wind, by a creature more attractive, to wit, a mercer with silks, patterns, and laces, from Paris: so the toilette was not complete at four, when a footman knocked at the door with "Madam, dinner stays."

" Then the cook must keep it back. I never can have time to dress; and I am sure no living woman takes less."

However, she soon came down, distended with an enormous hoop, glorious with brocaded skirt and quilted petticoat, and cocked up on red high-heeled shoes; bedizened, belaced, powdered, poma-tumed, pulvilioed, patched, perfumed, and every-thing else—except washed : yet less savage than the men in one respect; the commode and all the pyramidal, scaffolded heads had gone out; her hair was her own, and, though long, was compressed into a small compass; whereas the gentlemen had full-bottomed wigs that smothered their heads, contracted their cheeks, flowed over their shoulders, and befloured their backs.

My Lord Altham and two or three other gentle-men were there, and three ladies. Lord Altham, a little dark man with a loud voice, received her with great respect, and told her they waited only for his brother, Captain Richard Annesley.

" Nay, he will not come, methinks," said she. " He and I had words t'other day."

" Nay, then let the churl hang. Who waits ? "

A flaring footman appeared as if his string had been pulled.

" Bid them serve the dinner."

"I will, my lord."

For the conversation during dinner, see Swift's "Polite Conversation." You will be a gainer by the exchange; for the discourse at Lord Altham's board was half as coarse, and not half so witty.

Soon after dinner the host proposed "Church and State."

From that moment the ladies were evidently on their guard, and ready for flight.

"Parson," says my lord, "I'll tell you a merry story."

The ladies rose like one, and retired. My lord, having achieved his end, for at this time of night the bottle was his mistress, until it became his master, substituted a toast for his song:

> "The finest sight beneath the moon
> Is to see the ladies quit the room."

He then ordered the present bottles and glasses to be exchanged for others that would not stand upright, the stems of the glasses having been knocked off, and the decanters being made like a soda-water bottle. This ensured so brisk a circulation that, although they were gentlemen who had all "made their heads" in early life, the claret began to tell, as was proved by the swift alternations of superfluous ire, and hyperbolical affection, and peals of idiotic laughter; when, in

the midst of the din, an altercation was heard in
the hall : the disputants were three, and each voice
had its own key : first there was a sweet little
quavering soprano, appealing to a flaming footman ;
then there was a flaming footman, objurgating the
cherubic voice an octave lower ; then came the
commanding alto of Mrs. Betty.

" What is to do ? " roared Lord Altham.

" Why," said Mrs. Betty, seizing this opportunity, " 'tis a young gentleman that hath travelled
an hundred miles to see my lord, and my lord's
valet denied him, being stained with travel : but
'twas ill done, and him of kin to my lord."

" Of kin to my lord! Nay, then, Mistress
Betty, he is welcome to all here."

Betty, who had her cue from the English cook,
and who was already interested in the fair sorrowful young face and golden hair, made no more ado,
but led James into the room by the hand. The
numerous lights in the candelabra dazzled him at
first, and the fine clothes and perukes awed him ;
he hid against Betty's capacious apron, that descended from waist to ankle. Then he peered,
and saw Lord Altham standing up, looking half
pleased, half vexed : he gave a loud cry, as if his
heart was flying out of his body, stretched out his
arms, and flew to him. " Oh father ! father ! "

The sorrow he had endured, the joy and infinite
trust that swallowed all sorrow up at sight of his
father, both spoke in that one wild cry; it thrilled;
it startled; it sent Mrs. Betty's apron to her eyes
in a moment, and pierced the heart even of this
silly brutal lord.

"My boy! my sweet Jemmy!" he cried, and
sat down, and folded him in his arm, and kissed
him tenderly, with a mawkish tear or two.

The guests then stood up respectfully, and drank
welcome to the young gentleman. "Not forgetting
Mrs. Betty, that brought him to us," said the
chaplain, who had a sheep's-eye to her and her
savings: she was a Sassenach, and sure to have
savings; Irish savings were not.

"Father," said Jemmy, "they used me very
cruel at that school: bad luck to it! They were
always bating me, and the masther would not rise
a hand for me, bekase you sent him no money
for my schoolin' Why didn't you send him his
money?"

This, which would have made a Sassenach
father blush, did but divert my lord, and his
company. "I kept it for yourself, Jemmy," said
he.

"My lord is a great saver, sir. Long life to
him!" said another.

"He is putting it by to build a church," suggested the chaplain.

"'Twill be a church with a chimney, then," said Betty, who was somewhat free of her tongue. This sally was mightily approved by that unceremonious company. When the laughter ceased, the sweet little voice of Jemmy crept timidly in.

"Father avick, does my mother live here?"

Now this question made the company very uncomfortable. It quite staggered Lord Altham for a minute. But he burst out furiously, "Thou hast no mother."

"Nay, father; then what hath come of the gentlewoman that had red shoes, two pair, made for me in Ross; and the likely woman that brought me woollen hose she had made for me herself, and called me her child?" Then, seeing my lord silent, and much disturbed, he bethought himself, and said, "Well, if my mothers are both dead, I must love thee all the more."

Betty, who was watching Lord Altham's face very keenly all the time, now stepped forward, and took James away. She fed him, and then proceeded to ablutions. The cleanliness of his skin, dusty, but not grimed, surprised her; but, above all, his head. "Gramercy," said she, "not

one to be seen, and they swarm in my lady's.
To be sure, that same powder is a convenient
habitation."

She put him to bed; and, being a notable
woman, sat up half the night, and made him a
loose habit and a little hat. With this, and clean
linen, and a cambric tie, she brought him to Lord
Altham while Miss Gregory was abed. Lord
Altham was surprised and pleased, and took him
out in a chair, and had him shod on the spot, and
measured for a fine suit from top to toe. He was
petted by everybody, and especially by Miss
Gregory. This was a very clever young lady:
she was not going to risk Lord Altham's affections
by snubbing his son, a pretty, amiable boy. Mrs.
Betty's shot missed fire: Miss Gregory went with
the stream, and had two riding suits made, one for
James and one for herself, and she got him a pony,
and he was her cavalier. They were the glory of
Dublin and the Phœnix, and had often a crowd at
their tails. Their accoutrement was as follows:
each had a beaver hat, gold laced, looped, and
with a handsome feather: a coat and waistcoat
blazing with gold lace and gold buttons: only the
lady ended in a petticoat of the same stuff, cling-
ing close to her as a blister. She had also a little
powdered peruke like a man; her object being to

seem a smart cavalier by day, and a finicking fine
lady, hooped and furbelowed, by night. The only
drawback was that this exquisite costume brought
her mercer's bill to a climax, and he demanded
payment of the following trifles, and threatened
law. Fine Holland smock, one guinea; Marseilles
quilted silk petticoat, three pound six; hooped
petticoat, two pound five; Italian quilted ditto, ten
pounds; mantua and petticoat of French brocade,
seventy-eight pounds; English stays, three pounds;
Italian fan, five pounds; a laced head, of Flanders
point, sixty pounds; silk stockings, one pound;
a black-laced hood, and a French silk *à la mode*
hood, six pounds; French garters, one pound five;
French bosom knot, one pound twelve; beaver hat
and feather, three pounds; ditto for James, two
pounds; embroidered riding-suit of Lyons velvet and
gold lace, forty-seven pounds; ditto for my young
lord, nineteen pounds; sable muff, five pounds;
red shoes (English) two guineas; tippet, seven
guineas; French kid gloves, two shillings and six-
pence; with innumerable other articles, all for
outside wear, the body linen being in the proportion of the bread to the sack in Falstaff's tavern
bill. Many of these articles could have been had
for half the price, if the lady would have listened
to Dr. Swift, and bought Irish goods; but she

would almost rather have gone bare. No, she was Irish to the core; so everything she wore must come from England or the continent.

This bill, and the man's threats, brought on a fit of the vapours; another fashionable importation. She rode out with Jemmy one day, to shake them off, and they met a gentleman riding, in a scarlet coat, and a hat like a bishop's mitre. He drew up, and saluted Miss Gregory stiffly, and cast a sour look at Jemmy. " Odzooks," said he, " have you got that boy in the house ? "

" What matters it to you, sir," said the lady, firing up, " since you do never come there ? "

The officer explained that he and his brother, Lord Altham, had been out for some time. " To tell the truth, we are like cat and dog. Nought but want of money brings us together. You will see me now every day," said he, with a sneer: then, lowering his voice, " Madam, I desire some private conference with you. Will it please you to be at home this afternoon ? "

" Certainly, sir ; in one hour."

When he was gone, she asked the boy if he knew the gentleman. James answered, very gravely, that it was his uncle, Richard Annesley, and no friend to him ; " never gave me a good word nor a look in his life."

"Perhaps you are in his way," said she, with a laugh.

She gave Captain Annesley the *tête-à-tête* he had asked for, and he came to the point in a moment. Lord Altham and himself were both in want of money, and, in order to get it, had patched up their quarrels : parading Jemmy about the streets of Dublin was unseasonable, and just the thing to stop the business, or at least retard it. The money-lenders might hesitate, and say there was another interest to be thought of.

"Nay," said Miss Gregory, "that would never do ; for here I am threatened for £200 and more."

Captain Annesley worked on her cupidity, till she consented to part father and son : but she refused to do it with a high hand, or with brutal severity. She could never urge the father to turn his son out of the house. Richard Annesley, as artful as he was unscrupulous, offered her his house at Inchicore, and they settled that Lord Altham should be taken out there, and every means employed to separate him from James, till the money was raised. This artful pair now put their heads together every day, and the first thing done was to discharge Mrs. Betty. She went back to England, leaving James in the house. Next all the servants were discharged, except two, who were sent on to Inchicore; and an old woman left in charge of the house and Jemmy.

Miss Gregory so worked on Lord Altham, that he hid from James where he was going, stipulating only, like a sot as he was, that Richard should look to the boy, and see he wanted for nothing.

After all, the money-lenders hesitated, on account of the previous mortgages, and my lord remained in hiding with Mrs. Gregory and her daughter, and had to cut down his expenses, and live upon his rents.

James Annesley stayed in the house, hoping every day he should be sent for: till one day an execution was put in for rent, his riding suit was seized, and he was turned out into the streets, with nothing but what he carried on his back.

Then he began to wonder and fear. He ran to Mrs. Martha, whom he had neglected in his prosperity. She had left the town. He was amazed, confused, heart-sick. He wandered to and fro, wondering what this might mean. He had to sell his fine suit for a plain one and a very little money, and, when that was done, starvation stared him in the face. Deserted, and penniless, he had hard work to live. At first a playmate, one Byrne, brought him morsels of food in secret, and lodged him in a hayloft. Then he got into

the college, and used to run errands, and black
shoes. Vacation came, and even that resource
failed, and then he held horses, for a halfpenny or
a farthing, in Ormond Market, and was almost in
rags : no other ragged boy so unhappy as he, since
under those rags there beat the heart of a little
gentleman, and rankled the deep sense of injustice
and unnatural cruelty. Of late he had avoided
speaking of his parentage ; but one day, insults
dragged it out of him. A bigger boy was abusing
him because a gentleman, liking his face, had
selected him to hold his horse : the boy called him
a blackguard, a beggar, and other opprobrious
terms. "You lie," said James, losing all patience :
"I am come of better folk than thou. My father
is a lord, and I am heir to great estates, and have
been served by thy betters, and so should now,
if the world was not so wicked." These words
did not fall unheeded ; henceforth he was the
scoff of all the dirty boys in the place, and they
cried "My lord !" after him. One Farrell, that
kept a shop on the Quay, heard them at it, and
said to his shopman, "Why, I see no hump on
him : the boy is straight enough, and fair, if he
were cleaned." He called James to him, and
asked him why they called him "My lord." The
boy hung his head, and would not say at first, he

D

was so used to be jeered; but, being pressed, and seeing a kindly face enough, began to tell his tale. But Farrell interrupted him. "Lord Altham," said he, "I know him—to my cost. Well, I do remember one time I went to Dunmaine for my money, and got mulled claret instead on't; there was a child there, with my lady and his nurse." James said, eagerly, that was himself. "Nay, then," said Farrell, "why not seek thy mother, Lady Altham, if she be thy mother?"

"Oh, sir," said James, "I thought my mother was gone back to England. Dear, good sir, have pity on me, and take me to her, if she is in this wicked place."

"Child," said the man, "I know that my Lady Altham sojourned with her friend, Alderman King : but you are not fit to go there : come you home with me." So he took him home, and bade his wife clean him, and lend him an old suit of his son that was away at school. The wife complied, with no great cordiality; and Farrell sent a line about him to Alderman King, and then called at the alderman's house, and asked for my Lady Altham. "Nay," said the alderman, "my lady sailed for England a se'nnight ago. But, Master Farrell, what tale is this you bring me? Why, my lady never had a son."

"Oh!" cried James, as if he had been struck.

Farrell looked blank: but said, "Sure your worship is mistook."

"I tell ye, Master Farrell, she was eight months in this house, and discoursed of all her troubles, and she never breathed a word about a son of hers. Did she, Mistress Avice?" turning to his housekeeper.

"She did—to *me*, sir," said the woman, coolly. "My lady was my countrywoman, and opened her heart to me. She spoke once of her son, and said the greatest of her grief was she could never see him."

Here the alderman was called away, and Farrell took James home in tears. "Keep a stout heart, sir," said he; "your mother is gone: but I'll soon find your father, if he is above ground."

Farrell wanted to keep him, but his wife would not hear of it. "We have lost above £50 by that Lord Altham already. I'll have none of his breed in this house, bad scran to the dirty clan of 'em."

Now Farrell had a friend, a very honest fellow, one Purcell; so he told him the whole story one day, over a pipe. "Let me see him," said Purcell: "if I like his looks—why we can afford to keep something young about us. But I must see him, first."

So these two went to one likely place and another, and presently Farrell saw Jemmy in Smithfield, riding a horse, and pointed him out to Purcell. "Stand you aside," said Purcell, "and be not seen." He took a good look at the boy, and liked his face. "Child," said he, rather shortly, "what is your name?"

"James Annesley, sir."

"Whose son are you?"

"Alas! sir," said James, "prithee do not ask me. It makes me cry so. I'm a lost boy."

Then the honest man's bowels were moved for the child; but he would not show it all at once. "Are you Lord Altham's son?" said he, a little roughly. "Indeed, then, I am, sir," said the boy, and looked him in the face. "Then," says Purcell, still a little roughly, "get you off that horse; for, if you will be a good boy, I'll take you home with me, and," says he warmly, "you shall never want while I have it." Then Jemmy stared at him; and the next moment fell on his knees in the market-place, and gave him a thousand blessings: "For oh, sir," said he, "I am almost lost;" and he trembled greatly.

"Have a good heart, sir," said Purcell, and took him by the hand, all shabby and dirty as he was, and brought him home to his wife that was busy

cooking, being a right good housewife. "There,"
says he, "Mary, here's a little gentleman for thee."
So she looked at him, and smiled, and asked who
he was. "Thou'lt know anon," said he: "but
take care of him as if he was thine own." Now
she was not like Farrell's wife, but one that had
a good man, and knew it. "Go thy ways," said
she, and gave him a merry push, "and come thou
here no more till supper-time." Then he went
away, and she soon had a great pot on the fire,
and made the boy wash in a two-eared tub, and
put decent clothes on him; and drew all his
history from him with her kind words and ways;
and, when the honest man came home, he started
at the door, for there sat his wife knitting, in her
best apron, and aside her a lovely little gentleman
with golden hair, leaning on her shoulder, and
they were prattling together: and one was "my
child," and the other was "Mammy," already.
It was the happiest fire-side in Ireland that night;
and it deserved to be.

Here was a respite to all James Annesley's
troubles. He grew, he fattened, he brightened, he
loved his Mammy and stout John Purcell, and they
loved him.

Unfortunately, Farrell found out Lord Altham
at Inchicore, and went to dun him; and told him

about Jemmy. Lord Altham was shocked, and
promised to remunerate both Farrell and Purcell
as soon as he could raise money. Meantime he
blustered to Miss Gregory, and she must have
told Richard Annesley; for one September afternoon there walked into Purcell's shop a gentleman,
with a gun and a setter, and inquired, "Is there
not one Purcell lives here?"

"Yes, sir," said Purcell, "I am the man."

Then the gentleman called for a pot of beer,
and sat down by the fire, inviting Purcell to par-
take. When the gentleman had drunk a drop, he
asked Purcell if he had not a boy called James
Annesley. Purcell said yes, and the gentleman
said he desired to see him. Now Jemmy had been
ailing a little, and was in the parlour, with Mrs.
Purcell, in an arm-chair, by the fire; so Purcell
went in to tell him, and found him in tears.
"Why, what is the matter?" said Purcell. Says
the boy, "It is that gentleman: the sight of him
has put such a dread on me, I don't know what to
do with myself."

"Nay," said Purcell, "the gentleman is civil
enough. Come and speak to him." So he came
very unwillingly. The gentleman said, "So,
James, how do you do?" The boy answered,
stiffly, "Sir, I thank you, I am pretty well." The

gentleman said, "And I am glad you have fallen into such good hands." The boy said, gravely, "Sir, I have reason to thank God for it. They are kinder to me than my own kin." The gentleman said he must not say so, and asked him if he knew him.

"I know you well," said he, "you are my uncle, Richard Annesley." And, at the first opportunity, slipped back to his "Mammy," as he called her. He was all trembling, and she asked him why he was so, and he said, "That's a wicked man: he hates me; he hates me. He never came near me but to hurt me. I'd liever meet the devil. Some day he will kill me."

Whilst Dame Purcell was comforting him, and telling him nobody should harm him under her wing, Richard Annesley treated Purcell, and told him Lord Altham should recompense him: but Purcell declined that favour, and said rather contemptuously, "When he is man enough to take his own flesh and blood into the house, he knows where to find him: but I ask no pay: I can keep a lord's son, if his father can't, and I can love one, if his father can't: for there never was a better boy stood in the walls of a house."

Three months after this, Lord Altham had a short illness, and died. He was to be buried at

Christchurch, and the sexton told Mrs. Purcell the
afternoon before the funeral. They buried at night
in those days. Mrs. Purcell had not the heart to
keep it from the boy ; he turned very pale, but did
not cry. Only he would go to the funeral. Purcell
dissuaded him, and then he began to wring his
hands. Mrs. Purcell had her way for once, and
got him weepers to attend.

It was a fine funeral, by torchlight. Velvets,
plumes, mutes, flambeaux. One thing only was
wanting—mourners. The tenants of his vast
estates—his numerous boon companions—his wife
—his betrothed—his brothers, Lord Anglesey and
Richard Annesley—all drinking, or gaming, or
minding their own business. There stood by this
wretched noble's open grave only two that cared :
an old coachman, Weedon, and the poor boy he
had so basely abandoned. The rest were strangers,
brought there by hard curiosity.

When the coffin began to sink out of sight, the
tender heart of the deserted one almost burst with
grief and wasted love.

"OH, MY FATHER! MY FATHER!" cried the desolate child : and that wild cry of woe rang in ears
that remembered it, and spoke of it long after, and
under strange circumstances no one could foresee
at that time.

When he came back all in tears, Purcell said, "There, dame, I knew how 'twould be," and he was almost angry.

"But 'tis best so, John," said she: "dear heart, when he comes to be old, would you have him remember he could not find a tear for his father, and him no more?"

"Oh, Mammy, Mammy," said James, "only one old man and me to weep for him; those he loved before me, never cared for him," and then his tears burst out afresh.

A day or two after this a message came to James Annesley that his uncle wanted to see him, at Mr. Jones's in the market. The boy refused to go. "It is not for any good, I know," said he. But at last he consented to accompany Mr. Purcell, if he would go armed. Stout-hearted Purcell laughed at his fears, but yielded to his entreaties, and took a thick stick. James held him fast by the skirt all the way. In the entry to Jones's three fellows slouched against the wall. "Oho!" thought John Purcell.

Mr. Annesley met him, and Purcell took off his hat, and Mr. Annesley gave him good morning, and then, without more ceremony, called to one of the fellows to seize that thieving rogue, and take him to the proper place.

"Who do you call a thief?" said Purcell, sternly.

"Confound you," says the gentleman, "I am not speaking to you." Then he ordered the fellows again to take Jemmy away. But Purcell put the boy between his legs, and raised his stick high. "The first of you lays a hand on him, by God I'll knock his brains out." Hearing him raise his voice in anger, one or two people came about the entry, and the bullies sneaked off. "You a gentleman!" said John Purcell, "and would go to destroy this poor creature you were never man enough to maintain."

"Go you and talk to his nurse," said Richard Annesley, spitefully; "she knows more of him than you do."

"This is idle chat," said John Purcell. "He has neither father, mother, nor nurse, left in this kingdom, but my dame and me. Let us go home, Jemmy. We have fallen in ill company."

But from that day there were always fellows lurking about John Purcell's house; sometimes bailiffs, or constables or sharks disguised as such; and the boy one day lost his nerve and ran away: he entered the service of a Mr. Tighe, and sent word to Purcell that his life was not safe so long as his uncle knew where to find him, and he also feared to bring him and his Mammy into trouble.

For this cowardice he paid dear. He had been watched, and an opportunity was taken to seize him one day in the open street, by men disguised as bailiffs, on a charge of theft, and, instead of being taken to a court, he was brought to Richard Annesley's house. Richard Annesley charged him with stealing a silver spoon. The boy was quiet till he saw that fatal face, and then he began to scream, and to cry, "He will kill me, or transport me." Annesley's eyes glittered fiendishly. "Ay, thou knave," said he, "I have been insulted enough for thee, and my very title denied me, because of thy noise. Away with him!"

Then the men put him into a coach, and took him along by the Quay, screaming and crying for help. "They will kill me; they will transport me, because I am Lord Altham's son:" and people followed the coach, and murmured loud. But the men were quick and resolute, and, while one told some lie or other to the people, the others got him into a boat, and pulled lustily out to a ship that lay ready to cross the bar, for all this had been timed beforehand; and, once on board that wooden hell, he had no chance. He was thrust into the hold.

The law protected Englishmen from this, in theory, but not in practice. Some agent of Richard Annesley's indented James Annesley as his nearest friend, acting *at his request*, and the sole record of this act of villainy read like an act of plain unobjectionable business. He was kept in the hold, and his cries unregarded. The ship spread her pinions, and away. Then the boy was allowed to come on deck, and take his last look of Ireland. He asked a sailor boy where they were going. "Bound for Philadelphia," was the reply. At the bare word the poor little wretch uttered shriek upon shriek and ran aft, to throw himself into the sea. The man at the wheel caught him by his skirt, and had much ado to hold him, till a sailor ran up, and they got him on board again, screaming, and biting like a wild cat: the gentle boy was quite changed by desperation; for Philadelphia, though it means "brotherly love" in Greek, meant "white slavery" to poor betrayed creatures from the mother country.

Finally, after superhuman struggles, and shrieks of despair, so piteous that even the rugged sailors began to look blank, he went off into a dead swoon, and was white as ashes, and his lips blue. "He is dead," was the cry.

"Lord forbid!" said the captain. "Stand aloof, ye fools, and give him air."

"Oh, humane captain!" says my reader : but "Oh, good trader captain!" would be nearer the mark. This Richard Annesley, to save his purse, had given the captain an interest in the boy's life. The captain was to sell him over the water, and pocket the money. This fatal oversight elevated a human creature into merchandise. The worthy captain set himself in earnest to keep it alive. He fanned his merchandise, sprinkled his merchandise, and, when his merchandise came to, and with a stare and a loud scream, went off into heart-rending and distracting cries, he comforted his merchandise, and gave it a sup of rum and water, and hurried it down into a cabin, and set a guard on it night and day, with orders to be kind to it, but very watchful : this done, he gave his mind to sailing the good ship *James* of Dublin.

But next day he was informed that the merchandise would not eat, nor drink, but was resolved to die. "Drat him! drench him," said the stout-hearted captain.

"Drench him yourself," said the mate. "I'm sick on't."

Then the captain bade the cook prepare a savoury dish, and brought it down to James :

"Eat this, sir," said he, as one used to be obeyed. The young gentleman made no reply, but his eyes gleamed. The captain drew his hanger with one hand, and stuck a two-pronged fork into a morsel with the other. "Eat that, ye contrary toad," said he, "or I'll make minced collops of thee." The boy took the morsel. "So!" said the captain, sneering over his shoulder at the mate. The boy spat it furiously in his face. "May God sink thy ship, and burn thy soul, thou knave, that would'st steal away a nobleman's son, and sell him for a slave."

The captain drew back a moment, like a dog a hen has flown at, and had hard work not to cut him in two: but he forbore, and said, "Starve, then, and feed the fishes:" and so left the cabin. The mate, who was at his back all the time, told the boatswain young master was a nobleman's son, and was being spirited away, and there was "foul play" in it. Some remarks were made which it was intended the captain should hear. He took them up directly. "A nobleman's son," said he: "ay, but only a merrybegot: and so given to thieving, he will do no good at home. Why, 'twas his own uncle shipped him—for his good." This quieted the men directly, and, from that moment, they made light of the matter.

When James was downright faint with hunger,
the captain took quite another way with him;
went to him, and said he feared there was some
mistake, and he was sorry he had been led to take
him on board; but the matter should be set right
at landing. "No, no," said James, "I shall be
bound as a slave. May Heaven revenge me on my
wicked uncle! I see now why he has done this—
to rob me of my estate and my title."

"Indeed, I begin to think he is to blame," said
the captain. "But why take fright at a word,
sir? None can make you a slave for life, as the
negroes are, but only an apprentice for a time."

"I am beholden to you, sir," said James; "but
call it what you will, 'tis slavery; and I'd liever
die. But promise to send me back by the first
ship, and I will give you a hatful of money when I
come to my rights, and pray for you all my days."

"Ay, but if I do so, will you eat and drink, and
be of good heart?"

"That will I, sir."

"Then 'tis a bargain."

They shook hands upon it; and, from that hour,
were good friends. James was treated like a
guest: he ate and drank so heartily, that the
captain began to wince at his appetite; and, in a
word, what with the sea air, plentiful diet, and

a mind relieved from fear of slavery, the young
gentleman's cheeks plumped out, and became rosy,
he grew an inch and a half in height, and landed
at Philadelphia a picture of a little Briton.

The planters boarded the ship: the captain
threw off the mask, and sold him directly, for a
high price, to one Drummond.

James raged, and cried, and demanded to be
taken before a justice.

Then, for the first time, the captain produced
papers, all prepared by Richard Annesley, under
legal advice. The colony wanted labour, and was
ill-disposed to sift the evidence that furnished it;
it all ended in Drummond carrying his prize home
to Newcastle County.

Next morning, at five o'clock, James found himself engaged, with other slaves, black and white,
cutting pipe-staves, and an overseer standing by,
provided with a whip of very superior construction
to anything he ever saw in Ireland.

Being only a boy, and new at the work, he was
first ridiculed, then threatened, and, before the day
ended, the whip fell on his shoulders, stinging,
branding, burning his back much, his heart more;
for then this noble boy felt, with all his soul and
all his body, what he was come to : an ox—an ass
—a beast—a slave !

CHAPTER II.

In this miserable condition of servitude James Annesley remained nearly seven years, having been indented for an extreme period; and many a sigh he heaved, and many a tear he shed in solitude, thinking of what he had been, and what he had a right to be,. and what he was. But, being now a full-grown young man, tall, and very robust, he could do his work, and his misery was alleviated by caution; and, above all, by the blessed thought that his servitude was drawing to an end; since a white man could only be bound for a limited term.

But let all shallow statesmen, and pedantic lawyers, who trifle with the equal rights of humanity, be warned that you cannot play fast and loose with things so sacred. The mother country, in its stupidity, allowed its citizens to be made slaves for a time; the Pilgrim Fathers and their grandchildren, though no men ever valued liberty

E

more in their own persons, or talked more about
it, had not that *disinterested* respect for it which
marks their nobler descendants ; and so they, by a
bye-law or custom, enlarged the term of servitude.
This they contrived by ordering that, if one of these
temporary slaves misbehaved grossly, and above
all attempted escape, his term of servitude could
be enlarged in proportion, by judges who were in
the interest of the planters.

So the game was, when the white slave's term of
servitude drew near, to make his life intolerable :
then, in his despair, he rebelled, or ran for it, and
was recaptured, and reinslaved by this bye-law
passed in the colony.

"Where there's a multitude there's a mixture,"
and not every planter played this heartless dodge :
but too many did, and no man more barbarously
than this Drummond. By the help of an unscrupulous overseer, who did and said whatever he was
ordered, he starved, he insulted, he flogged, he
made his slaves' life intolerable ; and so, in a fit of
desperation, James started one night for the Delaware River : he armed himself with a little bill-
hook, for he was quite resolved not to be taken
alive.

In the morning they found he was gone, and
followed him, horse and foot. But they did not

catch him, for rather a curious reason : he had the ill-luck to miss his road, and got to the Susquehanna instead.

He found his mistake, when too late ; but he did not give up all hope ; for he saw some ships, and a town, into which he resolved to penetrate at night-fall : it was then about ten o'clock. Meantime, he thought it best to hide ; and, coming to two roads, one of which turned to his right, and passed through a wood, he turned off that way, and lay down in shelter, and unseen, though close to the roadside. Here fatigue overpowered him, and he went to sleep, fast as a church, and slept till four in the afternoon. Then he awoke, with voices in his ears, and, peeping through the leafy screen, he saw, with surprise, that there was company close to him : there was a man haltering a horse to a tree near him, and another already haltered ; a gentlewoman in a riding habit stood looking on, while another man drew provisions and wine from some saddle-bags, and spread a cloth on the grass, and made every preparation for a repast.

Then they all three sat down and enjoyed themselves, so that poor hungry James sighed involuntarily, and peeped through the leaves. The lady heard him, turned, saw him, screamed, pointed at

him, and in a moment the men were upon him
with drawn swords, crying, " Traitor ! Spy ! "

But James whipped behind a tree, and parleyed.
" No traitor, sir, but a poor runaway slave, who
never set eyes on you before." The men hesitated,
and he soon convinced them of his innocence. One
of them laughed, and said, " Why, then there's
nought to fear from thee."

The lady, however, still anxious, cross-questioned
him herself. His answers satisfied her, his appearance pleased her, and it ended to his advantage ;
they made him sit down with them, and eat and
drink heartily.

At last the lady let out they were fugitives, too,
and could feel for him, and she said, " We are
going on board a ship bound for Holland. She
lies at anchor, waiting for us ; and, if you can run
with us, we will e'en take you on board. But in
sooth we must lose no time." They started. The
gentleman had the lady behind him, and James
ran with his hand on the other horse's mane ; but
losing breath, the man, who was well mounted,
took him up behind him. Night fell, and then
they went more slowly, and James, to ease the
good horse, walked by his side.

But presently there was a fierce galloping of
horses behind them, and lights seemed flying at

them from behind. The lady looked back, and screamed, " 'Tis he himself; we are lost ! "

The men had only time to dismount and draw their swords, when the party was upon them, with a score of blades flashing in the torch-light. The men defended themselves, and James, forgetting it was no quarrel of his, laid about him with his bill-hook : but the combat was too unequal. In three minutes the lady, in a dead swoon, was laid before one horseman, her lover and his servant were bound upon their own horses, and James fared worse still, for his hands were tied together, and fastened to a horse's tail.

In this wretched plight they were carried to the nearest village, and well guarded for the night in separate rooms.

At day-break they were marched again, and James Annesley, in that horrible attitude of a captive felon, was drawn at a horse's tail through four hooting villages, and lodged in Chester gaol.

Law did not halt here : they were all four put to the bar, and then first he learned, by the evidence, who his companions were, and what he had been doing when he drew bill-hook in their defence. The lady was daughter of a trader in this very town of Chester. Her father, finding her in love with some one beneath her, had compelled her to

marry a rich planter. She hated him, and, in an
evil hour, listened to her lover, who persuaded her
to fly with all she could lay her hands on. The
money and jewels were found in the saddle-bags.
The husband was vindictive, the crime two-fold.
The guilty pair, the servant, and James, who was
taken fighting on their side, were condemned.

James made an effort to separate his fate from
the others. He told the judge who he was, and
what master he had run away from; declared it
was a mere accident his being there; he had been
surprised by the sudden attack on persons, who,
whatever their faults, had just been good to him.
The judge took a note while he was pleading in
arrest of judgment, but said nothing; and they
were all four condemned to stand on the gallows
for one hour with a rope round their necks, to be
whipped on their bare backs with so many lashes
well laid on; and then imprisoned for several years.

CHAPTER III.

Two little rivers meet, and run to the sea, as naturally as if they had always meant to unite; yet, go to their sources in the hills, how wide apart! How unlikely to come together, or even approach each other! Why, one rises south, and the other north-east; and they do not even look the same way, at starting. It is hard to believe they are doomed to trickle hither and thither, meander and curve, and meet at last, to part no more.

And so it is with many human lives: the facts of this story compel me to trace, from their tiny sources, two human currents, that I think will bear out my simile. The James Annesley river is set flowing; so now for the Joanna Philippa Chester, and old England.

She was the orphan daughter of two very superior people, who died too young. Her mother was a Spaniard, her father an Englishman, and

a lawyer of great promise. They had but this
child. She inherited her mother's jewels and
thirteen thousand pounds : her father, tormented
by some cruel experience in his own family, had
an almost morbid fear lest she should be caught
up by some fortune-hunter, and married for her
money, she being a black-browed girl with no great
promise of beauty at that time. During his last
illness he thought much of this, and spoke of it
very earnestly to the two gentlemen he had ap-
pointed her trustees. These two, Mr. Hanway and
Mr. Thomas Chester, hated each other decently,
but sincerely. Mr. Chester knew that, and, with a
lawyer's shrewdness, counted a little on it, as well
as on their attachment to himself, to get his views
carried out. He made them promise him, in
writing, that Joanna's fortune should be concealed
from her until she should be twenty-four, or some
worthy person, unacquainted with her means,
should offer her a marriage of affection ; she was
to be brought up soberly, taught to read and write
very well, and cast accounts, and do plain stitch-
ing, but never to sit at a harpsichord, nor a
sampler. She was to live with Mr. Hanway, at
Colebrook, till she was seventeen, and then with
Mr. Thomas Chester, her uncle, till her marriage.
Each trustee, in turn, to receive £100 a year, for

her board and instruction. Her fortune was all out at good mortgage, paying larger interest than is to be had on that security nowadays.

The £100 a year was of some importance to Mr. Hanway, and he was not at all sorry that Joanna Philippa was to be taught only what he and his housekeeper could teach her: that saved expense. He did teach her, an hour every day, and she was so quick that, at ten years old, she could read, and write, and sum, better than a good many duchesses. But the rest of the day she was entirely neglected: so she was nearly always out of doors, acquiring more health, and strength, and freckles than a girl is entitled to, and playing pranks that ought to have been restrained. She was, at this time, a most daring girl, and she always played with the boys, and picked up their ways, and, by superior intelligence, became their leader. From them she learned to look down on her own sex; and the women, in return, called her a Tomboy and a witch: indeed, there was something witch-like in her agility, her unbounded daring, and her great keen grey eyes, with thickish eyebrows, black as jet, that actually met, not on her brow, but—with a slight dip—on the bridge of her nose.

One summer afternoon, being then about eleven,

she had just ridden one of Farmer Newton's horses into the water to drink, according to her custom, and driven the others in before her, when she became aware of a gentleman, in black, with a pale but noble face, looking thoughtfully at her. It was the new vicar, a learned clerk from Oxenford. He smiled on her, and said, "My young madam, may I speak with you?" He knew who she was.

"Ay, sir," says she; and, in a moment, from riding astride like a boy, she whipped one leg over and was seated like a woman, and brought the horse out, and slid off down his fat ribs, and lighted like a bird at the parson's feet, and took her hat off to him, instead of curtseying. "Here be I," said the imp. "My dear," says the vicar, "that is not a pastime for a young gentlewoman." Joanna hung her head.

"Not," said the parson, "that I would deprive you of amusement, at your age; that were cruel: but—have you no little horse of your own to ride?"

"Nay, not so much as a Jenny ass. Daddy Hanway is—I know what he is, but I won't say, till we are better acquainted."

"Come, come, we are to be better acquainted, then."

"Ay, an' you will. Now may I go, sir?"

"Why we have not half made acquaintance. Madam, I desire to show you my house."

"Alack! And I am dying to see it. So come on," and she caught him by the hand with a fiery little grasp.

"Have with you then!" cried the parson, affecting excitement, and proposed a race to the vicarage: so they sped across the meadow. His reverence was careful to pound the earth, and make a great fuss, but not to distress the imp, who, indeed, skimmed along like a swallow.

"There," said she, panting, "there's none can beat me at running, in this parish, except that Dick Caulfield; Od rabbit him." The vicar allowed that refined expression to pass, for the present, and took her into his study. "Oh, Jiminy!" she cried; "here's books! I ne'er thought there were as many in the world."

"What, you are fond of books?" said he, eagerly.

"I doat on 'em; especially voyages. I have read every book in our house, twice over; there's the Bible, and 'Culpepper's Herbal,' and 'Pilgrim's Progress,' and the 'Ready Reckoner,' and the 'Prayer Book,' and a volume of the 'Spectator,' and the 'Book of Receipts, and the 'Book of Thieves.'"

" And which do you like the best of all those? "

" Why, the 'Pilgrim's Progress,' to be sure. 'Tis all travels."

" Strange," said the clergyman, half to himself; "that a girl born in a country village should be so fond of travels."

"Country village!" said she. "Drat the country village. I ran away from it once; but they caught me at Hounslow. But, bless your heart, I was only eight: better luck next time, parson."

" Nay, Mistress Joanna——"

"An't please you, call me Philippa. I like that name best."

" Well, then, Mistress Philippa, I am of your mind about travelling. My studies, and a narrow income somewhat drawn upon by poor relations, have kept me at home: but my mind hath travelled on the wings of books, as yours shall, Mistress Philippa, if you please. See, here's Purchas for you, and Dampier, Cowley, Sharpe, Woodes Rogers, where you shall find the cream of 'Robinson Crusoe,' 'Stout John Dunton,' and 'Montaigne's Travels,' short, but priceless. Here be 'Coryat's Crudities,' and 'Moryson's Itinerary,' two travellers of the good old school, that footed Europe and told no lies. Ay, Philippa, often as I sat in my study, or meditated beneath the stars, have I longed to

escape the narrow terms of this small island, and
see the strange and beautiful world: first of all, the
Holy Land, where still the vine, the olive tree, and
the cornfield, grow side by side; where the Dead
Sea rolls o'er those wicked cities, and Lot's wife,
in salten pillar, still looks on: to see Rome, that
immortal city where ancient and modern history
meet and mingle in monuments of surpassing
grandeur and beauty. Then would I run East
again, and behold the mighty caves of Elephanta,
monument of a race that is no more; the Pyramids
of Egypt, and her temples approached by avenues
of colossal sphinxes a mile long. Thence to the
Pole, and see its spectral glories, great temples and
palaces of prismatic ice, of which this new poet,
Mr. Pope, singeth well—

> 'As Atlas fixed, each hoary pile appears
> The gathered winter of a thousand years.'

Then away to sunny lands, where for ever the
sky is blue, and flowers spring spontaneous, and
the earth poureth forth pines, and melons, and
luscious fruits, without the hand of man,

> '—and universal Pan,
> Knit with the Graces and the Hours in dance,
> Leads on the eternal Spring.'

Then I would see the famous mountains of the
world; Ararat, where the ark rested, as the waters

of the flood abated; Teneriffe's peak, shaped like
a sugar-loaf, and, by mariners, seen often in the
clear glassy sky one hundred miles at sea; and
above all, the mighty Andes, so high that no
aspiring cloud may reach his bosom, and his great
eye looks out ever calm, from the empyrean, upon
half the world."

The scholar would have gone on, dreaming aloud,
an hour more; but his words, that to him were
only words, were fire to the aspiring girl, and set
her pale, and panting. "Oh, parson!" she cried;
"for the love of God, take hat, and come along to
all those placen:" and she crammed his hat into
his hand, and tugged at him amain.

"My young mistress," said he, gravely, "you
do use that sacred name too lightly."

"Well, then, for the love of the devil: I care
not: so we do go this minute."

Then he held up his finger, and, with kind and
soothing words, cooled this fiery creature down a
little, and put "Dampier's Voyages" into her hand.
Down she flung herself—for it was erect as a dart,
or flat as a pancake, with this young gentlewoman;
no half measures—and sucked the book like an egg.

He gave her the right to come and read when
she pleased: and, from this beginning, by degrees,
she became his pupil very willingly.

He played the viol da gamba himself; so he asked her, did she like music?

"No," said she; "I hate it." How many of her sex would say the same, if they did but dare.

Would she like to draw, and colour?

"Ay. But not to keep me from my travels."

It turned out that she had an excellent gift at drawing, and a fine eye for colour: so, with instruction, she soon got to draw from nature, and to colour very prettily; the only objection was, in less than six months from the first lesson, every roadside barndoor within distance presented a caricature, in chalk, of the farmer who owned it, and often of his wife and family, into the bargain. The number, and distance, of these "sculptures," as she was pleased to call them (why, I know not), revealed an active foot, a skilful hand, and a heart not to be daunted by moonlight.

The parson tried to break her spirit—with arithmetic. But no: she was all docility and goodness, by his side; she would learn arithmetic, or anything else, with a rapidity that nothing but a precocious girl ever equalled; but a daring demon, when he was not at her back.

In vain he begged her to consider that she was now thirteen years old, and must begin to play the gentlewoman: "I can not," said she: "gentle-

women are such mincing apes. The boys they
scorn them, and so do I, they make me sick.
Parson," said she, "I love you;" and she made but
one spring, and her arms were round his neck with
the same movement. "Grant me a favour," said
she, "because I love you. Have me made a boy."

The parson looked at her gazing imploringly
right into him with her great eyes; and was sore
puzzled what she would be at now. However, the
explanation followed in due course.

"Why," said she, "'twill not cost much, 'tis
but the price of a coat and waistcoast and breeches,
instead of these things," slapping her petticoats
contemptuously; "and then I *am* a boy. Oh!
'twill be sweet to have my freedom, and not to be
checked at every word, because I am a she."

"Why, what stuff is this, child?" said his
reverence: "putting thee in boy's clothes will not
make thee a boy.'·

"Yes, it will. You know it will; nay, to be sure,
there's my hair; but I can soon cut that."

"Now, Philippa," said her preceptor, "I cannot
have you cutting your beautiful hair—which is a
woman's crown—and talking nonsense. Hum!—
the truth is—ahem—when once one has been
christened Joanna Philippa, in the church, one is
a girl for ever."

"Alas!" whined Philippa, "and is it so? Methought it was the clothes the old folks put us in that did our business." Then, going into a fury, "Oh, why did I not scratch their eyes out, when they came to christen me a girl? Why cried I not aloud, No! No! No!—A Boy!—A Boy!"

"Well, we must make the best of it, my dear. I will read you what Erasmus saith, in his 'Gunæco-Synedrion,' of the female estate, and its advantages. Then you will see that each condition of life hath its comforts and its drawbacks."

The compass of my tale does not permit me to deal largely in conversation; otherwise the intercourse of this gentle scholar's mind, and this sharp girl's, was curious and interesting enough. It left Philippa, at fourteen years of age, very superior to the ladies of the period, in reading, writing, arithmetic, drawing, walking, leaping, and running; but far more innocent, in spite of her wildness, than if she had consorted with the women of that day, whose tongues were too often foul.

At this time the good parson fell ill, and, having friends in office, obtained leave to go on the continent.

He returned in two years, and found his pupil transformed into a tall beautiful girl; even her

F

black brows became her now, and dazzled the
beholder. But such a change ! She was now
extremely shy ; avoided the boys, blushed whenever they spoke to her, and played the prude even
with her late preceptor. She had a great many
new ideas in her head : need I say that Love was
one of them ? But, as there was nobody in the
parish that approached the Being she had fixed on
—young, beautiful, fair, brave, good, and that had
made the grand tour—her favourite companion,
after all, was the good parson: only she now approached even him with a vast show of timidity.
To tell the truth, she had just as much devil in
her as ever ; but, on the surface, was mighty
guarded, demure, and bashful.

And now, seeing her to be beautiful, and knowing
her to be rich, temptation entered the heart of
Jonas Hanway. Jonas was a respectable man ;
but he was a father ; and he thought to himself,
"Now, if my boy Silas and she were to make a
match on't, what great harm, so that it came
about of itself, and not of my tempting Silas with
her wealth. The Lord forbid I should ever do that."

So to bring this about as honestly as might be,
the old man indulged miss with a pony and the
very masculine riding dress fashion permitted to
women ; also a little purple velvet cap and white

feather, very neat: and set Silas to ride with her.
She used to pace out of sight demurely, then dash
out of the road into the fields, and away as the
crow flies over hedge and ditch, depositing Silas
in the latter now and then. She treated him
altogether with queenly superiority; and as for
him, he showed no admiration, nothwithstanding
the insidious praises of her old Hanway poured
into his dullish ears.

One day, when Mr. Hanway was out, this young
lady, who was now mighty curious, and always
prying about the house, gave the old gentleman's
desk a shake with both hands. She had often
admired this desk: it was of enormous size and
weight, and sculptured at the sides; an antique
piece of furniture. When she shook it, something
metallic seemed to ring at the bottom. She looked
inside, and there was nothing but papers. "That
is odd," thought Joanna Philippa. She shook it
again. Same metallic sound. Then, with some
difficulty, though she was a most sinewy girl, she
turned it over, and saw a little button, scarcely
perceptible. She pressed it, and lo! a drawer
flew out at quite another part of the desk. That
drawer dazzled her: it was literally full of sparkling jewels, some of them very beautiful and
valuable. She screamed with surprise; she

screamed again with delight. She knew, in a
moment, they were her mother's jewels, which
Mr. Hanway had told her were a few trifling things,
not to be shown her till her twenty-first birthday,
and then she was to have them for her own.

"Oh! thou old knave!" said she. She did not
hesitate one moment. "I'll have them, and keep
them, too, if I hang for it; for they are mine."
So she swept them all into her apron, and flew upstairs with them, and hid them : then back again
and put the desk straight.

That night she had them all on, one after
another, before she went to bed, and marched
about the room like a peacock, surveying herself.

Next day she took fright, and carried them out
of the house, and hid them in the thatch of an old
cart-house that was never used nowadays, so not
likely to be repaired.

On moonlight nights she would sometimes take
a little hand-glass out, and wear the diamond cross
and brooch, and parade with them sparkling in
the moonlight. Her bedroom commanded a view
of this sacred cart-shed, and she always took a
look at it the last thing before she went to sleep.

When temptation gets the small end of the
wedge in, how sure the rest is to follow.

In Jonas Hanway's case the wedge widened

"She would sometimes take a little hand-glass out."—*Page* 68.

after this manner. The time drew near when he must hand his ward over to her uncle Chester, and the very day came, when Silas must go to London to enter a friendly merchant's house, under circumstances too favourable for the opportunity to be thrown away for nothing.

It was under this double pressure on Mr. Hanway's conscience that the following dialogue took place between father and son upon the little lawn at the back of the house.

It was a fine spring day; the sun was shining hot after a shower. The gardener had been rolling the turf with a stone roller, and was now trimming the turf. Mr. Hanway had paced the gravel thoughtfully some time with his hands behind him, and Silas beside him, secretly longing to be out of the parish.

"And so, Silas," said the old man, regretfully, "in one hour you do leave your father and go to London."

"Ay, father," Silas replied, with the cruel cheerfulness of the young; "and I hope I shan't come back till I've made my fortune;" and then the old man stopped short and confronted him.

"Son Silas," said he, after a few moments' silence, "you might make it easier and quicker by staying at home."

"As how," asked Silas, with an eagerness that showed he was not indifferent to suggestions of that sort. But Mr. Hanway, who had been so ready when he ought to have hesitated, began to hesitate now—because it was too late, I suppose. He said:

"Nay, I ought not to tell thee that. It is very wrong of me. It is breaking faith with the dead."

Silas, who was a stolid youth in everything that did not touch his interest, replied very characteristically: "Why, you wouldn't keep your own son out of fortune to humour the dead! For shame, dad!"

Mr. Hanway shook his head, as much as to say he was not to be blinded by his hobbadehoy's egotism. He put the matter on a very different footing by a word.

"Nay, nay, 'tis thus," said he. "I see my son going to leave me, and a father's heart gives away. Boy, your cousin—my ward Joanna—she passes for a poor girl; but she is not—the Lord forgive me for telling thee—she is an heiress."

"That Tomboy an heiress! Sure you are jesting."

"No, Silas, · no. Her father was afraid some fortune-hunter might snap her up, so he bound old Chester and me, that be her guardians—he did bind us solemnly not to tell a living soul. Alas! 'tis a wrong act I am doing; but 'twill all be in the family; and I hope he will forgive me, and not visit me of nights—whisper, Silas! She is worth thirteen thousand pounds the day she marries, and her mother's jewels, that are worth three thousand more; they came from Spain."

"Father," cried Silas, "you take my breath away." Then with a doleful whine, "Why did you not tell me before?"

"For conscience' sake. I always hoped you two would pair by nature, being young and housed under one roof. And, Silas, bethink thee now, have I not given thee many a hint to woo her?"

Silas was fain to own this was so. "And," says he, "and so I have wooed the minx a bit, after a manner, now and then, to please you, not myself, I can tell ye."

"Good lad! good lad! Obedience to parents still brings a blessing."

Silas, an original observer, though on a very small scale, demurred to that wholesale judgment.

"It ha'ant brought me one then; on foot nor horseback neither. When I ride out with her to please you, she is ne'er content till she sees me in the mire; and the last time I walked with her I did but offer her a kiss, and she fetched me a slap

—made mine ears to ring for half an hour and more."

" And what did ye then, son Silas ? "

" Why, bade her go to the devil for a vixen and a Tomboy, as she is."

Jonas thought this a sinful waste of opportunities. " Ye silly oaf," said he, " ye should have kissed her twenty times directly."

" What ! and got twenty cuts on the head ? "

Jonas shrugged his shoulders contemptuously at this reasoning. Silas, fancying he had got the best of the argument, added, solemnly, " You'd be content with *one*. She hits like a horse kicking."

" Why, faint heart never won fair lady," explained the senior.

" Fair ! she is as black as a crow," observed the logical junior.

" Her feathers will make a peacock of thee, boy. Come, Silas, in one day she can make thee a gentleman for life."

" Why didn't ye tell me before ? " whined Silas, driven into a corner.

He then represented that it was too late now. His place was taken by the coach, and that would come up to the George inn, Colebrook, in an hour.

The pertinacious old man turned even this untoward circumstance his way.

" All the better, boy," said he. " Her heart will
be softer at parting. Don now thy best clothes
and woo her like a man. Tell her thou'dst give
up London and fortune for her. And see ! here's
a ring of price. Clap thou it on her finger as thy
betrothed. Maids do love rings dearly ; ten to one
she lets thee put it on ; and if so, why with a buss
'tis settled."

Silas was wrought on. " I'll do't," he cried ;
" I'll do't ; but mind, if she flings it in my face,
I go straight off to London."

" Ay, but she won't ; she won't." Then Silas
hedged. " If she won't have the ring, you ought
to let me keep it," said he.

" Ay, but she will ; she will."

So Silas donned his best clothes, resolved to win
Philippa, or else follow his valise to the coach.
When he was dressed his father saw him, admired
him, pronounced him inimitable, as far as mere
personal attractions were concerned ; but sore mis-
trusting his eloquence and tact in a matter of this
kind, armed him with the very words he was to
say, and so launched him at the unguarded Philippa, whom he had descried taking weeds out of
the gravel with her little hoe. As for the old
gentleman, he went to his own room and dressed
for dinner ; and that gave him an opportunity of

peeping through the window at the courtship unob-
served. The young couple had the lawn all to
themselves ; for whilst Jonas and his son were
conversing, the gardener had taken an observation
of the sun's altitude through his two hands, and
had made it dinner time or noon. Philippa's first
notice of her suitor's approach was a loud sigh,
rather theatrical than dramatic : she turned, and
there was Silas in his best clothes.

" What, Silas," said she kindly, " are you really
going ? " and her heart smote her a little for her
pranks.

" Ay," said Silas, affecting the deepest dejection
(by paternal order), " I am going to leave thee and
home."

" Oh ! how I envy you," cried the candid
Philippa. " To be a man, and carve your own
way to fortune ! "

" Ay, mistress," said Silas, a little off his guard,
" 'tis very inviting, and I have been wearying for
the day. But now the time has come, it seems I
know not my own mind, for fortune beckons me to
London, but love holds me here."

" Love of what ? " inquired Philippa, incredu-
lously—" gudgeon fishing ? "

" No."

" Love of lying about yawning six days in the

week, and sitting and snoring in church the seventh?"

Silas received this summary of his pursuits with stolid patience.

"No," said he; "try again."

"Excuse me; I am better employed."

"Nay, then, I'll tell thee. 'Tis love of a beautiful girl."

"Ther's no such thing in the parish."

"Ay! but there is, with eyes in her head as black as sloes."

It was not worth Philippa's while to misunderstand him. After that, she blushed a very little, and then laughed.

"Oh, are you there, cousin?" said she. "If 'tis me you mean, waste not another minute, but go straightway to London."

"What, am I not good enough for you?"

"That," said Philippa, curtly enough, "is a question I care not to answer. Enough, you are not the man for me."

"And who is the man for you?"

"I'll tell you. He must be young—and brave—and good—and fair-haired—I'll never wed another crow like myself—and six feet high—and above all, one that hath made the grand tour, and will make it again with me; and then," said she, leaning on her hoe, and falling into a half reverie, "the fair lands we see together will be more beautiful to me by his discourse."

She looked so lovely with her beautiful eyes upturned in rapturous anticipation, that Silas began to warm to his work.

"If that is all," said he, "I am your man. We will travel the whole earth together, as soon as we have got the money. Philippa, look at this ring. Is't pretty, think you?" Philippa glanced at it out of the tail of her eye, and said, "Indeed, 'tis well enough."

"Will you have it, Philippa?"

The lovely black eyes looked greedy, but feminine delicacy was on its guard; so a cautious answer was the result.

"Ay, if you like—some other time. When you are not talking nonsense."

"Nay, now or never, mistress," said Silas, armed with paternal resolution. "Come," said he, catching hold of her hand, "let me put it on thy finger, and give me a kiss for't."

Philippa drew back and began to pant a little at that. "I'll take no ring of thee in that way. Let me be, I say: I'd rather die than wed thee."

"And I'd rather die than not wed thee:" and

he still pressed her hand, and threw his arm round her waist, and drew her to him by main force.

"Ah! let me go," she screamed. "You are a churl, and a ruffian, I'll not be used so."

She struggled violently, and when nothing else would do, she tore herself clear, with a fierce cry, all on fire with outraged modesty and repugnance, and gave him a savage blow on the bridge of the nose with her little hoe: it brought him to one knee; and, with that, she was gone like the wind, and flung herself, sobbing, into a garden seat, out of sight.

Now this severe blow was not dangerous, but it made the lover's nose bleed profusely. It bled a great deal as he kneeled, half stupified, and when he got up a little way, it bled freely again: he thought it would never leave off. His love was cooled for ever. All he cared about now was not spoiling his new clothes: so, after awhile, he walked away very slowly, with his nose projecting, like a gander's; and he was scarcely clear of the premises, when Joanna Philippa, who had peeped, and seen him off, came back to her occupation, looking as demure and innocent as any young lady you ever saw. She was rather dismayed though when she found the grass incarnadined, and the gardener's turf-cutter literally drenched with blood.

While she was contemplating this grim sight,
and wishing she had not hit so hard, the old man
came at her all of a sudden, white with rage.
" Ay, look at your work, you monster," he cried,
" and the poor boy leaving us for good. You have
killed him, or nearly, and I'll trounce you for it."
He griped her by the arm, and raised his cane over
her head.

She was terrified, and cried for mercy. "Oh,
uncle, I did not mean. Oh, pray don't kill me !
don't kill me ! "

He did not mean to kill her, nor even hurt her ;
but, in his paternal rage, he struck her a great
many times about her petticoats, which made a
great noise. She screamed all the time ; only at
first it was " don't kill me ! " and then, " don't
degrade me!"

" There," said he, " let that teach thee not to
be so ready with thy hands, thou barbarous, ungrateful jade ! "

But now she confronted him, in silence, with a
face as white as death, and eyes that glared, and
her black brows that looked terrible by the con-
trast with her ashy cheek, a child no more, but
a beautiful woman outraged. She said nothing,
but gave him that one tremendous look, then fled,
with a cry of shame and anguish. She flew to

the cart-house, took out her jewels, and, in three minutes, she was gone. But nobody knew: for her cunning was equal to her resolution. She slipped into a wood that adjoined Mr. Hanway's premises, and going through that, got on the other side of a hedge, and so upon a road that led to London; but not by the great coach road, else Silas must have seen her from the coach.

She entered the city at ten that evening, and slept at an inn.

Next morning she sold one of her rings, and took a modest lodging, and bought some stuffs, and set to work to make a suit such as she saw worn by tradesmen's daughters of the better sort. All her fear was, to be captured, and her mother's jewels taken from her. They were all her fortune, she thought; and, besides, she loved them.

One day, just before the new clothes were ready, and being weary of confinement, she strolled abroad, and seeing a chocolate house, whipped on her mask, and entered it. While she was sipping her chocolate, a spark handed her the *Daily Post*, with a low bow, by way of preliminary to making her acquaintance. She thanked him so modestly, he hesitated; and let her read the paper in peace. It was a miserable sheet, with very little in it; but there was a curious advertisement:—

"*April* 26.—Lost, or mislaid, one pair large brilliant earrings, with drops of the first water; one diamond cross; three large bars for the breast (diamonds of the first water); large pearl necklace; brooch of sapphire and brilliants; one large ruby ring; one emerald and brilliants; one locket, set with amethyst and rose diamonds. If offered to be sold, pawned, or valued, pray stop 'em (*sic*) and the PARTY, especially if a young lady; and give notice to Mr. Drummond, goldsmith, at Charing Cross, and you shall receive 200 guineas reward."

The paper almost fell from her hands, at first: yet, with the fine defensive cunning of her sex, she sipped her chocolate quite slowly, feeling very cold all the time; and then she went home.

The advertisement was very well worded for others; but falling, unluckily, into her hands, it disquieted as well as terrified her. "My jewels!" said she: "not me. He means to steal them. Well, he shall never see them, nor me, again."

She carried her new dress to a shop that sold masquerade dresses, and she easily exchanged it for a seaman's holiday dress, a merchant captain's or mate's. She brought it home in a bundle. She purchased a trunk, and paid her landlady, and then she had only a crown left and her jewels.

She took a coach, it being now dark, and had

the hardihood to change her clothes in the coach. The seafaring man's dress fitted her so loosely, she had no trouble. The moment she had got into it, her native courage revived, and she was ready to dance for joy. "Now find your young gentle-woman, and her jewels," said she. "Nay, but I'll put the sea between us rather." She had noticed some clean looking lodgings, so she made the coachman stop there. When he let her out, he started at the metamorphosis; but she put her finger to her lips, and said, "Only a masquerading folly," and gave him her last shilling.

The landlady received the handsome young mate, all smiles, and they soon came to terms. In the morning she melted a jewel, and paid the landlady a week in advance. Then she took out her female costume, and pawned it. She pur-chased shirts, and good stockings of wool and cotton; and marched about with a little hanger by her side, but was mighty civil, not feeling desirous to draw the said hanger. She always gave a fine gentleman the wall.

She now asked the prices of jewels at many places; and, hearing of a good ship bound for America, she sold a ring, called herself a mer-chant's son, dressed accordingly, and sailed, a passenger, to Boston, in the bay of Massachusetts.

G

Her first intention was to be a woman again, as soon as she got there. But there was what they called in those days " a spirit " on board the ship, that is to say, a gasconading agent, working for the planters; he told her such a tale about the American colonies, and how any man could dig a fortune there, that she agreed to indent as servant and book-keeper, and see whether it would suit her; she thought it was no use being idle in man's clothes; indeed, she had too much energy. She was easily led into signing an indenture, the full effect of which she did not comprehend : yet she was sharp enough to read the paper, and bargain that she was to do no work, but keeping accounts and overlooking labourers, and this the agent wrote in, sooner than lose the prettiest young fellow he had ever seen : and, to make a long story short, a rich planter from Delaware acquired this prize, and carried her off to a first-rate farm near Willingtown.

There she remained a year, affording perfect satisfaction to her employer; reading every book she could lay hold of, taking in knowledge at every pore, flattering, and so winning the women, and watching the men like a very cat, to know their minds. This study amused her greatly.

She left the seeds of trouble behind her. At

seven o'clock that very evening she ran away, Mr. Hanway's gardener, whose cottage was on the premises, took in his turf-cutter, and showed it to his wife, all bloody. He laughed, and said, "Why, one would think they had been a pig-killing, with this here."

His wife, instead of laughing, gave a scream, and then fell a trembling. "Oh, dear!" said she, "we shall hear more of this." Then she told him she had heard some poor creature crying for mercy, and saying, "Oh! don't kill me! don't kill me!" and, after that, she had heard heavy blows. "Oh, John!" said she, "put it away from me, for I do feel sick at sight on't." So he went and put the turf-cutter away in the tool-house, just as it was. When he came back, he asked her if she knew whose voice it was that had cried for mercy.

"How can I tell, all that way off?" said she. "'Twas a woman's voice, for certain: alack! ask me not, John, I'm afeard of my own thoughts."

"Well, keep them to thyself, then: we have got a good place. Least said is soonest mended."

Next morning the news was that Joanna had run away. The gardener told his wife at breakfast. She shook her head. "Run away, poor thing! She'll never run no more. She'll never be seen no more, without you do find her, digging about."

"Hush !" said the man. "Hold thy tongue, we have eaten his bread a many years."

"I shall never bear the sight of him again, I tell thee."

"Well, keep out of his sight, then; he won't come after thee, I trow: but if ye go hanging of him, with your tongue, and losing me a good place, I shall twist thy neck, sweetheart, and then there will be a pair hung, instead of one."

These dark suspicions smouldered for many months. Mr. Hanway went to Mr. Chester, and told him the girl was a thief, and had run away with the jewels.

"A thief! Master Hanway?" said the other, coldly. "The jewels were her mother's, and coming to her."

"Ay, but she knew not that," said the old man, who was bitterly incensed against her. Not a word did he say to Thomas Chester about either of the violent scenes in the garden. Mr. Chester advised him to advertise, and drew the advertisement for him.

Months rolled on: all hopes of seeing Joanna again oozed away: both trustees were unhappy about it, and on ill terms; for Hanway thought his allowance ought to go on; but Chester ridiculed the idea: and so it stopped; since money could only be drawn under both signatures.

Presently there arose in the village a vague, horrid whisper of "foul play." It reached Lawyer Chester. He tried to trace it: it was impalpable at first; like a sudden smell of carrion. But this keen lawyer tracked it, and tracked it, and discovered that an old blind man, walking in his garden, which adjoined Mr. Hanway's, had heard a voice cry, "Oh, uncle! don't kill me! don't kill me!" and then several heavy blows. He learned, too, that the gardener's wife had lately thrown out mysterious hints, as to what would become of some people, if she were to tell all she knew. Then Mr. Chester began to fear a crime had been committed: only he could see no motive. But murders are not always motived: the passions slay, as well as the interests. Being a just man, and feeling that his dislike to Hanway might prejudice him, he carried his notes to a neighbouring justice, and left the matter in his hands.

This magistrate was young, and zealous: he had seen Joanna riding across country, and admired her: he went into the matter a little too much like a Crown solicitor.

Mr. Hanway was summoned to London, to

attend his son Silas, who had caught a violent fever. The magistrate in question heard of his absence, and took that opportunity to call on the gardener. He found the wife alone, and by coaxing and threatening soon got her story out of her. He took possession of the turf-cutter, which tool she and the gardener had avoided with horror ever since; and the sight of it, added to the other evidence, gave him a shock, and convinced him he saw before him the proofs of a bloody murder.

Everything was therefore prepared for the arrest of Mr. Hanway, on his return. But that return was delayed by a truly pitiable cause. Silas was insensible when his father came; and died a few hours after. The desolate father had a shell made for the remains, and brought them down to Colebrook. The sad burden was but just taken into the hall, when the officers of justice, who had rigorous orders, arrested the bereaved father, on a charge of murder.

He stared at them stupidly, and said, " Are ye mad ? "

They told him no : the evidence was strong.

" Is it so ? " said he, languidly. " Well, let me bury my child ; and I'll go to the gallows, or where you will : I have nought left to live for."

Then the officers of justice were puzzled what to

do. However, as it happened, the magistrate him-self came up; and, when he heard, he directed them to let the funeral proceed: but be careful the mourner did not escape.

The grave was already dug, and the clergyman waiting: so poor Silas was buried, attended by the whole parish, in strange silence, for their horror of the murderer was checked by their pity for the desolate father, to whom the charge of murder was, at that heavy hour, a feather-stroke, compared with his bereavement.

He went home alone: the officers kept a little aloof from him, and so did the people. He was examined in his own house, and confronted with the witnesses: the turf-cutter was also produced.

He told the simple truth: not a soul believed it: he was committed for trial, and a reward of fifty pounds offered to whoever should find the corpus delictæ, which was the one link in the evidence wanting.

Months passed on, and no corpus delictæ. At last some bones were found in a peat heath hard by, and brought to the justice, followed by a crowd.

"She is found! She is found!" was the cry. "The old rogue will be hanged now." And all day folk dropped in to see the bones of poor

Joanna. The parson and Mr. Chester, who were good friends, went together. Says the parson, "I know these bones well—— "

" There ! there ! " was the cry : " Parson can swear to 'em, that is enow."

" —— I know them," continued the parson, calmly, "for the bones of the moose deer, which ran in these parts, four thousand years ago. I do bid against the Crown for these. I will give five shillings ; and ten for the horns."

That very evening two young men came to the vicarage and told the maid, with a sheepish look, they had brought parson the gentlewoman's horns. They had dug a little farther.

But this did not shake the general impression that a foul murder had been done and artfully concealed. Mr. Chester, however, who had started the inquiry, now felt uneasy in his mind at what he had done : he called on Mr. Hanway, in prison, and found him piteously depressed. Mr. Hanway asked his forgiveness, if ever he had offended him.

" Nay, sir," said Chester, " I did never affect you much, nor you me ; but, in truth, you never wronged me, that I know of ; and seeing you in this plight, I blame myself, and would serve you. Come, courage, man. If she is alive, there is a way to find her."

" Would to God I knew that way."

" Advertise for her. Let her know your trouble, and that she is an heiress. That will be against the letter of her father's wish ; but not the spirit. Write the advertisement yourself, and I will see it sent abroad."

Then Hanway plucked up a little heart, and wrote a humble, touching advertisement, describing his peril. Mr. Chester took it, and, having read it, was fain to wipe a tear from his eye, and straightway dropped the judicial character, and shut his eyes to the evidence, and, resuming old habits, retained himself solicitor for the defendant. In that self-assumed character, he spared not his own purse, but scattered the advertisements far and wide, not in England only, but Scotland, Ireland, and every foreign country that spoke the English tongue.

CHAPTER IV

JAMES ANNESLEY remained in prison, awaiting his
sentence. He was not without hope ; but his fear
was greater : and this fear soon rose to agony ;
for the unhappy pair, whose kindness had brought
him to this, were led out to receive the first part of
their sentence within sight of the grated windows
of his cell. They had to sit under the gallows one
hour, with a rope round their necks, and then
received, the lover forty lashes, the woman thirty,
and the servant twenty-one, all on their bare backs,
and *well laid on.* Their groans and shrieks rent
the air, and froze James Annesley to the bone, for
he looked for his own turn to come next, and
behind the cutting lash frowned the grim prison.

A week passed, and a spark of hope was re-
viving, when one morning the jailor and another
officer came, and told him he must go with them.
His knees failed him, he groaned, and lay back
almost insensible. They gave him a drop of

brandy, and, seeing his mistake, told him to pluck up courage. " You are to be exposed every market-day, and not to be whipped, till somebody in Chester shall prove you were in the town, before you came in a prisoner."

He was so exposed every market-day for a month : a large paper was pinned on his breast, inviting all good citizens to testify what they knew of him.

On the fourth market-day, casting his eyes wistfully round, who should he see but Drummond : he had come all that way to buy horses, and was so intent on business that he noticed nothing else. James made signs to him, in vain ; he called to him ; he did everything to attract this cruel master's attention, whom he had run from. At last a man went for him to Drummond, and brought him up. Drummond started at first, then surveyed him with a cruel countenance. " What would you of me, young man ? "

" Do but take me home, and I will serve you faithfully."

Drummond, to torment him, turned on his heel, without a word. However, he went to the justices, and claimed him ; showed, by an entry in his pocket-book, when he ran away, and from what place, and knocked the indictment to atoms. In

twenty-four hours, James Annesley was riding
home at Drummond's back. When he got him
home, Drummond sued him for penalties and
damages: the penalty, five days for every day's
absence, came to a year; but the damages being
paid in service, came to two years and a half.

Upon this decision, James Annesley began to
fret, and pine away; and Drummond, who had
lost one or two that way, sold him to Jedediah
Surefoot, a flourishing planter, near Willingtown,
in Delaware. This was a beautiful place, and had
an extraordinary story, which was then fresh in
men's minds. William Shipley, a Leicestershire
man, was settled at Ridley, with his second wife,
Elizabeth Levis, of Springfield, in the county
Chester. She was a distinguished minister in the
Society of "Friends," and a remarkable woman.
Soon after her marriage, she dreamed a dream.
She was riding through a wild country, on what
errand she knew not; and mounted a lofty hill.
From this hill burst on her eyes a landscape of
surpassing beauty; a wide valley, green with
sloping lawns, studded with clumps of trees, and
settler's cabins. The sun streamed golden through
partial clearings made by the axe; even now it
tinkled unseen: and broad rivers ran, and little
brooks sparkled silver, and meandered to the

extreme limits of vision. She sat entranced upon her horse, and was speechless awhile with delight. Then she asked her guide what country this was.

"Elizabeth," said he, "it is thy home."

"Nay," said she, "my earthly home is Ridley."

"Not so," said he. "This sweet place cries out for thee, and for the Word. Submit thyself, then, to the will of Heaven, and come hither; so shalt thou do much good to the place and the people; and blessings shall be on thy house, and on thy labours in the Lord."

Elizabeth told this dream to her husband, with all the warmth and freshness in the world; and he made this sublime answer, "We are doing pretty well here," and the subject dropped.

Full three years afterwards, Elizabeth Shipley was invited to a meeting of Friends, between the Delaware and Chesapeake bays.

She rode alone, and without fear, till she came to the Brandywine river, and then, though the water was low, she took a guide: he led her some distance to "the old ford," and she got through, and went up the hill, by "the King's Road." At the top of the hill she checked her horse, and uttered a cry of amazement and delight; for lo, there was the paradise of her dream before her, ay, down to the minutest feature of the landscape, and the axe that tinkled unseen. She sat, like a statue, on her horse, just as she had done in her dream.

After this, she constantly entreated William Shipley to ride with her and see the lovely place. He thought it a waste of time : did not believe in dreams, though he durst not say so. So, at last, she said to him, "William, settle all thou hast in Ridley on thy children by thy first wife. I and mine will stand or fall by the place the Lord doth call me to."

The prophetess knew her lord and master; he came with her directly, to see Willingtown, and it struck him all of a heap. He examined it nearer, and found it was seated between the finger and thumb of two rivers, one impetuous, and admirable for turning mills, the other tidal, and navigable to the sea. "Why, Elizabeth," said he, "a man might grind his corn here with one hand, and ship it with t'other."

So, what with her faith in Power Divine, and his in Water Power, the Shipleys settled at Willingtown, now called Wilmington, and gave that rising place a wonderful impulse. William Shipley bought land between the streams, and set up mill and factory. Elizabeth became a shining light, and drew the cream of the Quakers thither, and even poor James Annesley profited a little by her virtues; for she preached and practised humanity to slaves, and Dame Surefoot, a simple motherly woman, was her pupil, though her senior; so there was no starving of slaves, nor frolicsome flagellation, on Surefoot's farm. Servitude was robbed of its fangs—though nothing could remove its sting—in the circle of which that pious woman was the centre.

But the beauty of the place, and the milder servitude, came too late for poor James Annesley. The long persecution of fortune, the almost unintermittent sufferings of his soul and body, had broken his spirit, and clouded his youth. He was worn out, dejected, hopeless. His mind might be compared to a ship, which has been so tossed, baffled, and battered, by storm upon storm, that at last it leaks, and sinks quietly in the golden ripple and placid sunlight of a calm.

He did his work well enough, but in dogged silence, and nothing ever came from him but sighs: his face was handsome, but full of misery. Dame Surefoot noticed this, after a time, and asked him one day what was the matter. "Nothing, madam," said he, "thank you." "Then why so sad? Most servants are glad to come to us from Drummond."

"And so ought I to be, madam. I will try to

be more cheerful. But three years more!" And
he groaned.

"What is three years?." said Mrs. Surefoot.
"Alas! young man, 'twill pass like a shadow.
You have got this new trouble, the vapours, with
keeping too much alone. I shall find you a companion; for you are a civil spoken young man."

So, that very evening, she went to her favourite—
when could any woman govern without one?—
"Philip," said she, "prithee speak to this servant,
James, and be good to him. He is well to look at,
and no idler; but so eaten up with sadness."

"Mayhap he is in love," said Philip. "I'll soon
find what ails him, mother."

This Philip was a black-eyed youth, as sharp as
a needle, who kept all the accounts, and sometimes
rode on business. He flattered the mistress finely,
and had got the length of her shoe, as the saying
is. The master valued him on other grounds: he
was saucy, but honest, and kept the books, though
rather complicated, with marvellous precision and
neatness. Thus valued on both sides, Philip, who
by-the-by was older than he looked, gave himself
considerable airs: and it was in rather a con-
descending tone he danced up to James Annesley,
and invited him to leave off sighing, and walk with
him into the town of Willingtown.

" Thank you, sir," said James, " but I prefer to meditate."

" To mope, you mean. 'Tis the worst thing for you : and I hate to walk alone. So be not churlish now. Why, man, we are countrymen."

" Sir, I shall be sorry company."

" But I shall be merry company. So come on."

" Well, if I must," said James, and went with him, reluctantly.

Master Philip chattered away for both, and stole a glance at his companion now and then. Young Annesley's replies were civil, but reserved. " You are no mill-clack," said Philip, ironically. " I am not," said James, humbly.

Philip carried an enormous basket. He had to bring groceries home, and salt, and medicinal herbs from Mrs. Dean, the Dutch widow; and coarse sugar, and a jar of vinegar. When all these were on board, the basket was very heavy, and James said, " I will carry that."

" Nay," said Philip, pretending to resist. " I carried it hither, and I will carry it home."

" That you shall not," said James, and laid hold of it, and fairly wrenched it from him.

" You are a rude bear," said Philip. " You have hurt my thumb."

" Where ?" asked James, catching at it to see.

H

" Somewhere," said Philip, and whipped it behind his back.

" Well, I am sorry for that," replied James. " I am much older than you, and stronger, and the least I could do was to carry your burden, since you put up with my dull company."

" Speak not to me. I'll never speak to you again, bear."

" And what else am I good for now, but to carry burdens ? "

" Oh, say not that, James. Alas ! why are you so sad ? You are young, you are well-looking—rather. What beautiful hair you have got ! I declare I did never see such hair : 'tis like silk. I'd never despond, if I had such hair as that, instead of my black stuff. You should flatter the women ; that is the way to get forward. Look at me. I get my own way in everything, and that is my strategy. Tell me, James, I won't tell a soul—Are you in love ? "

" No."

" But have you been ? "

" Never. I was but a boy when I was kidnapped, and sent over here ; and my heart has always been too heavy for those idle fancies."

" What, did you not come here of your good will ? "

" Consent to be a slave! who would be so
base?"

James said this with a certain majesty that
quelled his merry companion for a moment. He
drew instinctively a little farther off, and walked,
with thoughtful downcast eyes. Nor did he say
much more, in fact, but brooded over what his
companion had said. However, he chattered away
fast enough to Mrs. Surefoot, and they agreed that
James was not a sullen churl, but a fine, melancholy, interesting young man. Then they fell into
speculations as to why he had been kidnapped and
sent out. This wise conversation was uttered
within hearing of Maria Surefoot, a demure,
romantic girl of seventeen. She drank in every
word, but said nothing; only, thenceforth, James
became an object of vast curiosity and interest to
her.

One day that some very heavy work in loading
of timber was done near the house, James was
very zealous and active; and so athletic, that
Philip drew Mrs. Surefoot's attention to his
prowess.

"Yes, in truth," said the worthy dame. "Here,
Maria, run you and get him a can of wine, and
take it to him; he has earned it right well."

Maria soon appeared with the can, and went to

James : he was now seated on a bank, in sight, and, the brief stimulus of labour over, had fallen into his usual pensive state.

The girl approached him timidly and softly, and stood looking at him a considerable time. "Is she afraid to speak to him?" said Philip, pettishly.

"What should she be afraid of?" said Mrs. Surefoot.

The girl spoke to James, and he instantly rose, and removed his cap. She held him out the wine, blushing like a rose, and said, "Prithee, drink this; my mother sends it."

"I wish her every blessing," said James, piously; "and the same to you, Mistress Maria."

"You cannot wish me better than I wish you, James," murmured the girl, all in a flutter. "I have heard about you, and, if there is anything in the world I can do—for I pity you with all my heart." She turned, and went away in a tremor and confusion which did not escape the keen grey eyes of Master Philip. Dame Surefoot was older; so perhaps her eye could not seize all the minutiæ by which a girl's very body indicates when love has seized her.

The coast was no sooner clear than Philip ran out, and invited James into his office: "It is cooler there," said he.

"The girl approached him timidly and softly."—*Page* 100.

As soon as ever he got James into his office, he said, sharply, "What did Mistress Maria say to you?"

"I could not say, I paid no attention."

"I like not that young gentlewoman : she is a forward minx."

"Is she? You know best. You have been here longest. How cool it is here; and you have flowers in your window. What a luxurious boy! And what a many books!"

"Yes, I am the only one that reads much here. So our dame lets me have all the library. Are you fond of learning?"

"I love it, of all things. But, alas! I have been so ill brought up, and, whenever I got to my books, some cruelty or other came and took me from them. It is my grief and my shame that I, a gentleman's son, have the education of a porter."

"What, then," said Philip, "tell me, if I were to teach you, would that make you happier, and to leave off sighing so?"

"Indeed, I think it would. I burn with desire of instruction."

"Well, then, I will give you a lesson every evening. Then you will be out of the way of all these forward minxes."

"I trouble not my head about them. I would

liever be at the books with you. Let us begin at once."

Then Philip gave James a book to read, and he read it, but badly: gave him a letter to write, and he wrote it vilely.

"Come," said Philip, with a curious air of satisfaction, "I have a year's work before me, with thee."

He taught James, every evening after work, with a patience and an untiring amiability, that he had not shown in conversation, and James ploughed at it with all his heart, and was pathetically docile and grateful. Out of this arose, by degrees, a tender friendship, and loyal partisanship, that belongs to youth: and so, one day, being now such friends, Philip urged him by their friendship to tell him his whole story. He hesitated. "Philip," said he, "I never told it yet, but some ill luck did follow straight. No matter; sit by me, my one friend, and I'll tell it thee; ay, ever since I was four years old."

Then he told his story, but broke down once or twice; then went manfully on, the more so that, while he was telling it, a brown but shapely hand stole into his, and was seldom idle, but ever speaking as variously as a voice, with its gentle pressure of sympathy, and sudden grasps at danger: but when he came to his being kidnapped and swooning dead away in the ship, it trembled, and Philip turned his head away, and never looked towards him again, and by then he was flung into gaol and cast for death, the narrator discovered that Philip was crying.

"Oh, Philip!" said he, "do not you cry. Ah! how many a time I have cried over it all: but now my eyes are dry. Sweet Philip! how kind you are to cry for me. Ah, miserable me!" and, all of a sudden, Philip's tears drew forth his own once more, the first he had shed for years. They did him a world of good. "Oh, my dear Philip!" he cried, "you have saved me from despair: a cloud clears from my mind. Whilst I have one friend who will shed a tear for me, it were ungrateful to despair:" and he took Philip in his arms, and was going to kiss him heartily: but the boy panted, and put up both his hands, and said, "No, no! I am choking. Prithee, go get me a cup of wine."

James went accordingly, and the first person he saw was Mistress Maria; he asked her to oblige him with a cup of wine.

"Ay, that I will, James," said she, tenderly, and brought it him in a moment, and told him she must have the pleasure of seeing him drink.

" I will taste it, madam," said he ; " but, indeed, 'tis for Philip. He is not well."

" For Philip ! " said she disdainfully. " I hope the next time 'twill be for yourself."

James ran with the cup to Philip. Philip was not to be found.

" Was ever such a boy ? " said James. However, he left the cup of wine on the table : and the early negroes picked up that worm, as the saying is.

Next evening he went for his lesson, as usual. Philip was busy over a ledger, and only noticed him with a supercilious nod.

" Philip," said he, " I brought you the wine as fast as I could."

Philip never looked off his ledger. " You brought it so fast that I was gone to bed. You were too busy with Mistress Maria, to think of me, I trow."

" Nay, I did stay not two minutes with her."

" There—there—there—I thought as much ; you *were* with her."

" Foolish boy, have I the key of the cellar ! I asked the first I met."

" Well, I guessed she was the butler : so I did not drink a drop. Not a drop, sir."

" I am sorry for that."

" No, you are not."

" Yes, I am, Philip."

" Do not contradict *me*. I am very angry with you. You made me cry with your romance—that I do not believe a word of. Do not contradict *me*. —And I am not so fond of crying as you are; it makes me ill: and so now I'll just give you a piece of advice; for I see everything from this window; my nose may be in my ledger; but my eye is on you all; so tremble! I tell thee young women are the artfullest creatures: they are not like men, who get grey and cunning; girls are born artful: and two or three of these girls are setting their caps at you, after their manner. There's that Indian girl, Turquoise, she makes no disguise, being a savage; she lets all the world see she is ready to eat you up. Then there's the master's niece, great fat thing; she comes here six times for once she is wanted, and sits watching you, with her great grey eyes, like a cat watches for a mouse: she will catch you too, some day, if you take not the better heed: and then there's Mistress Maria, that is the worst of them all, because she is always here, and has so many opportunities. She is ever throwing herself in your way."

"Nay, nay," said James.

"Do you not meet her, in lonely places, whenever you take your walks without me?"

" Sometimes ; by pure chance."

" Chance ! foolish man : that shows how little you are fit to cope with them."

" Very well, Philip," said James : " since you give me the benefit of your age and experience, I'll give *you* a piece of advice. Do not you trouble about me ; for I am not in love with any young woman, and never was. What I love is the liberty I have lost, and the country I have been banished from. Love is not for a slave. If ever I get home again, I may fall in love ; but I think it will be a dark woman : they have always been my best friends. So never you mind me. 'Tis you that are in danger from those girls, not I."

" Me ! ha ! ha ! "

" Ay ! why your head is full of them. I never knew a boy of your age talk so much about women, nor think so much about them."

" Do I talk as if I love them ? "

" No ; but you do study them ; and abuse them beyond reason : and those are the men that are caught the first, I've heard."

" Well, this is idle chat. Come, sit down, and I'll give you your lesson, James. Now then. How dark is your sweetheart to be ? Copper, like Turquoise ; or lamp-black, like Chloe ? "

" Thank you, Philip. I prefer a white skin.

But her hair, and her eyebrows, and her eyes, I care not if they are as dark as—— "

" The devil's," suggested Philip.

" Nay, yours will be dark enough for me. They are the blackest ever I saw—long life to 'em."

Philip coloured high, with pleasure ; and then said, with arrogance, " Come, sir, this is idle chat. Let us to something more profitable, if you please."

The snubbed scholar submitted with a smile. He was getting used to Master Philip's caprices ; they amused him.

James Annesley's spirits improved ; his fine eyes began to beam at times, and colour to come into his cheek.

Mistress Maria, on the contrary, began to sicken and pine ; and the vigilant Philip determined to be her doctor, and prescribe her change of air. One morning he asked an interview with the master and mistress : they were breakfasting in the parlour. Philip was admitted.

Now Jedediah Surefoot was not like his wife, who treated her servants as her children ; he was humane, but very short with them ; Philip stood in awe of him, and had prepared a little speech beforehand. " Master," said he, " I think a good servant should tell his employer, in time, if he sees anything going on that might take an ill turn : so I am come to tell you something."

" Then why not tell it at once ? " said Jedediah.

" Nay, sir, only for fear you should be hasty, and blame him who is guiltless in the matter. The truth is, master, and I hope you will forgive me, and set it down to my zeal and duty, if I do make so free, but it is about my young mistress."

" Ay," said Jedediah, frowning, "and what canst thou have to say about her ? "

" She is sick, sir; and will be while she bides here."

" Why, the air is wholesome enough. I never was better in my life than I am here."

" 'Tis not the air that is amiss, sir, saving your presence. 'Tis the mind."

" Speak plainer, thou jackanapes, if thou hast ought to say at all."

" Nay, then : Mistress Maria hath cast her eyes on James Annesley, and 'tis for him she is love-sick. Would you cure her 'tis but to send her elsewhere for a year. Change, and the sight of other men, will soon restore her."

Jedediah was taken all aback by this revelation. " Patience," said he, " can this be so ? "

" Nay, Jedediah," said she, "I hope not : but

Philip is not one that lies. Alas! what is to be done?"

"The first thing to be done is to know the truth."

He called a negro, and bade him clear the room, and bring an easy chair into it. This done, he sent the negro to his daughter's room, and ordered her to come and sit in his arm-chair by the fire : when he heard her step on the stairs, he turned his wife and Philip out by another door (for the room had two), and left that door ajar. "Now bide you there," said he, "and still as mice."

He then went and ordered James Annesley to bring in billets of wood and fill the great basket in the parlour. This done, he stole back on tip-toe to his wife and Philip, and shook his fist at them, to keep their uneasy tongues quiet. They were on thorns, both of them, the mother for her daughter, and Philip for his friend. "Master," he whispered, "think what you do. James is a good young man. He will never be so unfaithful as to seek her out and offer love to her; but seeing her all alone, and sick for love of him, 'tis too much for flesh and blood. Why, 'tis like the devil, to tempt a weak mortal so."

"Hold thy tongue, jackanapes," was the stern reply.

"Nay, but I cannot. This goes against my conscience. Do as you will, sir, but I wash my hands on't." And he was walking off, with dignity.

A rude hand was laid on his collar, and Jedediah, in a stern whisper, said, "Would'st go and tell thy friend James, and put him on his guard? Budge but one inch, and I'll have thee whipped, and soundly, the first this three years."

Then Philip turned very pale, and began to shake like a leaf. His quick spirit saw the terrible mistake he had made, and all the possible consequences flashed on him at once. What more likely than that James should commit a folly in an unguarded moment; and then the stern old man would punish him; and oh, agony! he would have been the traitor to betray his unfortunate friend; ay, and that friend would know it. Such was the distress this cost him, that beads of perspiration rose on his brow though his body was cold all over.

And the miserable suspense was so long: it seemed an age before they heard James come into the room and put down his heavy basket of wood; and then the time he was placing the billets in the large basket: and all passed in silence till the billets were placed.

At last a soft female voice said, "Thank you, James; you are very good."

"Nay, madam," James was heard to say, "'tis little to do for you, and you in sickness; but I hope you are better, Mistress Maria."

"No, James," sighed the young girl, "and never shall be, till you are my doctor."

"I, madam!" said James, "why, I have no skill."

"'Tis not the skill, but the will that lacketh. You dull, insensible man, see you not 'tis your unkindness that is killing me? Nay, dissemble no more. Oh! that I could hate thee as I ought, for slighting my affection. Alas! James, what is it in me that displeases you? I am young; they say I am fair; am I not better worth thy love than that Indian girl, that is for ever hanging about thee, and so I hate her. Speak to me, James, for mercy's sake; do not make me woo thee in vain, and sue where I have a right to command. Oh, how I shall hate you now, if you are ungrateful. Hate you, alas! I cannot: thou hast bewitched me. I love thee to distraction; for pity's sake, speak to me."

James was much troubled and abashed. "Madam," said he, "for Heaven's sake bethink you. A slave is not a thing to love, nor to be loved. You are young, you are lovely; and I wonder that I can be so much your friend as to affront you. But you spoke of gratitude: do I owe none to your good mother, who has softened my slavery? What would her feelings be, and your father's, too, were I to be a traitor, and rob them of their only child? No, madam, I have not the excuse of passion; and I will not be a villain in cold blood."

"My parents! Hypocrite! You are a coward, and dare not love above you. Wretch, I hate the sight of you. Begone to your Indian."

"Nay," said James, "I'll begone to my good Philip. He is my truest friend."

"Ah! and tell him how I have disgraced myself."

"Not me; and, madam, I will prove to you I was born a gentleman."

"Leave me, sir," said the girl more gently. He bowed and left her.

"James!—James!—James! Come back. You might say you do not hate me. You might tell me you are sorry for me."

"I am, madam. I pity you from my soul."

"Pity me? I scorn your pity. You must choose between love or hate."

"I will never love you, madam, if I can help it; and I will never hate you, after what you have said to me—till you give me cause."

So ended this strange interview. James retired,

with a respectful bow; and the young lady, as soon as he was gone, had a cruel fit of sobbing.

Philip's face was now radiant with unhoped-for triumph, and poor Mrs. Surefoot's red with maternal shame, and the tears streaming. As for Jedediah, he looked terribly disturbed and gloomy. "Not one word of this, to any soul that breathes: that is my order," said he. "If you disobey me, look to it."

Then Philip urged the temporary retirement of Mistress Maria. The good woman, who was like butter in Philip's hands, sided with him. Not so Jedediah. "Banish my daughter for a servant!" said he. "Think of some other way."

"May I?" said she. "Then, sweetheart, if I might have my will, I'd part them as becomes us. 'Twas rare fidelity and modesty. Oh, Jedediah! I know what Mistress Shipley would say: Give the young man his liberty, that pines for it, and hath earned it of us by his good deed."

"Now you talk sense," said Jedediah; "I will think on't."

Then Mrs. Surefoot went, all in a hurry, and told Mrs. Shipley her trouble, and Mrs. Shipley gave her religious comfort and advice, and highly approved Jedediah's giving James his liberty. "'Tis the least he can do," said she, "and a new

suit to boot. If the young man is willing to try
his fortune in these parts, I will give him an axe
and a hoe, and a meal a day for three months, and
William shall let him a few acres of wood for
nothing the first year, and thereafter for a payment in kind. We have planted many a poor
man so, that now doth well enow."

But whilst Mrs. Surefoot was in Wilmington,
one McCarthy, a planter in the same district, and
a thorough trader in all lawful articles, flesh and
blood included, came in and found Jedediah
strangely ruffled for one of his placid sect.
McCarthy wanted to sell him some produce, but
Jedediah answered fretfully, " Another day, friend :
I am in sore trouble : the minx ! the Jezebel ! My
peace is disturbed. My very stomach upset."

" Then do a bit of trading," said McCarthy,
" that will comfort you : there is nothing like it.
Now, what shall it be ? Have you got any servants to sell, or sheep ? "

" No," said Jedediah : then suddenly replied,
" Hum ! I've only one I can part with, and he's a
pearl."

" A pearl ! Don't try that on me, man. You
aint the man to part with the pearl first, and keep
the oyster shells."

" Family reasons, neighbour. 'Tis James Annesley. I cannot part with him for less than three hundred dollars. 'Twould be a sin.''

"Three hundred dollars! Oh, *Je*-rusalem!''

"Neighbour," said Jedediah, "prithee, in thy trading, make not so free with that sacred city, where is neither buying nor selling."

"Then I'll keep out of it as long as I can," said candid McCarthy. "I'll give one hundred and fifty dollars for him."

"I can't take that. 'Twere a sin."

McCarthy put on a look of alarm. "Oh, if you are going to talk religion, while you are doing business, you'll have the skin off my back;" and he beat a feigned retreat.

Jedediah was alarmed. "Stay," said he, "thou man of haste—and Belial."

"Then take a fair offer, thou man of pious words and cruel hard bargains."

The results may be divined. They came to terms for one hundred and seventy-five dollars; the money to be paid and the servant taken in one week. For Jedediah gave no credit, and McCarthy, though wealthy, had not the cash in his pocket, but was about to receive a large sum. This stroke of business did not transpire that day; but next morning Mrs. Surefoot carried it to Philip, with a deluge of feeble regrets.

Philip was struck dumb by this sudden blow: for a long time he was too much surprised and shocked to comment on Jedediah's conduct and character. So Mrs. Surefoot babbled on uninterrupted. "What will Dame Shipley say? She will discourse on it till I shall wish I had ne'er been born. I am a miserable woman. The world is too hard for *me*. But, alas! I'm a wife, and sworn to obedience; and he is a good husband, and a good man; but what he hath bought for money that he never will give for naught; the Lord forgive him, and me, for not knowing how to manage him as Elizabeth does her good man, for all he is as hard as flint by nature."

Philip repaid her twaddle with a swift glance of scorn, then asked her, with affected composure, when McCarthy was to be expected. She told him in five days, without fail, and meantime Maria was to keep her chamber.

Soon after this Philip fell ill, and kept his bedroom. Mrs. Surefoot visited him often, and sent James to Katey Dean for simples. Philip got worse, and yet insisted on doing his work. At his request a couch was sent up to his little room, and he lay on his back and still kept the accounts, though groaning with pain. James became very anxious, and was always running up to see how he was, and sat gazing at his pale face piteously, and often implored him to say if there was anything he could do for him. Generally, Philip answered rather pettishly, and told James not to come there wasting his time. But one day, seeing James gazing at him with the tear in his eye, and a look of wonderful affection and sorrow on his noble, though simple, face, the boy gave a great gulp and whined out, in rather a tearful way, "James, do not you be a fool. What is the man snivelling for?" James hid his face in both hands, and groaned aloud.

"Come near me," said the boy, "and I'll tell you a secret. Will you keep it faithfully?"

"Ay, that I will."

"Then you must know, I am not ill a bit; I am only feigning."

"What! Alas! thy poor white face."

"Chalk, stupid. I tell thee, when you are all a-bed, I rise, and dance about the place, and shake my fist at you all, especially at that old knave Jedediah, and that dish of skim milk, his wife, that has got a man, and lets him be her master, instead of making him her head slave, as I would."

Philip's laugh and sparkling eye amazed James Annesley, and he cried out, "Oh, thou dear, good, sweet, wicked boy, for playing so with the hearts

that love thee; let me kiss thee;" and he rushed
at him to embrace him : but Philip caught up the
inkstand in a moment, and threatened him; "let
me be," cried he, "I hate to be slobbered. Sit
down, thou foolish, and talk sense."

"Nay," said James, "talk it thyself, and tell
me why thou art such a dear, good, artful young
fellow, to sport with the feelings of those that
love thee; and, moreover, 'tis unlucky to feign
sickness."

"Here's an ungrateful toad," said Philip; "why,
'tis for thee I do it."

"For me, Philip?"

"Ay, thou innocent, for thee. Oh, James, I
could not abear to be parted from thee." Philip
said this with a world of tenderness, and then hid
his face in his hands and blushed like a rose.

James's face showed that he was sore puzzled.
Philip, who could change his mood like lightning,
darted off into his favourite tone of lofty assump-
tion. "Why, thou coxcomb," said he, " dost thou
really think thou art fit to go to a new master,
without me at thy back? Come, James," added
he, patronizingly, " you are a good, worthy young
man, but you know you are somewhat of a milksop. You are not fit to go alone. You cannot
beat the men, nor flatter the women. I can do

both, especially make fools of the women, and turn 'em to butter with my tongue; and I know not how it is," continued he, assuming now an air of philosophical meditation, " but custom governs us strangely; once get into the habit of taking care of a child, or a dog, or a James Annesley, or any foolish, helpless sort of a pet, and in truth, you get so used to it, you can't let it go alone; you still come clucking after it, like a hen after her duckling. Is it not laughable?"

"No; for I am as fond of thee, Philip, as thou art of me."

"That you may easily be: for I am not fond of you at all: but I am warmly, and sincerely, and truly, accustomed to you, sir: and so I can't part, I won't neither; I'll kill everybody dead first, and die myself. But there's no need of that; I've got the key to that hunks: Avarice, James, avarice! Come, no more idle talk; but be a good lad: obey thy friend and protector, and let's to work. Give me that piece of chalk. So. Now go you to Jedediah, and ask him to see me alone, before I die. Tell him I have somewhat to say I would not trust even to our dame."

James did as he was bid; and Jedediah, in the course of a few hours, when he had nothing more remunerative to do, went to Philip's room. He found him lying pale and exhausted, with a little table by him. He sat down by him, and said he hoped that he was better.

"Master," said the boy, "I shall never be better. I have got the complaint my father died of, and in a few days I shall leave you. What vexes me is, you will lose a faithful servant."

" 'Tis a sore dispensation to *me*."

"And you will have to bury me; and that is like flinging money away. Nothing comes of it."

"It cannot be helped," said Jedediah, with a little groan.

"Not by you; but I think I could help it. Why should you lose·the money you paid for me, and the money for the coffin and all?"

" 'Tis a sore dispensation. But it cannot be helped."

"Yes, sir, it can. McCarthy comes here to-morrow, to buy slaves." Jedediah nodded. "He got the better of you, in that sale of wood."

Jedediah groaned.

"It's your turn now. I'll seem well, or nearly, when he comes: you shall say, ' James Annesley will fret, without his friend: ' then McCarthy will buy us both: and I shall die on his premises, not yours."

Jedediah's little keen eye flashed. He subdued

it, and said, "But I doubt me whether that would be fair trade. What thinkest thou? Is it lawful to spoil the Egyptians?"

"It is a Christian duty. And think of me, master. I shall die miserable, if you have to bury me, and lose so much *money* by me."

"Nay, I will not have thee die unhappy. That were cruel. Thou hast been indeed a faithful servant, and I'll humour thee in this thing."

"Good master, kind master! Then I pray you go at once to Mistress Maria's chamber, and fetch me her pot of red. Ask her not for it, or she'll deny you, and swear to't. 'Tis in the drawer of her table whereon stands her glass."

"My daughter, paint her face?"

"Ay, and her lips and all, at odd times. Fetch it me, sir, privately; for without it McCarthy will see the trick, and never buy me."

Jedediah went straight for the cosmetic, looking black as thunder.

Philip chuckled with delight. "Aha!" said this sweet, harmless boy. "I have lent that minx a dig into the bargain."

McCarthy came with money in both pockets, and was taken into Philip's office. Philip wrote him a receipt.

McCarthy eyed the penmanship, and the books.

" Sell me this one," said he to Jedediah, more than half in jest.

" You may as well, Master," said Philip, " for you know how fond I am of James. I shan't stay anywhere long without him."

" Do not baulk his fancy," suggested McCarthy. " I'll give ye fifty dollars more for this one."

Jedediah, after a well-feigned hesitation, consented, and in less than an hour the two friends' bundles were in McCarthy's light waggon, and they were marching behind it.

With them, to their infinite surprise, walked Jedediah Surefoot, a short thick riding-whip in his hand.

The fact is, his daughter had slipped out, taking advantage of her mother being at Willingtown, and he was afraid she had resolved to have a tender parting with James, or some worse folly: and, who knows, exasperated at being sold instead of rewarded, James's good faith might melt before a second temptation of the sort. So he said grimly, to his late servants, "I'll set ye on your way." He stalked along with them in silence. They thought he would go a mile, and then give them his blessing; but no : mile after mile, this kill-joy stuck to them, and was irksome, for they both wanted to talk, and congratulate each other on being still together.

At last Philip lost all patience, and resolved to make the intruder smart : he whispered James to fall back a little, and suddenly putting on his saucy swagger, that was quite new to Jedediah, he said, "Come, old man, hand forth my vail."

"Thy vail, boy?"

"Ay. Do you think I shall let you bite my worthy master there, and not have my nibble? Two gold pieces I demand. Give them, or I'll reveal the bubble to McCarthy, and have thee trounced, thou dealer in man's flesh : thou hypocritical knave, that would'st rob a church, and go to prayers before the deed, and after."

Jedediah was stupified at first, by this sudden hail-storm of insolence : but amazement soon gave way to rage. He gave a roar and rushed at Philip. Philip screamed and tried to escape ; but could not ; he clutched him fiercely by the collar, and raised his whip on high ; but it never came down; for, at Philip's first scream, James rushed on Jedediah with equal fury, and seized his arm, and caught him by the throat so felly, that, in a moment, his face was purple. Then James seized his whip, and mad with rage himself, whirled him round in a circle, and thrashed him furiously ; then put his foot to Jedediah's stomach, and, with one amazing thrust, spurned him head forward to the ground, that he rolled over, and the dust rose round his helpless body, like a cloud. This done, he flung his whip at him where he lay.

Philip clung, sobbing and trembling, to his arm.

James stood like a Colossus, his feet wide apart, his eyes glaring.

"Nay, be not alarmed, sweet Philip," said he. "He is no master of ours; but only a knave I have taught a lesson. None shall lay whip on thee, while I am by."

He coaxed and encouraged him, and they walked slowly on; but Philip, in walking, still clung to James's strong arm, and trembled.

When he was a little better, he looked up, and gazed on James, with quite a new sentiment of admiration, and said, "Oh! how grand, and strong, and brave, and beautiful you were. I did not think 'twas in you."

Having thus delivered himself, he lowered his head again suddenly, and clung to James's arm again.

"Nay," said James, "I am not a brave man: my want of courage was the first cause of all my misery. Child, 'twas only rage, not courage: no matter; I have but one friend; I'll not see him abused."

"Bless you, James!" He suddenly took James's

hand, and kissed it with a gentle devotion he had never exhibited before. "Dear James," he said, "I cannot bear a blow. 'Twas for a blow I left my home and all my friends."

"Ay, indeed! Pluck up heart, now, and tell me all about that."

"Tell thee my story? not for all the world."

"Why, I told thee mine."

"Ay: you have nought to blush for. I'd rather die, than tell thee mine. What have I done? I have put a barrier between me and the man I——, nay, heed not what I say. I am ill. I am sick. I have been frightened. I shall faint. I shall die."

"Nay, nay," said James, "take not on so, for nought. Is this he who called me a milksop?"

"Ay," said Philip, weeping. Then, with a piteous effort at his little hectoring way, "and will again, if I pee-pee-please."

"Meantime," said James, "I'll bestow thy valour in yon cart:" caught up the weeping Hector in a moment, and carried him in his strong arms, striding away, till he overtook the cart. "Master, poor Philip hath been ill of late, and he is aweary. May I put him in the cart?"

"And welcome. There is room for thee an' all."

"Nay, sir, I will not weight the good horse."

In a very few minutes there was a good deal of talking and laughing in the covered cart. Master Philip was amusing his new master, and taking the length of his foot.

"Dear heart!" thought Annesley, "what a strange boy 'tis. He changes like the wind."

Late at night, they reached McCarthy's, a large farm, about sixty miles from Philadelphia.

CHAPTER V

McCARTHY was a widower, and the house was kept by his daughter, a lady of very striking appearance. She was very tall, and commanding, and fair. Some thought her beautiful: others were repelled by the extreme haughtiness of her features, with which her deportment and manners corresponded.

The two friends, of course, talked everybody over, with whom they were likely to come in contact; and they differed about Mistress Christina McCarthy. James thought her the most beautiful woman he had ever seen. Philip screamed "What ! ! ! ! ! ! ! ! ! ! ! a nose like a man's; foxy eyebrows, white eyelashes, and a cold, cruel eye. She is not a woman," said this candid critic: " she is a cat."

"I never heard thee praise a woman yet," objected James.

"That is their fault, not mine," retorted Philip, who had long ago resumed the upper hand. " You

will be pleased to avoid that cat, like poison," said
Philip: "and, if she runs after you—and I hear
she has had a dozen beaux already—you will come
to me for advice, or our friendship is at an end,
sir. I shall have my eye on her."

The effect of Philip's espionage was this: he
discovered that Christina McCarthy passed James
and him as if they were dirt, her lofty affections
being fixed on a big mulatto slave. Such an
attachment was repugnant to the feelings of white
men, and contrary to law. They kept it very close,
in consequence, and nobody on the farm dreamed
of such a thing, until this Argus-eyed Philip came,
and found it out, by their secret glances, and
signals, and a deal of subtle evidence.

He told James of it, and made merry over the
lady's hauteur.

"That is so like the jades: whenever one of
them knows herself baser than all the rest, she
puts on a mask of transcendent pride, to throw
dust in folk's eyes. But they cannot throw dust in
mine."

James hoped it was not true: "for 'tis dis-
graceful," said he, "and contrary to nature: and,
poor man, she is his only child."

"Don't contradict me," said Philip. "I tell you
'tis so: and I'll show you the law." He had

picked out a copy of the State laws, on purpose to ascertain the probable fate of this haughty beauty, whose superb carriage had roused a most vindictive feeling in Master Philip.

James was not so curious in love affairs as Philip, and saw nothing to justify the libel. The lady passed often before his eyes, a model of cold dignity and feminine reserve. He scouted the notion, and almost scolded Philip for his uncharitableness towards women.

But one evening, having done his work, he took "Plutarch's Lives," which Philip had borrowed for him from the master, and lay down under the stockade, to read it. He was so absorbed in this book, and lay so still, that the little birds came about him, and did not mind him: the dusk came on, and still, with his young eyes, he went on reading, till suddenly he heard footsteps on the other side of the rails, and, after the footsteps, voices.

Now James was outside the rails, but these speakers were inside, and well hidden by the shadow of some lofty trees. This, in fact, was the favourite rendezvous of Christina and the mulatto Regulus. James knew the young lady's voice directly, and, though they spoke low and hurriedly, he heard enough to show him they were

K

lovers, and that she was going to elope with the fellow, as soon as she could lay her hands on a large sum of money her father was about to receive for the sale of another plantation. James listened with horror, and asked himself what on earth he should do. At last these ill-assorted lovers parted: that is to say, Regulus went off, leaving his young mistress to follow at such an interval of time as might lead to no suspicion. Then James thought he would not tell the old man, but would at all events try first to show the young woman her folly: he ran hastily to a gate, penetrated the wood, and came swiftly through the trees, to her, for he saw her white dress still standing there. Seeing him come straight to her so fast, she took him for Regulus come back with news, and she was so unguarded as to say, " Why, what now, my dear Regulus ? "

A strange voice answered her, at whose first tone she uttered a faint cry of alarm. " 'Tis not Regulus, madam; but one who has more real good wishes towards you than he has."

Christina trembled violently; but defended herself. She drew up haughtily, and said, " Why, 'tis James Annesley. How dare you speak to me ? What are you doing here at this time ? Have you been here long ? "

"Long enough to learn something that astonishes, and pains me, and I hope I may be in time to prevent it. Madam, I saw you and Regulus together."

"Wonderful! And now you see me and another of my slaves together. I was giving Regulus an order: and now I give you an order. Go home, and sleep the liquor off that hath made thee so bold as to speak to me; begone, or dread the whip, thou malapert."

James stood his ground. "Before I go tell me what I ought to do. I am your father's servant, madam, not yours. Both you and I, we eat his bread. Ought I to let him be robbed of his daughter, and his money, and never breathe a word?"

Then she began to pant, and said, "What mean you?" Then he told her that he had overheard every word that had passed between her and Regulus.

"Indeed!" said she, with an attempt at defiance, belied by her short breath. "Repeat it, then," said she, ironically.

"I will," said he gravely: and he did repeat it, and at such length, and with such exact fidelity, that, as he went on, shame and infinite terror crawled over her; her knees smote each other, and her haughty frame cringed and writhed, and she sank half down upon a wood pile that was near, and her white hands fell helpless, one in front of her, and the other by her side: never was a proud creature so stricken down in a moment.

Then this good young man pitied her, and hoped to save her. He said, "Madam, for Heaven's sake, look at the consequences. What good can come of it? If you fly with Regulus, and take your father's money, you will be caught one day, and set on the gallows, and be publicly whipped: for I have seen one as young and fair as you served so."

A moan from the crushed woman was the only comment.

" And if you steal nought, yet marry a mulatto, 'tis against the law, and your children will be illegitimate, and you will lose your father's estate, and break his heart."

Christina interrupted him. "Oh, say no more, James, for pity's sake. I have been mad. Oh! what a precipice! James, do not thrust me over. Do not tell my father, for mercy's sake."

"Not if you will promise to forego this mad design. Sure that mulatto must have bewitched you. That one so fair as you should cast an eye of love on anything so foul."

She caught at this directly. "Ay," she cried,

" 'twas witchcraft, and no other thing. But you have opened my eyes, good James—too late—too late ! " and she burst into a flood of tears.

" That depends on yourself : if you will swear to hold no more converse with that mulatto, I shall not feel bound to utter one word of what I know."

" James," said the lady, " you are my guardian angel ; you have saved me from a crime, and from an act of phrenzy I now look back upon with horror. Do but continue your good work. Advise me at every step, and all will be well."

James was surprised into consenting to that : and she then begged him to conduct her home. " Alas ! " said she, " I can scarce stand." She leaned on James's shoulder, and went very slowly and feebly. This gave her time to say some of those vague things with which such women think to excuse their follies. " If you knew all, you would pity me, even more than you condemn me." And again, with her white hand leaning on his arm, she said, " How sorcery blinds us ! " And what with this, and her gentle pressure of his hand at parting, she disturbed even this Joseph's mind a little, and set him thinking it would not be very hard to cure her of her insane caprice.

Next day she sent for him openly, and told him her plan. " I shall keep out of his way ; I shall

not move from my own apartments; or, if I do,
you shall be with me: and now here is a letter
I will beg you to take him. Read it first before I
seal it."

The letter ran thus :—" An accident has frus-
trated our design, for the present. My father has
not yet brought the money into the house. I hurt
my foot last night, and shall not, I fear, be able to
come to our rendezvous for some days. Burn this
before the face of whatever person I may send it
by, or I shall think you do not mean fair to

" The Writer."

James highly disapproved this letter, and told
her so. " Why," said he, " it cannot fail to keep
hope alive in him."

" Exactly," said she : " and so he will not blab
of my folly."

" No more he will, if you break off all connection
with him. And why write at all ? Such a letter
is worse than silence."

However, she talked him over, and convinced
him that she was resolved, in a cowardly and artful
way, to detach herself gradually from the deplorable connection, so that he half consented to take
the letter. Then she took a slice of cake out of
her closet, and a pint of rich wine, and sat close to

him while he drank it, and showed him such signs of favour, that he was the more inclined to believe she would readily detach herself from Regulus : so he consented to take the letter.

The mulatto eyed him keenly ; took the letter, read it, burned it before his eyes ; and said, " Tell her what you have seen me do ; that is all."

Christina now showed James so many marks of favour, and so open, that Philip took him to task. " My poor mouse," said he, scornfully, " are you going to let that cat catch you so easily ? " When that produced no effect, he remonstrated, advised, scolded, and, at last, quarrelled with him down-right, and would not speak to him.

Now James was really rather smitten with Christina ; her tenderness and cajoleries, following upon her haughty demeanour, had wonderfully tickled his vanity, and even grazed his heart ; but he was not so far gone as to part with Philip's friendship. So one day he came to him, and said, " Dear Philip, do not you quarrel with me, in a mistake. I will tell thee the truth about Mistress Christina ; but first you must swear to me, on the big Bible, never to reveal one word of that I tell thee."

Philip turned pale at this : but took the oath, and then James told him all.

He was more alarmed than surprised. "I knew she was naught, the minute I clapped eyes on her. Look at her white lashes, and her cold, cruel eye. The unnatural beast! that would rob her own father, and wed with a brown! And what sort of a man are you? Why went you not straight to her father, like an honest man? What had you to do to go to her, and get cozened, you silly goose? Are you a match for that artful jade, think you?"

"Nay, she seems very penitent, and keeps away from him; and—whisper, Philip. If I chose, I could take the brown's place, as you call him, any day: and, really, 'tis a temptation."

"You love the wretch?"

"Nay: not quite love. But she is fair, and she was so haughty, and now is so tender. I own I think more about her than I ever did of any woman yet. To be sure, I am very proud of saving her, and that makes the heart soft towards the fair creature I have rescued from 'a precipice.'"

Philip's face turned green, and his lips pale. His face was distorted and discoloured with the anguish these words cost him; and he sat mute as a statue.

James did not happen to look at him, and went maundering on. "The only thing I like not is

"From words, they came to blows."—*Page* 139.

that letter to Regulus. What think you of it, Philip?"

Philip, though sick at heart, made a great effort, and said, faintly, "The letter was writ to show him he must temporise, but not despair. Prithee, James, leave me awhile: I have work to do. Come in an hour, and we will see what all this really means."

He went, and then Philip began to sigh and moan at the confession James had made; and, for a long while, he could think only of his own misery, at being supplanted in James's heart. But of course his hatred of this rival soon led him into a keen and hostile examination of her conduct, and the consequence was a new and more disinterested anxiety, which led him to put a very keen question to James the moment he entered the room. "Has the mulatto shown you any enmity?"

"None whatever."

"Yet he sees his mistress bestow favours on you. Then all is clear. She has told him. You are their dupe. How that woman must hate you!"

"Nay," said James, smiling conceitedly, "that I'll be sworn she does not."

"What, not when you have come between her and her fancy, and do keep them apart? Think you, when once a woman hath loved a woolly

mulatto, she can so come back to wholesome
affections? She hates you; and spends her days
and nights scheming to destroy you. Oh, those
cunning lashes, and that cruel eye! They make
me tremble for you. Let me think what she is
about at this very minute." He resumed, after
a pause, " She will draw you on to offer her some
innocent freedom; then fly out, and accuse you
of wooing her. Who will believe you—a slave—
when the young mistress swears ? "

"I'll not give her the occasion."

"How can you tell? And if you do not, why
then she will get rid of you some other way. You
shall be stabbed in the back, some dark night, and
never know who struck you : but I shall know, and
I shall kill *her*—before I die."

So strong were Philip's fears, that he armed
James with an enormous knife, and made him
promise never to go to any lonely place without it.
James assented, to quiet him; but, in his heart,
made light of these extravagant fears. On the
other hand, he felt piqued by Philip's insinuation
that the mulatto and his penitent were duping
him; so he used often to get up in the dead of the
night, and make his rounds with stealthy foot, to
watch. The effect of this vigilance was, that one
moonlight night, coming softly round a corner, he

found Regulus under the young mistress's bedroom window, which window was open, the weather being warm. James collared him directly. "What do you do here, at this time of night?"

"I do what you do," said the mulatto.

"Not so," said James; "for I guard my master's goods against a knave."

"Knave thyself, and meddler, and fool," cried the mulatto, whose rage had been simmering this many a day.

From words, they came to blows, and struck each other hard and fast, without much parrying: in the midst of which Christina put her head out of her window on the first floor, and looked steadily down at them. After a few moments of self-possessed observation, she said, in a keen whisper, "Kill him!"

In this combat, the white struck at the face, and the black at the body: by this means the black's face was soon covered with blood, but the white man was most hurt, and felt instinctively that he should soon be overpowered; so he closed with his dark antagonist; they wrestled fiercely, but it ended in James throwing him, and falling on him: the ground was hard, and the fall of the two heavy bodies on it tremendous; it drove the wind out of Regulus for a moment, and James got him by the ears, and pounded his bullet head on the ground.

Christina now screamed loudly; a window or two were opened; night-capped heads popped out, and the combatants separated by mutual consent, and retired, glaring at each other.

James had not gone far, when he was seized with a violent sickness; and, after that, he crawled to his bed, bruised and seriously hurt by the body blows he had received. Next morning he was too stiff and ill to go to his work.

Philip heard a vague report that James and the mulatto had been fighting in the dead of night, and sent a message directly to James, desiring to speak to him. The servant came back and said he was too ill to leave his bed. Philip was much concerned at this, and, after a slight hesitation, went and knocked at the door of James's room : he slept over the stables. A faint voice said, " Come in." Philip lifted the latch. He found James lying on the bed, just as he had come from the battle; and his face two or three colours. Philip had intended to scold him; but this was no time. He came softly to him, and said, " Alas! my poor James, how is it with thee ? "

" But badly, in truth," said James, still in a faint voice.

"How came it about?"

He told him the truth.

"Ah!" said Philip, sadly. "Jealousy. How men do love ill women! That old cat—thirty, if she is a day—to have two lovers, and two nations after a manner, fighting for her o' nights beneath her very window. Did she see you?"

"Indeed she did."

"And smiled, I'll be bound, at what would make a good woman scream to part the fools. Did she say nought?"

"She said, 'Kill him.'"

"Kill whom?"

"The black, I do suppose."

"I am not so sure of that." And Philip fell into a reverie. It was broken by James going suddenly back on something Philip had said. "I do believe thou art right," said he, "and finding him under her window, I felt a sort of jealousy as well as wrath at his continuing to tempt her: if 'twas so, I am rightly served: but flout me not for't, Philip, for I think I am sped."

"Now, Heaven forbid. Where is thy hurt?"

"All over me. I made a great mistake. I kept beating him about his bullet head; but he still belaboured my ribs. Oh! I am all pains and aches; it hurts me e'en to speak."

"Alas! alas!" said Philip, and laid a cool consoling hand on the hot brow: then he suddenly
ground his set teeth, and said, "Curses on them
all : I will end this to-night ; no later."

James asked him what he meant. He refused
to say ; but the fact is that he was resolved to go
that very night to McCarthy, who was then on a
visit to his brother, five miles off, and tell him the
whole story. Knowing that James would remon-
strate, he kept his resolution to himself, and went
off for the present to prepare a composing draught
for his patient, after the receipt of Patience Surefoot.
He made the decoction, in which, I believe, dried
flowers of the lime-tree were a principal ingredient;
and, while he was thus employed, a negro came in,
and, with a congratulatory grin, told him there
was a gentlewoman wanted to see him. He came
out, and beheld Maria Surefoot on horseback. He
stared at her. "Philip," said she, "I have ridden
fifteen miles to bring thee this." She handed
him a copy of the *Philadelphia Post*. "Sweet
Philip, tell him I loved not wisely, but truly."
Then she looked all round for James ; but she
knew it was better for her not to see him : the tears
started from her eyes ; but she turned her horse's
head, and away home without a word, little knowing that she had honoured her sex, and adorned
God's creation, by that simple act.

Philip took the paper back to his room, and sat down to see why she had brought it all that way. Maria had marked an advertisement.

"His Majesty's frigate *Bellona*, commanded by Admiral Vernon, is now lying in Delaware Bay, short of hands, whereby able seamen and apprentices can now obtain double pay and good victuals."

Philip saw at once the value of this hint, and did justice to Maria's unselfish love, which disappointment had purified, instead of turning it to hate, as it does your selfish passions. But having James by his side he was hardly prepared to run the risk of flight. James had already suffered cruelly by an attempt of that kind. Yet it was a great temptation : he vacillated. He held the paper in his hand, and pondered the pros and cons.

And now I have a truly extraordinary circumstance to relate : the paper, a single sheet, contained only twenty advertisements altogether ; one was, as I have related, marked for Philip to read. But there was another one not marked, and Philip's eye fell on it by accident. Yet this advertisement set Philip's eyes staring, and, soon, as he read it, the paper began to shake in his trembling hands.

"I, Jonas Hanway, now lying in jail, charged with the murder of my ward, Joanna Philippa

Chester, take this way to let her know my evil plight, and beg her, for pity's sake, to come back, or write of her welfare. Poor Silas, that made the mischief, is in his grave, and nought awaits her here but my true repentance, and the kind affection of my co-trustee, Mr. Thomas Chester, under whose care she now is, if only she could be found. And, for a further inducement to return, I do now, with my co-trustee's consent, inform her that she is heiress to a fortune of thirteen thousand pounds or more, which knowledge was withheld from her by her father's express desire, lest any man should wed her for her dower, and not for true love of her : but now 'tis thought best to let her know the truth, lest she should throw herself away. The said Joanna is now nineteen years of age, tall, and active, and of singular beauty ; hath eyebrows black as jet, and do meet so remarkably as, in an Englishwoman, must needs draw notice. She hath been traced to London, and it is thought she hath crossed the seas. Whoever will give information respecting her, shall receive a reward of

"FIVE HUNDRED GUINEAS.

"She had her mother's jewels with her. But they are now her own.

"From my sorrowful prison at Staines, January, 1739–40."

Advertisement!—It was a cry from a Prison, and a cry from home, that knocked at her very heart. She uttered a responsive cry herself, as if the prisoner's cry had sounded in her ears; and then she devoured the words once more, feeding on every syllable in great amazement. But presently the letters grew hazy; her filling eyes saw them no more, and, in their place, came the pleasant meads of Colebrook, the English landscape, humble, but sweet, the grey old church, with the swallows twittering round : her dear parson's scholarly face, the white-headed children before each cottage, clad with rose and eglantine. Then her heart gushed to her eyes in a stream, and the wanderer lay softly back in a chair, quite motionless, and let the sweet tears flow.

Then came the desire to act; to fly home, and save that poor bereaved father, and live amongst her folk. How should she manage it? she had jewels secreted about her, any one of which was worth more than a slave's ransom. Why not go to McCarthy; tell him who she was, and offer him a diamond ring for her liberty? Why not? because he might have her seized, for wearing man's clothes, and throw her into prison for life, so severe was this colony in that matter. No; she

L

could not endure the shame ; nor run the risk.
She would take one of his horses, and ride by
night to Philadelphia ; and make terms with him
through some other party.   One thing alone she
did resolve—not to lose an hour, but to be gone
that very night.   One day lost, and the prisoner's
life might pay for it.   Yes, she would go, and take
James Annesley with her.   She took up the sleeping draught, and went to his room.   She made
him drink it, and then covered him up warm, and
took his hand in hers.   "James, dear," said she,
"I am a happy—creature.   I have news from
England : sad news, after a manner—yet sweet :
and I am going home."

"Going !—Ah well : God's blessing and mine go
with thee."

"Why, thou foolish man, I go not without thee.
This very night we ride to Philadelphia, and
thence to England."

James shook his head sorrowfully.   "There is
no escape for a slave.   I have tried it."

"Ay, all alone, and on foot, without money or
means.   But 'tis different now.   I shall command
the expedition ; I, who, by your leave, possess the
two capital gifts of a commander, which are forecast, and courage ; forecast, by which I do foresee
all possible accidents, and provide for them ; and

courage, whereby I overcome and trample under
foot those petty dangers that scare a mere ordinary
man like thee.—What's this?"

"What is what?"

"I smell a smell I never could abide. 'Tis a
cat. I know 'tis a cat. There! there, she is—
coiled in the mouth of that sack. I shall faint, I
shall die."

"Why, here's a coil about poor Puss. 'Tis the
stable cat, and loves to come here."

"Well, she goes forth, or I."

"Open the door then, and fling thy cap at the
poor harmless thing."

"I call not foul things harmless, especially when
they are all claws. I like not your cats, even
when they are called Christinas."

While Philip was driving out the "harmless,
necessary cat," James criticised him. "Why, 'tis
like a girl, to be afear'd of a cat. But indeed you
are more like a girl than a boy, in many things.
You hate women more than is natural, and you
turn your toes out in walking; and you carry your
hand so oddly when you walk."

"Mercy on us, how?"

"Why, you turn it out sideways, and show
the fingers. I walk with my thumb straight
down."

Philip turned very red, but said, pertly, " All
which proves that I was born of a woman. Now
you were born of a goose. I'm man enough to be
your master, and this very evening you shall ride
with me to Philadelphia."

" You are my master, and I own it," said
James : " my master, by superior learning, wit,
and daring, only the courage comes and goes most
strangely. But, good my master, for all that, I
cannot ride with thee to-night."

" Oh, say not so, James. Why not ? "

" I could not sit a horse, for my life."

" Alas ! how unfortunate we are. James, think
me not unkind ; but I must go to-night ; with thee,
or without thee."

" You must go without me, then ; for indeed
I am not able."

" But perhaps you may be by nightfall. Have a
good sweat, and a good sleep ; and I'll come again
at dusk ; for, oh, James, I *must* go ; and I am loth
to leave thee."

Then Philippa retired, and went and made some
slight preparation for the journey she had resolved
to take : but, in the midst of it all, her hands fell
helpless, and her heart revealed itself to her. She
could not go. Love burst through all self-decep-
tion at last. She loved him ; had loved him long ;

and now loved him to distraction. Leave him on his sick bed, and among enemies: no, not for a day. She had honestly intended—if he could not come—to fly to Philadelphia, sell her jewels, and buy him of McCarthy: but, now it came to the point, she burst out crying, and found she could not leave him in trouble, no, not for an hour. "Nay," said she to herself, "but I will come at night, and hector him, and taunt him, and coax him, and try all my wicked arts to get him to go with me: then, if he cannot, I will pretend to go without him, but I'll slip back softly, and lie on the mat at my darling's door. None shall come to hurt him but over my body."

Meantime, James received another unexpected visitor. There was a gentle tap at the door; and Mistress Christina glided in. He was surprised, and tried to rise and receive her; but she put up her white hand, that he should not move. Then she sat down by him, and, with the most cajoling tenderness, expressed her regret at what had occurred. "Why," said she, "will you trouble about that man whom you know I have discarded?"

"He was there to tempt you, madam."

"More likely through jealousy; seeing me favour you, perhaps he suspected me of speaking

to you at all hours.   But once more, James,
trouble not about him.   Has he hurt you ? "

"Nay, madam, not much," said James : "a few
bruises, that I am to sleep away.   He got as good
as he gave, I know."

"That is true," said she, gravely ; "he is much
cut about the face, and you have knocked out one
of his front teeth."

"I will knock his head off next time."

"I will give you leave to kill him—*next time*,"
said the lady, calmly.   "Meantime, prithee get
well—for my sake.   I'll send you something to do
you good."   She then kissed her hand to him, and
went softly out.

Before she had been long gone, Philip's potion
began to work, and James fell into a fine sleep and
a violent perspiration.

Presently there was another tap at the door, and
as the sleeper did not reply, Chloe entered, with a
large basin of strong soup prepared by the white
hands of Christina herself.   Chloe was followed by
the late discarded cat, returning now with lofty
tail, sniffing the savoury mess.   Chloe, finding the
patient asleep and perspiring, had the sense not to
awaken him ; only, as she thought it a pity the
soup should cool, she put it down by his bedside,
calculating that the smell might waken him, as it

would her. To keep it warm, she put "Plutarch's Lives" over it, and then retired : it was about four o'clock.

Now, if James was asleep, Puss was not. He turned about the leg of the table, sniffing; and at last sprang boldly on to the bed, and from the bed to the table. Here he found an obstacle in Plutarch. Plutarch covered the soup, not entirely, but too much for Puss to get a nose in. He sat quiet a few minutes, then he applied his fore paw and nose and made a sufficient aperture. Then he found the soup too hot. Then he sat on the table a whole hour, waiting. Then he arose and gradually licked up nearly half the soup: then he retired quietly, and coiled himself up.

James still slept on his balmy sleep, till just before sunset. Then he was awakened by a violent knocking.

He looked up, and there was the poor cat in violent convulsions, springing up to an incredible height, and hammering the floor with his head, when he came down.

James got up, unconscious of his late pains, and threw some water over him. He thought it a fit : but, after a few violent convulsions, came piteous cries, and the poor creature stretched his limbs, and died foaming at the mouth.

James soon discovered the cause, in the stolen soup.

His blood ran cold. He fell on his knees, and thanked God he was alive. But how long? what would not hate so diabolical as this attempt? He seized his knife, and prepared to sally forth.

At this moment he heard a whistle under his window.

"Ah!" thought he, "a signal of assassins." He instantly dragged his bed and other things to the door, to impede an attack from that quarter, and then went cautiously to the window. To his great relief it was Philip, who had given that signal. He opened the window directly. "Oh, Philip! They have tried to poison me!"

"Ah!—who?—who?"

"Christina herself. Sent me soup. The cat stole some, whilst I slept, thanks to your medicine, —you are my preserver,—and see, the poor cat is dead." He took the cat's body, and flung it out. Philip recoiled, with a cry of horror. "Come forth!" he cried. "Come forth! or they will murder thee yet. Oh, my love, come forth to me."

"I will, I will. And, in a moment, he tore away the bed and other things from the door, and ran down to Philip. Philip had lost not a moment, but was getting the two best horses out. James helped him. Without a word more they saddled and bridled them, and Philip sprang into the saddle; his black eyes were gleaming with a strange fire.

"Take that dead beast before thee," said he; "and I'll give thee liberty and vengeance."

They galloped off, over the soft ground, Philip leading, and took the road for Philadelphia.

They did not venture to speak till they got clear of McCarthy's premises, but then James told Philip of Christina's visit and cajoleries, followed by murder.

Philip said, "'Twas in her eye. Ah! thou foul cat, but I'll be even with thee;" and Philip ground his teeth audibly, and his eye shot fire in the moonlight. "My poor James," said he, "that would not harm a mouse!"

About five miles from McCarthy's, they passed his brother's farm. They passed it a hundred yards or so, and then Philip drew the rein, and haltered his horse to a gate, and made James do the same. "Now take that dead Christina in thy hand," said he, bitterly, "and follow me." He marched up to the farm, and asked for William McCarthy.

"What want you?"

"We are two servants of his, come with news of life and death."

"You shall find him at supper with the rest."

Philip walked boldly into the noisy supper-room, followed by James. "Silence all!" said he, with a voice like a clarion : and the room was still in a moment.

"Master, have you money in your house?"

"Ay," cried McCarthy, half rising, and turning pale; "more than I can bear to lose. But 'tis in the safe, boy. None knows of it but my daughter."

"Am I your daughter? Yet I know it. Your daughter has a mulatto to her lover, and they have planned to rob you of your money, and fly."

"The proof!" roared McCarthy.

"The proof is this : James there overheard Christina and Regulus plan the robbery : he taxed Christina with it; and she tried to cajole him; but, failing in that, and knowing he would tell you, like a faithful servant as he is, she this day essayed to poison him."

Here there were some exclamations. "Ay, sir," continued he; "the cat, by God's mercy, stole a little of the soup, while he slept : now look at that cat's body, and judge for yourselves."

The cat was instantly examined.

Philip did not stop for that. "Now, master, take your weapons, and to horse this moment, and save your goods, if there be yet time." Mr. McCarthy, and his brother, and two or three men, ran out. Philip turned to the others, and, folding his arms, said boldly, " Sirs, ye are Christian men, and white men like ourselves ; is it your will that good servants of your own flesh and blood shall be poisoned, like rats ? " There was a roar of honest disclamation. "And all because Christina McCarthy is so lost to shame as to wed a black and rob her own flesh and blood. Then, sirs, to your justice we two commend our cause. There is the poisoned beast, to prove our words, and half the poisoned soup in this good young man's room over the stable. Punish them with everything short of death. James and I will keep away a little while ; for, if we testify, the judge might hang her. Give you good e'en."

Having delivered this bold but artful speech, he retired with James, and, the moment he got outside the door, whispered him, " Now run for't, or they will keep us to testify in their courts." They ran off like the wind, untethered their horses, and, springing into their saddles, rode rapidly off, keeping the side of the road at first, to dull their horses' hoofs. They rode all night, and, with the earliest

streak of dawn, entered the fair town of Philadelphia.

McCarthy and his party, twelve in all, caught
the mulatto and Christina in the very act of
levanting with McCarthy's money. They made
short work of them : bound Regulus to a tree,
and flogged him within an inch of his life, with
Christina tied to a chair close by, and the dead
cat in her lap. Then they drummed the mulatto
out of the district, and sent Christina to a farm in
Massachusetts, to clean pots and pans in the
kitchen for a twelvemonth and a day.

CHAPTER VI.

PHILIP, being commander, sent James to one inn, and went to another himself. He said that was most prudent, to avoid discovery: but his real motive was different. He had a very difficult game to play. His wit, however, proved equal to it. Remembering that his father was a lawyer, he inquired for an old lawyer, a grey-headed one: he stipulated severely for grey hairs. When he had found his grey-headed lawyer, and liked his countenance, he did not make two bites of a cherry, but told him all, and showed him the advertisement.

The lawyer easily got her eighty gold pieces, on the security of her diamond cross, and gave her a room on his own premises, where she could dress herself in any costume she liked, without being reported.

Meantime, James Annesley was not idle: he saw a notice up that Admiral Vernon's ship was short of hands, and he went and engaged himself to

serve on board her ; he promised to bring a much
smarter fellow next day, meaning his mate Philip.

When they met in the evening, he told Philip
this, and Philip was much vexed at first. " Oh !
why will you do things without asking me ? "

However, on reflection, she acquiesced, and, with
true feminine tact, altered all her plans, to meet
this unexpected move. She told James she would
go on board the ship; but in another capacity.
She had friends and money, and would work for
both. Only, for a day or two, he must not expect
to see much of her.

The lawyer sent the horses to McCarthy, and
advised him not to trouble any more about the
servants, as they were under his care, and he
might have to go into the poisoning business, if
they were molested.

Soon after this, a young lady in her mask called
on Admiral Vernon at his lodgings, and asked him
if he would take her home in his ship.

" Zounds, madam, no," said the admiral ; " no
petticoats aboard the King's ship."

" Alas, sir ; say not so : do but cast your eye
over this advertisement. Indeed 'tis no common
case ; 'tis a matter of life and death, my going in
your ship." The admiral read the advertisement,
and cried out, " What ! Accused of murder ?

Gadzooks! what fools these landsmen be! Are you indeed the gentlewoman they seek?"

"Ay, noble Admiral. Deign to regard my foul eyebrows, that are all published to the world so barbarously in this advertisement:" and the sly puss removed her mask, and burst on the sailor in all her sunlike beauty. At this blaze, he began to falter a little. "'Tis pity to deny you; but why not go in the first ship of burden?"

"Sir, none sail this week, and they are too slow for my need, and, in truth, I'm afear'd to be drowned, if I go in any other ship but the one you do command. Oh, Admiral! you are too brave to deny the weak and helpless in their trouble."

"Madam!" said the Admiral, "you mistake the matter. 'Tis of you I think. I am a father; and a ship of war is not the place for young gentlewomen."

"But, sir, I am discreet, and know the world: and I can wear my mask, and keep close. Oh, noble sir, have pity on me, and let me sail in your good ship." Then, with her lovely eyes, she turned on, what I, labouring to be satirical, call the waters of the Nile. Then the Admiral rapped out the usual oaths of the sea and the century, and said she had done his business; "a sailor was never yet proof against salt water from a woman's eye."

He then told her where his ship lay in the Bay
of Delaware, and his day and hour of sailing: she
must come out in a boat, and he would charge an
officer beforehand to see her safe a-board.

Philippa returned to her lawyer in high spirits,
and sent him to James, with a note in her own
hand, directing him to go on board the English
flag-ship next day at six in the evening, and she
would follow the day after, before the ship sailed.
James did as he was bid. At noon next day a
boat brought a lady in her mask, alongside; and
James, who was looking out anxiously for Philip,
saw her taken on board, with her boxes,—for she
had found time to shop furiously,—and handed
respectfully to her cabin; but James did not
recognize her, nor dream this tall gentlewoman
was little Philip.

At two p.m., the Admiral was seen coming out;
the yards were manned directly, and he mounted
the quarter-deck, with due honours, and the next
minute the pipe was going, and the men's feet
tramping to the capstan, whilst others hoisted a
sail or two; and the anchor was secured: and the
ship bowed, and glided, and burst into canvas, and
the busy seamen all bustled, and shouldered poor
James out of the way, with salt curses, as he ran
about the ship asking wildly for Philip, and de-

scribing him to coarse fellows who only jeered him.

One faint hope remained; Philip might be down below: but the next day dissipated this; Philip never showed his face, and this puzzled and grieved James Annesley so, that even the prospect of Liberty and Home could not reconcile him to the loss and seeming desertion of this tender and faithful friend.

The officer in charge of the new hands now called on James to do some very simple act of seamanship. He bungled it, and there was a good deal of hoarse derision; to which he replied, at last, a little sadly, but with good temper, "Men are not born sailors; are they?"

An officer at the other side of the deck heard this reply, and was struck with the voice, or the face, or perhaps with all three, and called to him. He came respectfully, and removed his cap.

"Sure I have seen that face before," said the officer.

James started, and said, "I have seen yours, sir; but where?"

Said the officer, "I'll tell you that. Is not your name James?"

"Indeed, sir, it is."

"Son of Lord Altham that was."

M

"Yes, sir; but how—oh, 'tis my kind school-fellow."

"Ah! I am Mat Matthews, that set you on your way to Dublin. I took a good look at you that day: and I seldom forget a face I look at so; but what means this disguise, in Heaven's name? You have been reported dead, in Ireland, this many a year. Where have you been? Is this a frolic, good sir, or hath Fortune used you crossly?"

"Sir," said James, "I'll tell you in a word, but a word full of misery: my uncle Richard kidnapped me, and sent me to the plantations; there have I been a slave this many a long year, and even now escaped by a miracle."

"A slave! You! a lord's son, a slave! Kidnapped, and by Richard Annesley, say you? Why, 'tis he now holds your father's lands and titles. Perdition! Here is foul play! The knave! 'Twas to steal your lands and titles he spirited you away."

"Indeed, sir, I always did suspect it. Such villany was never yet done for love of God."

"Sir," said Captain Matthews, "sit you down: and not another rope shall you handle in this ship." He ran, with his heart in his mouth, to the Admiral; and his warm-hearted Irish eloquence, burning with his school-fellow's wrongs, soon fired the honest sailor. They agreed that this was the real Earl, and his uncle a felon, whom the sight of the true heir would blast. "And now I think on't," said Matthews, "Arthur Lord Anglesey is dead, and Richard Annesley has succeeded to *his* lands and titles too; so that there is one of the greatest noblemen in England and Ireland a sailor on board this ship—and a very bad one."

"That may not be," said the Admiral; "overhaul the wardrobe straight, and rig him like a lord, as he is, and make us acquainted." He added, with a touch of delicacy one would hardly have expected, "I'll not see him in his sailor's jacket, nor seem to know he hath been brought so low."

CHAPTER VII.

IT was a beautiful moonlight night : the great ocean was calm, and the light airs so gentle, that snow-white studding sails were set aloft to catch them.

The Honourable James Annesley in a suit of blue velvet laced with silver, gold-laced hat, and jewel-hilted sword, paced the deck, and admired the solemn scene, the incredible sheen of the rippling ocean kissed by moonbeams, the ship's gigantic shadow, that ran trembling alongside, and the waves like molten diamonds, that sparkled to the horizon.

His tide had turned : finery on his back, a hundred gold pieces in his pocket, that Matthews, a man of large fortune, had insisted on lending him ; a popular admiral conveying him home, an honoured guest.

Yet it seemed there was something wanting ; for, after he had enjoyed the scene awhile, he sat

"This sigh caught the quick ear of a young lady."—*Page* 165.

down upon a gun, and meditated ; and his meditation was not gay, for soon he heaved a sigh.

Now this sigh caught the quick ear of a young
lady who had not long emerged upon deck. It
was Joanna Philippa Chester, who never showed
herself by day, but took the air at night, and even
then had always her little mask in hand ready to
whip on. Joanna was farther still from complete
happiness than James was ; her breast was torn
with doubts, and fears, and shames, for which my
reader, who has only seen her fitful audacity in
boy's clothes, may not be quite prepared. She was
now all tremors and misgivings, and paid the
penalty of her disguise. Under that disguise she
had fallen deep in love with James Annesley; yet
inspired him with no tenderer feeling than friendship for a boy. That knowledge of the heart,
which an inexperienced but thoughtful woman
sometimes attains by constantly thinking on its
mysteries, told her that between love and friendship there is a gulf, and that gulf sometimes
impassable. Philip might stand for ever between
James and Philippa.

And, besides this, for a girl to wear boy's clothes
was indelicate ; it was condemned by law, it was
scouted by public opinion. James Annesley, even
in his humble condition, had shown a great sense

of propriety; and she felt, with a cold chill
running down her back, that he was not the man
to overlook indelicacy in her sex, much less make
an Amazon his wife: and now, as she had learned
with her sharp ears, the story he had told her was
confirmed, and he was the real Earl of Anglesey,
and all the less likely to honour a Tomboy with
his hand. For three whole days she had longed
and pined to speak to him; yet fear and modesty
had held her back. She could not bear to be
Philip any more; yet she dreaded to be Philippa,
lest she should lose even Philip's place in his
regard.

Even now, the moment she saw him seated,
with the moon glittering on his silver lace, and
his jewelled sword, and his dear, shapely head
lowered in pensive thought, her first impulse was
to recoil, slip down into her cabin again, and
torture herself with misgivings, as she had been
doing all the voyage.

But love would not let her go without a single
look. She turned her eyes on him, that soon
began to swim with tenderness, as she looked at
him. She stole a long drink of ineffable love, and
the next moment she would have been gone; but
he sighed deeply, and she heard it. Then the
habit of consoling him, and her yearning heart,

were too much for her. By a sudden impulse she
whipped on her mask, and stole towards him.
She trembled, she blushed; but all the woman
was now in arms to defend that love which was
her life.

He heard her coming, looked up, and saw a tall
young lady close upon him, dressed in the fashion,
with a little silk hood, and a mask that hid all
but her mouth. He rose, removed his hat, and
bowed ceremoniously. She curtsied in the same
style.

"Forgive me, sir," said she, " I fear I interrupt
your meditations."

"Most agreeably, madam."

"Methought I heard you sigh, sir."

"I dare say I did, madam."

"I was surprised, sir, for I hear you are a
gentleman of quality, going home to high fortune,
after encountering her frowns. Sure that should
make her smiles the sweeter."

"Madam, it may be so: but my enemies are
powerful: I may find it very hard to dispossess the
wrongful owners."

"And 'twas for that you sighed."

"Not at all, madam. I sighed for the loss of a
dear friend."

"Alas! What—dead?"

" Now, Heaven, forbid ! "

" False then, no doubt."

" I hope not : but I am sore perplexed; for he never failed me before."

"He ? What, 'twas only a man then, after all?"

" 'Twas a boy, for that matter ; but what a boy ! you never saw his fellow, madam. His head was all wit; his heart all tenderness ; his face all sun-shine. He brightened my adversity; and now, when Fortune seems to shine, he has deserted me. Oh, Philip ! Philip ! "

" Philip ! was that his name ? "

" Yes, madam."

" Is he a dark boy ? "

" Yes, madam, yes."

" About my height ? "

" Oh no, madam, not by half a head."

Philippa smiled at that, and said, " Then, sir, you shall sigh no more on his account, for I happen to know that same Philip is here, in this very ship."

" Is it possible ? God bless you for that good news, madam. Oh, madam ! pray bring him to me, for my heart yearns for him. Why, why has he hidden himself from me ? "

" Nay, sir, you must have patience. The boy is not so much to blame. He is in trouble, and

dare not show his face on deck. I wonder whether
I may tell you the truth ? "

" Yes, madam, for Heaven's sake ! "

"Well then, the truth is—ahem—he is here
disguised as a woman."

"You amaze me, madam."

"And if you were to accost him as Philip,
'twould be overheard, and might be his ruin : if
you can be so much his friend as to fall into
this disguise, and treat him with distant civility,
while he is on board the ship, I'll answer for him
he will come to you, not to-night, but to-morrow
night at this time."

James Annesley eagerly subscribed to these
terms.

Next evening he paced the deck impatiently, and,
in due course, a young gentlewoman came towards
him, with Philip's very face, but blushing and
beaming.

James ran to meet her : devoured her face, and
then cried, " It is ! it is ! oh, my sweet Philip ! "

The young lady drew back instantly in alarm,
and said, " Is this what you promised ? Call me
Philip again, or offer the slightest freedom, and
you shall never see me again. My name is
Philippa."

" So be it, thou capricious toad. I am too

overjoyed at sight of thee, to thwart thy humours. Thou wert never like any other he that breathes."

"I shall be more unlike them than ever now," said she. "Methinks my disposition is changed, since I put off my boy's attire : and the worst of it is all my courage hath oozed away."

"It had always a trick of coming and going, Philip."

"Philippa, or I leave the ship."

"Well, Philippa, then."

"What sort of a gentlewoman do I make ? "

"Nay, if I knew not the trick, I should take you for the most beautiful woman I ever saw."

Philippa blushed with pleasure. "And you look beautiful too," said she. "Fine feathers make fine birds."

He then scolded her gently, and asked her why she had deserted him.

"Well, I'll tell you the truth," said she, and delivered him a whole string of fibs.

She met him next evening, and the next, and so mystified him by her beauty and her bashfulness, that he questioned Matthews and the Admiral about the young lady, but Matthews knew nothing, and the Admiral pretended to know nothing, she having sworn him to secresy.

Philippa was offended at his curiosity, and sent

him word he had done very ill to ask other persons about her: she should not come on deck for ever so long.

She kept her word, though it cost her dear: even when they touched at Jamaica, and everybody else landed, she kept her cabin. But when they left Jamaica, she took another line. She came openly on deck now and then in the daytime, and removed her mask.

The effect may be divined: the officers of the ship treated her like a Queen, and courted her with all possible attentions; these she received with singular modesty, politeness, and prudence: and her heart being sincerely devoted to one, her head was not to be turned.

James Annesley looked on with wonder, and a dash of satire, to see men all but kneeling to a boy: but he soon got jealous, and the other men opened his eyes, and he began to ponder over many things. The truth flashed on him, and Philippa saw it in his face. Then she coquetted with her happiness, and, when he begged a private interview, she put him off.

But when they passed Lizard Point, she came to her senses, and gave him his opportunity.

He was much agitated; she was more so, but hid it better. "Tell me the truth," he cried.

" You were always Philippa, and I a blind fool."
She hid her red face in her hands, and replied
with the charming directness of her present sex.

" Oh, why did I ever wear those abominable
clothes ? "

" Nay," said James. " Why did you ever doff
them ? for, see now, you have killed the friend of
my bosom."

" I'm glad of it," said she, with one of her shows
of spirit.

" And will you give me nothing in exchange
for him ? "

" Alas, James ! " she cried, " what can I give
you that you will love as you did him ? *I hate
that boy.*"

" Nay, do not hate him; but for him I had
never known the greatest, truest, tenderest heart
that ever beat in woman. Oh, Philippa, you saved
me from despair, you saved me from servitude : I
never could love another now you are a woman ;
be my bosom friend still, but by a dearer title ; be
my sweetheart, my darling, my wife."

" Ay, that or the grave," she cried: and the
next moment he held her curling round his neck,
and cooling her hot cheeks with tears of joy.

They landed at Portsmouth, took a kind leave

of the Admiral, to whom they owed so much, and, accompanied by Captain Matthews, dashed up to Staines with post horses, four at every relay. When they came near to the town, she bade the driver post to the prison. She demanded to see Jonas Hanway. He was called into the yard, and, at sight of her, gave a scream of joy, and they had a cry together, and forgave each other. She feed the jailor to send to the proper authorities, and take the necessary steps for his liberation. Then she went on to Thomas Chester, who lived outside the town by the river side : but Matthews left them in the town, and went on to London, on his way to Ireland. He had inherited large estates, and was about to leave the King's service.

Thomas Chester, though a man not easily moved, gave a loud shout when his niece ran to him : he folded her in his arms, and thanked God aloud, in a broken voice, again and again.

When they were a little calmer, he said to his man, "Send abroad, and let them ring all the church bells for three miles about ; I'll find the ale : and thou, Thomas, bring in our young lady's things. She is mistress of the house."

Then they went out, and found two boxes, and one James Annesley, seated peaceable. "And who is this ?" said the old man, staring not a little.

" 'Tis only my—my James," said she, as if every young gentlewoman had a James; but the next moment her cheeks were dyed with blushes. " Dear uncle, he has been my friend and companion in servitude, and some do say he is the——"

" Whoever he is, he hath brought me thee, my sweet long-lost niece, and must lie at my house this happy night." So he received James cordially, and put off all inquiries till the morrow. The next morning James told him, of his own accord, he loved Philippa, and was so happy as to have won her affections. He also spoke of his wrongs, and said he was Lord Altham's son, and dispossessed by the uncle, who had kidnapped him ; and he should go into Ireland at once, and hoped to punish his uncle, and make Philippa Lady Anglesey. He proved himself in earnest, by starting for Ireland this very day. The parting with Philippa was very tender, and left her almost inconsolable, being their first real separation since they knew each other.

So the wise old lawyer let her have her cry out. Next day he told her what the young man had said.

" Alas ! " said she: " he is gone on a wild-goose errand, I fear: and, as for me, I would not give one straw to be Lady Anglesey; to be Mrs. James is heaven enough for me: and, alas! if any ill befall him in that savage Ireland, I shall always think 'twas because I was not by him as heretofore; and you will have but one more trouble with me—to bury me."

"Niece," said the old man, "craving your pardon, you are pretty far gone."

"Never was woman farther," said she, frankly. "I am fair sick with love. My James carries my heart and my life in his bosom, go where he will:" and she leaned her head prettily on the old man's shoulder.

"Hum!" said the lawyer, and dropped that subject, not possessing even its vocabulary.

He waited a reasonable time, and then cross-examined her. "My young mistress," said he, "have you told your sweetheart you have thirteen thousand pounds? and, now I think on't, 'tis nearer fourteen thousand, by reason of your folly in going and getting your own living, instead of spending it."

"Have I told James? No; not yet. I found out my father's will, by that advertisement, and, since he wished it kept secret, I have held that wish sacred."

Mr. Chester told her she had done well. Lord

Anglesey had been long in possession; and it was
not likely he would be ousted without a fearful
litigation, in which her little fortune might easily
be swamped. " No, Philippa," said he, " still go
by your father's will, and by my lights, and let us
not risk one shilling of your fortune. Your husband can never be a pauper, while that remains in
your hands." She caught that idea in a moment,
and gave her solemn promise.

The first letter from Ireland served to confirm
her uncle's wisdom. James wrote to say that he
had been to a dozen attorneys, and they all refused
to take up his cause against a nobleman so powerful as Lord Anglesey, and who had been years in
possession, without a voice raised against his title.

However, a day or two after writing this, James
Annesley fell in with a long-headed attorney, called
McKercher, who listened to his story more thoughtfully than the others, and went so far as to ask
him for a list of the people he thought could bear
out his statements. Having got this, Mr. Mc-
Kercher found Farrell and Purcell, and, by means
of them, one or two more not known to James
Annesley; and they established the kidnapping.

Then McKercher began to think more seriously
of the case. He called on Mr. Annesley at his
lodgings, and found him and Matthews taking a

friendly glass, and talking the matter over. Mc-
Kercher made three, and said over his glass that
the kidnapping was certainly a fine point; but it
would be worthless without direct evidence to
Mr. Annesley's parentage, and money would be
required, to ransack the county of Meath for evidence, and for other purposes; for money would
certainly be used against them freely.

The warm-hearted Matthews offered a thousand
pounds directly, to begin : thereupon McKercher's
eyes glittered, and he hesitated no longer : all
three went out to Mr. Matthews's house that day
in cars of the period; and next day rode on his own
horses to ransack Meath and Wexford for evidence.

They found some little evidence, and McKercher secured it : but there were two enemies in the
field before them. Death was one, Lord Anglesey
the other. This nobleman had got a fortnight's
start, in rather a curious way. Admiral Vernon
anchored off Jamaica a few days. It got wind
that he was bringing home the real Lord Anglesey.
The *Daily Post* announced it, and the *Gentleman's
Magazine* copied, as indeed may be seen in the
Gentleman's Magazine for February, 1741.

Death, the other antagonist, had been unusually
busy since James Annesley crossed over the bar
of Dublin. Lady Altham—dead. Mrs. Avice,

N

to whom she had spoken of a son—dead. The chaplain who he believed had christened him—dead. His sponsors, male and female—dead.

But McKercher was not to be baffled: he hunted up the old servants of Dunmaine House, and, from one to another, he began to create that pile of testimony which even now stands on record to prove this obscure man the Napoleon of all attorneys, living or dead. He, and James, and Matthews, rode hundreds of miles after evidence; till one night Annesley was fired at from the edge of a wood, and two slugs whistled close by his head.

They all spurred away, in great alarm.

When they had got to the town they were going to, tactful McKercher set to work that moment and printed bills, describing the attempt, offering a thousand pounds reward, and, by subtle insinuation, accused Lord Anglesey of the crime: he got up what we now call a demonstration; showed his handsome client to the public, on a verandah stuck over with bills thus worded:—

"THIS IS THE HEIR. COME, LET US KILL HIM, THAT THE INHERITANCE MAY BE OURS."

For all that, he sent Annesley back to England directly. "It is too pretty a suit to be abated by a bullet," said keen McKercher.

James Annesley returned to Staines, and found
the roses leaving Philippa's cheek. Ere he had
been back a week they bloomed again.

McKercher circulated his bills in Dublin, with
a guarded account of the attempted assassination,
just keeping clear of an indictment for libel. One
of the bills was sent over to Lord Anglesey by a
friend.

That nobleman, at this period began to lose
heart. His estates were large, but encumbered:
he had been, for years, amusing himself with
trigamy; and trigamy had entailed its expenses.
All the ladies had to be dressed as if there was but
one Lady Anglesey; and you may see, by Miss
Gregory's bill, that those noble brocades, though
cheaper in the end than the trash we call silk, were
dear at first. Then the three ladies had children,
and one of the three was so ill-bred as to indict my
lord, and had to be bought off.

Then he had Charles Annesley and Frank
Annesley on his back. Francis Annesley, an
English barrister, claimed a large portion of the
estates, and filed his bill in England. Charles
Annesley had a large claim under Earl James's
will, which claim Richard, Lord Anglesey, had lately
compromised for a third, and then, with his usual
perfidy, evaded the compromise, whereon Charles

obtained a decree with costs, and a sequestration, under the terms of which Charles now received all the Irish rents, and paid himself his share. The earl, therefore, was in the power of Charles Annesley for his very subsistence.

On the top of all this came James Annesley, armed with McKercher, and hard cash, of which his lordship, like many other Irish proprietors, had mighty little, compared with the value of his estates.

Thus attacked on all sides, and influenced probably by some reasons not easy to penetrate so long after the event, he began to falter: and being at his house in Bolton Row, which house the writer of these lines (be it said in passing) occupied, for some years, a century later, he sent for his London solicitor, Giffard, and directed him to try and effect a compromise with Jemmy, as he called him.

Giffard was too cautious to commit his client to writing, in a matter so dangerous, but he intimated to McKercher that he had something important to say, if McKercher would come to London. McKercher wrote back very courteously to say he was very busy collecting evidence, but would wait on Mr. Giffard in a fortnight. In anticipation of this conference, Lord Anglesey told Giffard on what terms he would resign his estates, and live in France. He even went so far as to engage a French tutor.

Meantime, James Annesley was a guest of Mr. Thomas Chester, and a favoured suitor for his niece's hand. The old lawyer liked James, and, at this time, hardly doubted he was the real heir to the late Lord Altham, and he intimated plainly that if Mr. Annesley would allow Philippa's dower, whatever it might be, to be settled on herself, they might marry as soon as they choose, for him.

Young Annesley smiled at this stipulation. "I hope to settle half the counties of Wexford and Meath on her, besides," said he. So one Sunday morning the lovers were seated in a pew, with their heads over one prayer-book, her dear old tutor delivered certain ephemeral words that seemed to this happy pair to have a strange vitality, compared with the immortal part of the Liturgy. Said he, in a sonorous, yet kindly voice, "I publish— the banns—of marriage—between the Honourable James Annesley, bachelor, of the parish of Dunmaine, in Ireland, and Mistress Joanna Philippa Chester, spinster, of this parish. This is the first time of asking. If any of you know cause or just impediment why these two persons should not be joined together in holy wedlock, ye are now to declare it."

While these words were delivered, Philippa's face was a picture: her eyes lowered, her cheeks mantling with a gentle blush. The words rang strangely in those lovers' ears.

How tight custom holds civilized men and women, and flies them but with a string: both had led adventurous lives, had been slaves in a distant colony, and this demure lass, with long black lashes lowered, had played a fine caper in boy's clothes. Yet there they must sit at last, over one prayer-book, in Staines church, and hear their banns cried in one breath with two more couple that had never budged out of Middlesex.

Let the reader now contemplate this pretty picture, and James Annesley's prospects, a rose-coloured panorama. In Ireland, his interests pushed by that rarest of all friends, an able and zealous attorney; in London, his arch enemy losing heart, and preparing to accept an income, and retire from the disputed estates to Paris. In Staines, his hand in his sweet Philippa's, and holy wedlock, the sacred union of two pure and well-tried hearts, awaiting him in one little fortnight; even that fortnight to be spent in sight of Paradise; and the gate ajar.

Writers are human; and I feel myself linger here, for it grieves even hardened me to have to plunge again into the misfortunes of the good : but now are my wings of fancy clipped, hard Fact holds me with remorseless grasp, and I am constrained to show how all this bright picture was shivered in a day, and by the man's own hand.

CHAPTER VIII.

MR. THOMAS CHESTER had retired from the law, with a comfortable fortune. He was now a bit of a sportsman : rented of Sir John Dolben the right of fishing the Thames for some distance, and of shooting over a part of the manor ; and paid half Sir John's gamekeeper. He was a man that respected the rights of others, and stickled for his own. He did not mind a stray cockney fishing his perch, roach, and gudgeons, with the hook, for that was fair sport ; but he was bitter against all who poached on his water with nets, for he said, "They rob not me only of my fish, but my fish of their lives ; tis not sport, 'tis larceny."

Annesley had often heard him say this. One day Annesley came out with his gun to Redding, the gamekeeper, and they were about to go out together shooting waterfowl ; this was the only sport to be had, for it was the 1st of May.

As they were about to start, Redding cast his

"'My father! they have murdered him.'"—*Page* 185.

eyes round and saw one Thomas Eaglestone and
his son casting a net from Sylvester's meadow.
" There is that old rogue again," said he. " Let
us have his net." He set off to run, and Annesley
ran after him, to help. Redding came up first,
and collared Eaglestone. But he, to save his net,
threw it half into the river: then young Eaglestone seized the cord, cut it, and jumped into the
river. Annesley snatched at the net, and his gun
went off. Old Eaglestone cried, " Villain, you
have slain me," and fell, scorched and bleeding, on
the ground, and never spoke more. The boy
swam away to the other bank, and the smoke of
the gun drifting away revealed the man lying in
the agonies of death, and Annesley and Redding so
stupefied and appalled, that they did not move
hand or foot, but gazed with terror at each other,
and at their bloody work.

They had but just realized that the man was
shot, and in the agonies of death, when young
Eaglestone was heard to cry across the water,
" My father ! they have murdered him."

Then Redding seized Annesley by the arm,
" Heard you that ? They will hang us," and set
off instantly to run; which cowardly and im-
prudent course Annesley, who was quite unnerved,
unhappily imitated, scarcely knowing what he did.

They got to Redding's house; and Redding laid his
hand on all the money he could, and fled the
country: but Annesley would go no farther. He
said, " I have slain an innocent man; and let me
die for it." He sat a little while, with his head
and his hands all of a heap, and then fell on to the
floor in a fainting fit. There were three women in
the house; they raised him, and just then the
constables were seen coming with young Eaglestone. What did these wise women do, but drag
him upstairs, and hide him in a sort of partition
between two floors; and there the constables, who
had sure information he was in the house, found
him without any trouble. This hiding told heavily
against him, both then and afterwards. In such
terrible cases courage is the better part of discretion.

They found him in a state so deplorable, that
they set him in a chair in the yard, and sprinkled
his face with water; and he was some time before
he could command his limbs and walk with them
to the justice.

A number of people followed the officers, and
when they came upon the bridge, James stopped,
and said, " Have I no friends here ? " Then there
was a cry of " Ay ! " for indeed he was already
respected in that part. " Then," said he, " I do

implore you throw me over the bridge, and end me; for I have slain an innocent man, and shall never more know peace."

The justice sent them to Sir Thomas Reynell, and he heard the evidence, and committed him.

They had five miles to go, and all drank together on the road, and things were said over the liquor that afterwards affected the case.

As for James Annesley, he fell now into a dull resignation, and his regret was greater than his fear, except for Philippa. He gave one William Duffell a crown piece to go to Philippa, and beg her not to believe one word she should hear, except from his own lips. "Speak comfortably to her, good William, or this will kill her too:" and then for the first time he began to cry and bemoan himself.

Duffell sped on his errand; but others had been before him. Remorseless Rumour came open-mouthed to Mr. Chester's house, and told Philippa James Annesley had murdered a man.

She was as white as a sheet in a moment and trembled: but her faith supported her. "'Tis false!" said she. But tongue followed tongue, and, as the vulgar always exaggerate and add, a crop of lies were engrafted into the little bit of truth, and threats, and oaths were said to have preceded the firing of the gun. Even Philippa's faith was giving way under repeated attacks, when Duffell came in with that comfortable message.

She cried out, as if he could hear her, "Believe thee a wilful murderer? That I never will. Unfortunate thou always wast. But guilty never." Then she said she would go to him on the instant. "Where is he?"

"IN THE CAGE AT HOUNSLOW."

She was with him in less than an hour; and, with the two pale faces close together, he told her how it had happened. She believed him; she consoled him; she treated it as a simple misfortune, for which he must grieve, but could never be punished, and she left him greatly encouraged. But her words were bolder than her heart, and, when she reached home, the great restraint she had put upon herself, for love of him, gave way, her body overpowered her great spirit, and she had faintings one after another that laid her low. Though prostrated herself, this noble girl dictated words of comfort to her unfortunate lover every day, and Thomas Chester carried them. Mr. Chester exerted himself to bail James Annesley, and appeared likely to succeed, when suddenly one Giffard, a London solicitor, appeared for young Eaglestone, and objected with such ability and weight, that Sir Thomas Reynell said he must consider the matter and take advice. Then Mr. Chester saw that Annesley was to be prosecuted vindictively; and he conceived some grave suspicions, and began sadly to fear the final result of this unhappy business.

What I have now to relate will show the reader his suspicions were well founded.

CHAPTER IX.

IT was eleven o'clock on the 2nd of May. The Earl of Anglesey lay in state, receiving visits in bed. On the sheets beside him lay his peruke superbly powdered, and adorned with a Ramilies tie. A servant held a small glass before him, and while he talked to his visitors, he tinged his cheeks with carmine, and put on his patches, as openly as if these things were essential parts of a toilet.

His conversation was mighty vapid, affected, and lisping, until his courier, Lawler, knocked loudly at the door, and said, "I must speak with my lord on the instant."

"Ask him where he comes from?" said my lord, laying aside his affectation.

The man burst into the room, and answered, "From Staines, where you left me to watch James Annesley; and, my lord, I bring strange news."

"Fling a bottle of scent over him, and leave us in private," said Lord Anglesey.

This was done, and Lawler told him James Annesley had killed a man at Staines, and was now in the cage at Hounslow.

"What fool's tale is this? I can't be so fortunate."

"Nay, my lord, 'tis the truth: but some say 'twas accident, others say 'twas done of malice."

Lord Anglesey's eyes glittered: "So say I, and I will prove it, if money can do't."

He gave the man a gold piece, and dismissed him: dressed himself in half an hour instead of two hours as usual, and went at once to his attorney Giffard, told him the good news, and that all thought of a compromise was at an end. "Go down to Staines on the instant," said he, "and tell me can we hang that knave." Giffard went down, and saw young Eaglestone and others, and reported that John Eaglestone could hang or transport James Annesley. "Then," said Lord Anglesey, "you must be his lawyer, and I will find the money, if I pawn my diamond ring."

Giffard did not much like the business, but he undertook it, sooner than lose his noble client. He advised Lord Anglesey on no account to appear in the business, or he would prejudice the

prosecution, and he himself saw young Eaglestone, and easily moulded him to Lord Anglesey's
purpose, by rousing his cupidity, and also his
desire of vengeance for his father's slaughter.

Thus the Crown was used as an instrument of
private vengeance. Yet who could object? Only
the son and his attorney were seen. The ruthless
man who bribed the witnesses and spurred the
law was in the dark.

But they were not to have it all their own way.
James had written post-haste to McKercher. He
handed over the other business to his clerk, Pat
Higgins, and came at once to Hounslow; saw the
prisoner, found Giffard was in it, whom he knew
to be Lord Anglesey's attorney, saw Anglesey
behind Giffard, and his very first move in the case
was one that had never occurred to Thomas
Chester, nor to any other friend of Annesley's,
though many were coming about him now. He
put Lord Anglesey under a system of espionage as
complete and subtle as ever Fouché brought to
bear on a man; and he told nobody but Philippa,
and bound her to secresy. This done he proceeded
to the legitimate defence, and left no stone un-
turned. But he could never get at the most
dangerous witness, young Eaglestone. Giffard
kept him too close.

He encountered Giffard once or twice, and always treated him with profound respect; separated him entirely from his client, and charmed him with his good temper and urbanity. "Ah, sir," said he, "if you knew Mr. Annesley, his goodness, and his misfortunes, you would regret the severity you are compelled to show him."

"I regret it now," said Giffard.

Just before the trial, Philippa, who was all zeal and intelligence, secured a piece of evidence to prove that the boy Eaglestone had not been so confident the gun was fired purposely, until Giffard came on the scene. But, with all her efforts, that was all she could do for her lover now. How different from former times, when she was a boy !

She spoke of her helplessness to McKercher, with tears in her eyes, and told him it had not been always so.

"Helpless, madam !" said McKercher: by the hoky, beauty is never helpless. You have found him a witness that I'd never have heerd of may be, and ye can do him a good turn at the trile, if you have the courage to come."

"The courage to come !" cried she. "I have the courage to die for him, or die with him. Of course I will be there, with my hand in his all the

time, to show that there's one who knows he is not
a murderer."

"Ah, if they'd only let us," said McKercher,
with a sigh. "But I'll have you on the bench,
ony way, an' I'll find some way to let the jury
know they'll have to strike at his head through
your heart, alanna:" and the warm-hearted
sharper was very near crying.

The dreadful day of the trial came at last.
Philippa was seated on the right hand of the
judge's seat, but on a lower bench. She was
dressed, by McKercher's advice, in black silk,
with a small head-dress of white lace, and no
ornament but a diamond cross on her bosom.
There she sat in a frame of mind beyond the pen
to paint. This was her first court of law; her
first trial. The solemnity, the ancient usages, and
all the panoply of justice, struck upon her young
mind in one blow with the danger of him whose
young life was bound up in hers: and for this
reason I shall briefly describe this trial from her
point of view; and the reader who has imagination will do well to co-operate with me, by putting
himself in her place, as well as in the place of
the accused.

First there was the usual hardened buzz of

lawyers, to whom this terrible scene was but an every-day business. Philippa heard with wonder and horror. What! could men chatter when a life, and such a life, was at stake?

Then came in the judge, in ermine and scarlet, and all stood up. Philippa eyed him as a divinity on whom her darling's life depended.

Then the prisoners were brought to the bar, Redding having surrendered. Philippa uttered a faint cry, instantly suppressed, and her eye and her lover's met in a gaze that was beyond words.

But here the proceedings were disturbed for a moment, by the entrance of a gorgeous gentleman, in scarlet and gold, powdered peruke, and Ramilies tie, who stalked in, and seated himself by the judge. This was Lord Anglesey, come to gloat over the criminal, and keep the witnesses for the prosecution up to the mark. He stared on the public as on so many dogs, and on James Annesley with a bitter sneer. James was all in black velvet, with weepers, as one who mourned the death he had caused.

Silence having been obtained, the prisoners were arraigned, and the indictment charged against James Annesley, labourer, that he, not having God before his eyes, but moved by the instigation of the devil, on the 1st of May, with force and

arms, in and upon one Thomas Eaglestone, feloni-
ously, wilfully, and of malice aforethought, did
make an assault, and that he, the said James
Annesley, with a certain gun, of the value of five
shillings, being charged with powder and leaden
shot, did discharge, and shoot out of the said gun,
by force of the gunpowder as aforesaid, and him
the said Thomas Eaglestone in and upon the left
side of the belly of the said Thomas, did strike
and penetrate, giving to him, the said Thomas,
on the said side of his said belly, one mortal
wound, of the breadth of one inch, and of the
depth of four inches, whereof the aforesaid Thomas
then and there instantly died. The indictment
then repeated the nature of the act, describing it,
in the usual terms, as wilful murder, and against
the peace of our Lord the King, his Crown and
dignity.

The virulent terms of the indictment, being
new to poor Philippa, made her blood run cold;
for it seemed to her that the Crown thirsted for
his blood, and would not stick at any exaggeration
to hang him.

The Clerk of Arraigns now put the usual question, in a loud voice, "How say you, James
Annesley, are you guilty of this felony, or not
guilty ?"

James Annesley, thus called upon before judge, jury, enemy, and sweetheart, showed unexpected qualities. Though a man of unsteady nerves when hurried, he lacked neither dignity nor courage—give him time—and what little bile he had in his nature was stirred by the sight of the man who had kidnapped him as a child, now hunting him down as a man. Instead of simply pleading not guilty, he objected to the terms of the indictment. "I observe, my lord," said he to the judge, respectfully, but firmly, "that I am indicted as a labourer. Now 'tis well known that I claim the earldom of Anglesey and great estates, and am likely to make good my claim elsewhere. This word ' labourer' therefore can never have come from the mind of the Crown. Kings are gentlemen ; they do not insult the gentlemen whose lives they seek. Surely there is some private malice behind the Crown."

This observation being received in dead silence, he asked his lordship to let him be tried within the bar, in respect of his quality.

"Certainly, Mr. Annesley," said my lord. But he thought to himself, "I shall have to hang you all the same."

Then both prisoners were allowed to sit within the bar.

Then the jury were sworn, and Serjeant Gupper

opened the case in the close dry way of a counsel
who feels that the facts can be trusted to do the
work. He stated that the Eaglestones were fishing
in a meadow that belonged to one Sylvester, and
that Annesley and Redding came on to the ground,
and first threatened Thomas, with foul language,
and then shot him; and, even after that, threatened
John; but he escaped across the river, and brought
the constables after the prisoners, who, well knowing their guilt, had fled : but Annesley was found
hidden in Redding's house, and dragged forth, and
afterwards offered the boy money not to come
against him : but he said, "I will not sell my
father's blood."

When this neat outline was delivered with
perfect sobriety, everybody looked at the prisoners,
and Annesley in particular, as dead men.

The counsel for the Crown called John Eaglestone first. He swore to the preliminary matter,
which was, indeed, undisputed, and declared that,
while Redding was collaring his father, Annesley
threatened the old man's life, with a ruffian-like
oath, if he did not give up his net; and then, not
waiting for the old man's answer, *shouldered* his
gun and shot him dead, and afterwards threatened
him with the butt end of his piece, but he escaped
by swimming, and ran instantly for the constables.

He swore also to the hiding of Annesley, and his subsequent attempt at bribery.

Philippa, at this stage, felt all the bitterness of death; and could scarcely sit upright.

In cross-examination John Eaglestone was asked whether he had not given a different account to three persons, Duffin, and Dalton, and Thomas Chester. He looked staggered a moment, but boldly swore he had not.

McKercher then showed his teeth. Counsel, carefully instructed by him, drew from the witness that he was now living with one Williams, whom he had not known before this trial, was called his servant, but dined at his table.

Counsel.—"Of course you have seen my Lord Anglesey at Williams's?"

The Court here interrupted, and said the question was improper.

A juryman, however, asked this boy a very pertinent question, whether there was no jostling or struggling for the net between Annesley and him. He said, "No."

Many other witnesses were called for the Crown; but they were all at some distance, and only proved the killing. Fisher, indeed, one of these witnesses, said that he saw Annesley snatch at the the net, and then the gun went off.

This rather contradicted Eaglestone, and gratified the juryman aforesaid.

This Fisher, though a witness for the Crown, admitted, under cross-examination, that, within two hours of the event, young Eaglestone had told him he believed the act was not done designedly.

Counsel for the Crown then commented on the evidence, dwelt upon the sanguinary threats that had been proved, and not disproved on cross-examination, and demanded a verdict.

This closed the case for the Crown.

The Court then called on James Annesley in these terms : " Mr. Annesley, you are indicted in a very unhappy case. What have you to say ? "

James Annesley then surprised his friends again. He rose like a tower, and spoke as follows : " My lord, I am quite unable to make a proper defence, having been kidnapped when a child by him, who now seeks my life under the disguise of a public prosecutor, and so I lost the education I was entitled to by my birth."

He paused long on these words, and turned his eyes so full on Lord Anglesey, that every soul in court turned too, and looked at him. A shiver ran through the court. It was indeed a remarkable combination; a remarkable situation. In fact, considering that the defendant here was to be the plaintiff in a great civil suit, if he could save his neck, and that the nobleman who sat by the judge in England, to see him hanged, was to be defendant in that suit, should this indictment fail, the situation was, perhaps, without a parallel in all time.

James Annesley resumed: " My lord, you have heard a true and deplorable accident, falsely and maliciously described in this court, with a view to stopping lawful proceedings in the Court of Exchequer in Ireland. The simple truth is that neither I nor my innocent fellow prisoner were trespassers. He is gamekeeper to the lord of the manor. It was his duty to seize a poacher's net, and I ran with him to help him. The deceased threw the net half into the river. The boy jumped in, to swim across with it. I stepped to seize one of the ropes that trailed on the ground, and the gun went off, to my great surprise and grief, and killed a poor man, whose name I did not then know, and he never wronged *me*, and I had no malice against him, nor ground of malice.

" My lord, and gentlemen, mine has been a life of strange misfortunes ; but, believe me, whatever your verdict may be, it must always be my greatest grief that I have caused the death of an innocent man."

These words, delivered with great decency and

touching resignation, drew tears from many eyes
besides Philippa's, and even the judge bowed his
head slightly in sober but profound approval of
the prisoner's concluding sentence.

Redding, called on for his defence, said that he
had seized the net, in discharge of his duty. That,
when the man fell, Mr. Annesley did not know that
he had shot him, and would not believe him till he
turned up the flap of the man's coat, and found
the wound: and then Mr. Annesley showed such
grief and concern, that he felt sure it was as pure
an accident as ever happened in this world. The
judge then retired for some refreshment, and there
was a buzz of conversation, and by the time the
judge returned, everybody in court understood the
relation of the parties: the lovers both in black,
and that shameless peer, who would hang the
young man in England, to stop his lawsuit in Ireland; and the judge sitting in his place, between
the defendant's true lover and his enemy.

THE EVIDENCE FOR THE DEFENCE.

They proved, by documents and evidence, that
Sir J. Dolben was lord of the manor, and Redding
his gamekeeper, with full powers to seize nets, etc.
Then, by Dalton, who was Philippa's witness, that,
on the day of the killing, young Eaglestone had

said distinctly he believed it was done undesignedly. Then, by two more respectable witnesses, that he had said the same thing next day.

Then they traced his change of mind to Giffard.

Then they went on, and connected Giffard with Anglesey.

Then they went further, and proved that Anglesey was constantly with Williams, and that Williams was keeping young Eaglestone *like a gentleman.*

Thereupon Anglesey turned pale as ashes, and fidgeted on his seat, and Philippa, looking like a woman at the jurymen's faces, turned red, and her eyes flashed, for she saw them cast looks of disgust and contempt at him.

Then they brought two medical men of high character, who had probed Eaglestone's wound, and declared the shot had gone not downwards, but upwards, and, indeed, at a considerable angle, and that the blisters at the *back of the body,* caused by the shot, were several inches higher than the wound. This evidence agreed with Annesley's account and Fisher's, and not with Eaglestone's testimony that the gun had been shouldered.

This closed the defendant's case.

The judge summed up briefly. He said that the sting of the indictment lay in John Eaglestone's evidence. The other witnesses for the Crown had proved nothing but the killing, which was super-fluous, since the prisoners admitted it. That, as to Eaglestone's evidence, it was highly damnatory, but unsupported by any other witness, and contra-dicted in one vital part of it by the two surgeons; in another respect, viz.: as to whether the act was intentional, the same witness was contradicted by himself, and in the worst possible way; for, while the act was fresh in his memory, he had said repeatedly that it was accidental; and it was only when his mind had been worked upon by some person or persons not present at the act, that he had come to say it was intentional. Against Red-ding there was not the shadow of a case. Against Annesley, the charge of murder had failed; but they must consider whether it was manslaughter, or chance-medley. If they thought the gun went off accidentally, it was chance-medley.

The jury, being invited to retire and consider their verdict, said, through their foreman, there was no need for that, as they had made up their minds long ago, and thereupon brought it in chance-medley, which was, in fact, a verdict of acquittal.

The Court then discharged the prisoners on the spot, and in five minutes Philippa and James were

rattling down to Staines in a chaise and four,
which McKercher, who knew he had made the
the verdict safe, had provided, and ribboned the
horses; he followed in a chaise and pair with
Redding.

James and Philippa sat hand in hand all the
way, with hearts almost too full for words; and
the church bells rang for his escape as they had
for hers.

Philippa flung her arms round McKercher that
night and kissed him, and blessed him, so that
the good-hearted sharper shed a tear. He told her
all the blood in his heart was at her service; and
what he had done for James that day in England
was child's play compared with what he would do
for him in Ireland.

He was off to Ireland next day; but he left a
sting behind him. Ere he had been gone a month,
out came a volume, called "Memoirs of an Unfortunate Young Nobleman," in which, under the thin
disguise of "Anglia" for "Anglesey," "Altamont"
for "Altham," and so on, a full and interesting
account was given of James Annesley's wrongs,
and Lord Anglesey's vices, including his trigamy,
and other matters not relevant to James Annesley's
concerns.

Lord Anglesey, at this time, was in a stupid,

sullen state. He had left the court disappointed,
rebuked, and exposed. He stormed at Giffard for
his defeat, and quarrelled with him, and would only
pay half his costs. Whereupon Giffard sued him.
Anglesey employed a solicitor. He subjected Giffard to interrogatories. McKercher heard of them,
and subpœnaed Giffard for the Irish trial. Anglesey, though he swore he would run his sword
through McKercher at the first opportunity, dared
not indict his publisher for the "Memoirs," though
libellous. He lay quiet, even when the *Gentleman's
Magazine* came out with the whole substance of
the book, and made him a by-word throughout
the nation.

Nevertheless, this stirred him up an unexpected
friend. Charles Annesley wrote to him, and said,
"This is a very serious matter. We had better
lay aside all differences, and make common cause
against this upstart, James Annesley." Lord
Anglesey replied that he did not know which
way to turn; he had drained himself already, in
trying to unmask that imposter in Ireland, and
hang him in England.

Charles Annesley replied that he would find ten
thousand pounds that year, sooner than see the
estates and title transferred to this upstart, by
perjury and lying romances.

Thus encouraged, Lord Anglesey drew largely on Charles Annesley, and went into Ireland, and employed agents of all sorts, and poured out money like water.

His presence and influence were soon marked by a sinister event. Pat Higgins, McKercher's clerk, returning to Dublin with valuable notes of evidence, disappeared, together with his papers. McKercher, whose own corrupt practices were bloodless, vowed he had been bought by Lord Anglesey's men and sent out of the country. But he was never heard of again, and it is the general opinion in Ireland now that he was made away with by persons in the employ of Anglesey.

McKercher now got leases signed by James Annesley, and put his lessees into possession of several farms in Meath. Anglesey ousted them by force, and Campbell Craig, one of the tenants so ousted, who was a tool of McKercher's, served a writ of ejectment on Lord Anglesey in the Irish Court of Exchequer. This brought the matter to an issue, and the cause was set down for trial. Though the actual property in litigation was small, all the Irish estates of Lord Anglesey depended on the verdict in Craig *v.* Anglesey: of that the parties were agreed.

But meantime James Annesley had fallen into

deep dejection of spirits. The malicious prosecution had done him good; it had stirred up his
resistance ; but, now a jury had acquitted him, he
could not forgive himself for having killed a man.

McKercher comforted him, rallied him, but all
in vain. He actually wanted to drop the proceedings against Lord Anglesey. "He will beat me,"
said he : "I shall never thrive. I have shed
innocent blood."

McKercher was first sorry, then angry, then
alarmed. He wrote seriously to Philippa about
him, and she wrote back directly, "Send him to
me."

In anticipation of his arrival, Philippa made
Mr. Chester buy James a horse ; and she had a
riding dress made so masculine, that she could
speak her mind more freely in it. She had also a
country dress for walking, made ; and, when he
came, she encountered his melancholy point blank
with hilarity. "Your spirits want a *philip*, sir,"
said she, "and I must give them one." She rode
with him, she walked huge walks with him, she
would not let him mope or pine. She was Philip
one moment, all vivacity and cheerfulness ; Philippa the next, all tenderness ; and neither out of
place. Her resolution, with her wit, and her
tenderness, attacked his despondency with so many

weapons, and such minute pertinacity, that at last she drove the dark cloud away, and the man plucked up heart again to fight his enemies, and love his sweetheart as she deserved: and here I cannot help observing that, if this man's misfortunes were almost unparalleled, so his good fortune, in finding so rare a woman as this to love him, was almost as singular. I believe that at this juncture she saved him from the mad-house. Well, she had her reward; she saw the colour creep back to the beloved cheek, the brilliancy to the dull eye: she saw the shapely head held up again, and, at last, she heard the beloved tongue bless her for what she had done.

But a deep mortification was in store for poor James Annesley: and one that took him by surprise, and tried his temper and his heart in the very furnace.

Mr. Thomas Chester had been for some time growing rather cold to him; but, seeing him so down-hearted, had not spoken his mind: but he now took an opportunity, and had it out with him. He said, "Mr. Annesley, if you had come to me as a poor gentleman, of no pretensions, I think I should have said to you, ' Show yourself willing to make a livelihood, and you shall have my niece, since matters have gone so far between you.' But

P

you call yourself the son of Lord and Lady Altham, and others say you are not so, for my lady never had a son."

"I assure you, sir, on my honour——"

"And I assure you, on my honour, that you do not remember the circumstances of your birth, any more than I do mine. Therefore, sir, by the kindness that is between us, I beg of you not to abuse your influence with my niece, by urging her to marry you, unless you can make good your pretensions. I could show you it would be unwise to take any other course, on account of the singular powers Mr. Hanway and myself possess under her father's will: but I prefer to appeal first to your honour and delicacy."

James Annesley, though wounded to the heart, replied, with perfect dignity: "Mr. Chester, after the stain that has fallen on me, I have never asked my dear Philippa to marry me; but, since you offer her to me on condition that I can prove my birth before a jury of my own countrymen, I take you at your word; and so be it. And, sir, I bear you no ill-will for this. You are an honest man, and Philippa's true friend, and to be her friend is to be mine."

"That is very handsomely said, young man," said Mr. Chester.

Annesley thought over this for an hour or two; and, after dinner, he burst out before Philippa: "Sir, you have roused me from my lethargy. I value Philippa's hand more than I do the lands and title I have been robbed of. I shall start for Ireland to-morrow."

"So soon?" said Philippa.

"Ay, sweet one," said he: "and, if I am not the true Earl of Anglesey, I will never trouble you again, nor your good uncle."

Philippa turned pale, and knit her black brows at Mr. Chester. "Uncle," said she, "you have been saying something to him."

"No more than my own conscience says to me," replied Annesley, before the old lawyer could speak a word.

James Annesley stood firm, and parted from Philippa tenderly, but hopefully, next day. Philippa was inconsolable, and kept her room. When she did reappear, her uncle saw, with regret, that he had lost her affection.

She scarcely spoke to him, never volunteered a remark, and treated him with a bitter coldness that distressed him. However, he felt sure he had done his duty, and his niece would see that, too, some day. So he remained firm. But he was uncomfortable, to say the least. She went about

the house pale and gloomy, knitting her magnifi-
cent brows, and never speaking, nor smiling, except
when she got a letter from James, and then it was
as if the dead had come to life; ardent kisses on
the paper, eager devouring of the contents, eyes
streaming; and then away to some secret place,
to read it again all alone.

At last he made an appeal to her one day. He
said, gently: "Philippa, let me ask thee a question.
Dost thou really think Thomas Chester is thine
enemy?"

The girl hesitated, and then said, " Why,
n-n-no."

"Thou knowest he is not, but loved thy father
dearly, and loveth thee. Then would it not become
thine years to say, 'This is an old, experienced
man, who loves me. Let me not condemn him
hastily, lest I fight against my own good.'"

The sullen eyes began to fill at that: but never
a word.

However, he said no more; for he saw the shaft
had gone home.

But two days after this came a letter to say that
the trial, after several postponements, was to be
that day month, by special appointment; and that
McKercher was hopeful, though not confident. The
assassination, or spiriting away, of Higgins, with

his notes, the fruit of two months' research, was very unfortunate.

The letter had been a week coming.

Philippa brought it to Mr. Chester, and coolly putting her arm round his neck, as if their attachment had never been interrupted, she said, " Uncle, dear, please you read that."

So he smiled, well pleased at being " Uncle dear'd " again all of a sudden ; and he read the letter. " Well," said he, " at all events it will end his suspense and yours."

" Uncle, dear," said the young lady, "you asked me, did I doubt your affection ? Well, of course you cannot love as *he* doth ; but I do think you love me a little, in your way. But that I shall soon know ; for I shall put it to the proof. Uncle, dear, if you love me, go with me straightway to—Dublin."

He started, and then said, " That is as if you should say, 'Sweet uncle—I know you love me —take me into the pit of torment.'"

" Oh, fie ! fie ! "

" What else is litigation ? If I take you to Dublin, you will be in court, as you were at the Old Bailey, sore against my wish : and here 'twill be ten times worse ; for you will hear him taunted by counsel, and exposed by a score of witnesses, and defeated in the end."

The young lady smiled superbly. " Uncle," said she, " you are learned in the law, no doubt ; but most unlearned in women's hearts : each word you have spoken, it is a chain of steel, and draws me to Dublin by the heart.   Had you but said, ' He will surely win, and can be happy without thee for a time,' I had yielded : but, when you tell me he shall be defeated and shamed over there, then am I here on hot coals, and cannot bide.   Know that I love him as men cannot love.   I grudge him no triumph all to himself, no solitary joy.   But trouble—and I not have my part ! shame—and I not blush with him !   Nay, but I tell you, not one sup of grief, sorrow, shame, or any mortal ill, shall *ever* reach his lips but I *will* have my share on't, by the God that made me ; ay, made me for no other use that I know of, but to console my darling, that is the very pearl of goodness, and the butt of misfortune from his birth."

She clasped her hands with angelic fervour, and was gone, with the words.

The old lawyer looked after her admiringly, but sadly.   " She is too good to last," thought he. " I fear she is like her father, and will ne'er make old bones."   Then he fell into one of the long reveries a thoughtful old man is subject to, since the past offers a larger landscape to him than to the young.

He had been thus an hour and more, when in came a swift foot ; he looked up, and there stood— Philip, in the very clothes he had last worn at Wilmington ; he had put on, with them, his old audacity, with which, however, a hot blush was doing battle.

"Now, uncle," said he, sharply, "how is it to be ? Will you go to Dublin with Philippa, that is a poor timid creature, afraid of men and mice and everything, or shall Philip go alone ? Philip, that fears nought, and feels like Alexander the Great at this moment ; the Lord be praised for doublet and hose."

Mr. Chester interrupted her. "Thou brazen toad, come hither, and let me look at thee. What, is this indeed the disguise thou didst prank thyself in out there ? "

"Ay, uncle, and will again,—if you are unkind. Come now, good sir. Time flies. How is't to be ? "

Mr. Chester uttered a groan of resignation. "Needs must, when the devil drives," said he. "Go you upstairs this minute, and doff that masquerade. To-morrow we will set forth, and be in Dublin this day week, God willing."

CHAPTER X.

PHILIPPA was welcomed with surprise and rapture by James Annesley.

McKercher wore a blank look, that did not escape Philippa, but he recovered himself, and was rather violent in his expressions of satisfaction. Nevertheless his original face of utter dismay imprinted itself on her memory, and puzzled her for some time. She told him she should be present at the trial. He assented, with a great show of warmth, and, having assented, began to raise one objection after another.

" It will be the longest trial ever known."

" No longer for me than for him."

" The court will be crowded to suffocation."

" What strangers can bear, I can."

" 'Twill be a bitter fight this time."

She did not deign a reply.

" 'Tis pity you should hear him taunted by their counsel and their witnesses."

"I have borne to hear him charged with murder."

"There will be hard swearing: they have forty witnesses."

"When I know all that malice can say against him, then I shall be the better able to comfort him."

Her face, with its native power and indomitable resolution, lent double effect to her words. McKercher gave in, and said, with a sort of admiring sigh, "Och, sure thin, go which way it will, he's a lucky man."

She was too lofty to affect to misunderstand him. She said, simply, "It is the one piece of good fortune in his hard, his cruel lot;" and then a gentle tear stole down the lovely cheek, and McKercher was subdued entirely, and, keeping his misgivings to himself, made it his business to get her and Thomas Chester excellent seats at the trial. It was one of great expectation. When Philippa entered the court, a very large and commodious one, the floor was already crowded with the public, and, before she had been there ten minutes—for she went early—all the seats about the bench, and below the bench, were filled with Irish peers and peeresses, gorgeously dressed, and the gallery crowded with citizens and their wives.

Presently the claimant entered with his friends; not dressed in black, as at the last trial, but in a rich suit of purple velvet, and a gold sword-hilt. He wore an air of composure, but Philippa could see that he was flushed with excitement.

A sort of doubtful murmur ran round the court when he took his seat; but several of the ladies whispered in favour of his personal appearance, which, indeed, was captivating.

Lord Anglesey and his friends came in soon after, and he took his seat; but first he looked round the court, and exchanged bows with all the most distinguished persons present.

His eyes and James Annesley's met, and James turned a little pale at the sight of this implacable foe. He remembered the day he was kidnapped. The earl, more self-possessed, stared at him with a sort of over-looking air; and after that ignored him utterly. The general feeling was in favour of Lord Anglesey. They were great worshippers of rank in Ireland, and his lordship's rank was established: the chances were this claimant was an upstart.

Everything betokened an extraordinary battle. The prodigious number and various dresses of the witnesses on both sides, and the number of counsel engaged, thirteen for the claimant, led

by Mr. Marshall, second Serjeant, and fifteen for
the defendant, led by prime Serjeant Malone, the
ablest counsellor of that day, either in Ireland or
England.

And now the judges were announced. Hooped
dresses rustled as that brilliant assembly rose, and
no less than three judges entered, in their scarlet
and ermine, to sit on this important case; for it
was a trial at Bar.

The jury's names were called: they were all
gentlemen of good position; there was a baronet
and a right honourable amongst them; and the
only objection to any of them was that a couple had
unexpired leases under Lord Anglesey. McKercher,
however, declined to object to them on that score.
Their swords were girded on them in court and the
trial began.

Mr. Serjeant Marshall opened the case of the
plaintiff's lessor, which I shall ask leave to call
the claimant's case.

It was one that lent itself to a rhetorical open-
ing; but the learned serjeant took the other
great line; in a speech which is worth study as
a model of condensation, and strong sobriety, he
articulated his topics, and marshalled an army of
facts to prove—1. That James Annesley was the
son of Lord and Lady Altham. 2. That the

defendant had kidnapped him, and sent him out of
the country, and, failing in that attempt to get rid
of him, compassed his death in London, by a
prosecution the character of which he should not
describe, but leave it to the witnesses.

But able speeches of counsel are no rarity, and
this trial offered something not only rare, but
marvellous ; two piles of evidence, each as high as
a tower, and each contradicting the other in nearly
all the particulars directly affecting the issue.

They proved by *Mrs. Cole* and by two servants,
that in 1714 Lady Altham had expectation of
offspring, and *Mrs. Heath*, her gentlewoman, knew
it.

Then they advanced a step, and proved by *John
Turner*, seneschal to successive Earls of Anglesey,
that, in the spring of 1715, Lady Altham was
manifestly expecting her confinement; and a year
or so after he saw her teaching a child to walk.
By *Bartholomew Furlong*, a peasant farmer, that
in 1715 her condition was notorious; that, as
ladies of rank never nursed their own children,
he applied personally to Lord and Lady Altham
for his wife to be the nurse, and came to terms
with them, subject to Dr. Brown's approval. But
Dr. Brown did not approve of Mrs. Furlong.
This was confirmed by *Dennis Redmond*, a groom

at Dunmaine, 1714–16, who said the doctor selected for wet nurse *Joan Landy*, a cleanly bright girl, that lived on Lord Altham's land.

By *Dennis Redmond.*—That early in the summer of 1715, *Mrs. Heath* sent him to Ross—three miles from Dunmaine—to fetch Mrs. Shiel, a professional person, since dead; and he brought Mrs. Shiel to Dunmaine on a pillion, and that same day a son was born.

By *Joan Laffan*, chambermaid.—That she was in the *house* when this son was born.

By *Mary Doyle* and *Elinor Murphy.*—That they were in the *room* when this son was born.

By *Captain Fitzgerald.*—That he, being quartered at Ross, Lord Altham asked him to dinner, and to *tap the groaning drink.* (What we call caudle.) Then he came to Dunmaine House, saw the baby in the nurse's arms, and gave her half a guinea. Had seen the same nurse in court that day. "I took notice of her, sir, because she was very handsome, if you will have the truth of it."

By *Alderman Barnes*, of Ross. — That Lord Altham dined with him in Ross, on the alderman's return from a visit, and said over the bottle, "Tom, I'll tell you good news. I've a son by Moll Sheffield." Whereupon he shook his head in disapproval. " Zoons, man!" says my

lord, " why, she's my wife ! " Then I begged his
lordship's pardon, for I remembered my Lady
Altham was daughter to Sheffield, Duke of Buck-
ingham.

Redmond Doyle, *Murphy*, *and Laffan*, servants
in the house at the time, and *Christopher Brown*,
servant to Anthony Cliff, at Ross, swore to the
subsequent christening, accompanied with a bonfire,
and such carousing that " some of them were
drunk in the ditches to the next morning." They all
named as the sponsors three persons who were
since dead, Anthony Colclough, Councillor Cliff,
Madame Pigot, and the clergyman, dead, too.

To cure this excess of death, they proved by
Southwell Pigot, *Esq.*, it was always received in the
Pigot family that Lady Altham had a child.

They proved by *Joan Laffan* that this child was
nursed by *Joan Landy* at her own house, a cabin ;
and that the said cabin was embellished on this
occasion, and a coach-road made to it by which
Lady Altham went daily to see the child. That,
in due time, Master James was weaned, and then
came into Dunmaine House ; and there she,
Laffan, was his dry nurse and sole attendant.
That in February, 1716, Lord and Lady Altham
parted in angry manner about Tom Palliser,
" whose ear," said she coolly, " I saw cut off,"

and Master James pointed to the blood on the floor. Laffan and Redmond both swore that they saw the actual parting; and Lady Altham cried, and begged to have James. But Lord Altham would not let her.

This witness went on and swore that Lady Altham retired to Ross, and the Dunmaine servants took James to her clandestinely, which was confirmed by *Lutwych*, a shoemaker, at Ross, who swore Lady Altham ordered child's shoes of him and bemoaned herself. "I had better be the wife of the poorest tradesman in Ross, for then I could see my child every day; but now I can only see him by stealth."

To conclude their evidence about the deceased Lady Altham they followed her to Dublin, and *John Walsh, Esq.*, swore she had cried to him over her husband's cruelty, but had thanked God "for an indulgent father and a promising young son, who would be a prop to her old age;" and *Mrs. Hodgers*, who let lodgings in Dublin, deposed to a solitary conversation, in which Lady Altham, finding her to be English, gossipped with her, and told her she had a son.

They followed James from Dunmaine to Kinna, Carrickduffe, and other places where Lord Altham had resided, and proved by several witnesses he

had been always dressed, powdered, booted, and
horsed like a nobleman's son till he was more than
ten years of age. Then they proved Lord Altham's
entanglement with Miss Gregory, and also his
poverty, to account in some degree for the boy
being deserted at that time. In proof of his
poverty, one witness swore that *when he kept
hounds one hound would eat another.*

They then opened a vein of indirect evidence
founded on the words and deeds of Lord Anglesey,
the defendant. They grafted this into the case
very neatly, thus :

They proved by several witnesses that Lord
Anglesey was constantly in communication with
Lord Altham, and often at Dunmaine and other
places, and they made it clear that Lord Anglesey
knew for certain whether James Annesley was or
was not his brother Altham's lawful son. This
done, they proved by *Laffan* that she knew defendant well, and that he came home to Dunmaine
a few months after the parting, and asked after
Jemmy, and she told him my lady had begged
hard for him, but my lord would not let her have
him. Then the defendant swore an oath, which
she repeated verbatim, when questioned, and at-
tested that blessed name to which all Christians
bow, that *he* would have let Lady Altham have the

boy, and take him to the devil; "for," said he, "I would keep none of the breed of her."

Having grafted this branch they grew it high.

They called *Dominick Farrell* and *John Purcell*, the latter lamish, and with a staff, but sturdy still.

Foreseeing the terrible difficulty under which I now labour, I stuck close to Purcell's sworn evidence in those earlier scenes he figures in. So please turn back to those scenes, and imagine every word you find there sworn to in open court before the principal actors in the scene—the child, now grown to man's estate, and the barbarous uncle, both glaring at each other, also before Philippa and her eyes that poured black lightning at her lover's treacherous enemy, and before the excitable Irish crowd, that roared and raged like wild beasts at Purcell's every other sentence. He told how he had taken the claimant off a horse in Smithfield, and carried him to his wife, etc.; the first visit of Captain Annesley to his house, when the boy was all terror, but Richard Annesley all politeness, Lord Altham's death, Richard Annesley's changed behaviour, and attempt to kidnap him. He told his tale simply, yet well; anybody could see, by his emotion and earnestness, he was not inventing, but living a real romance over

Q

again.   Once or twice, in relating his sturdy
answers to Lord Anglesey, he involuntarily struck
his stick down upon the table, and so pointed his
speech : but, when he came to the first attempt at
kidnapping, and told how he put the boy between
his legs, and dared that craven lord and his three
bullies, with his single cudgel, he suddenly waved
his staff round his head with a gesture so impul-
sive, that a roar of admiration and sympathy burst
from the crowd, followed by a buzz that interrupted the proceedings for some minutes.

Tenderer feelings were aroused among the tenderer : for, upon this, all the scene came back to
James Annesley, and he made an eloquent motion
of his hand towards the champion of his child-
hood, and then buried his face in his handkerchief.
Many tears were shed all round.

Asked to identify poor little Jemmy, if he could,
John Purcell pointed at once to James Annesley,
and said, with manly emotion, "That is the gentleman.   I KNOW HIM AS WELL AS I KNOW THE HAND
NOW UPON MY HEART."

This witness's cross-examination only led to
fresh triumphs. He was asked with a sneer
whether all those persons could not have taken the
child from him had they really meditated violence.
He replied, " No, SIR," and struck the table with

his staff. "I'D HAVE LOST MY LIFE BEFORE I'D
HAVE LOST THE CHILD."

At this there was a loud huzza, and the very
peeresses about the bench waved their handkerchiefs to the honest fellow, and Philippa could
have hugged them for that.

Having admitted he had afterwards seen him in
a livery, he was asked if he still thought he was
Lord Altham : he replied, frankly, that it had
staggered him ; "but still I thought so in my conscience : FOR MIGHT MAY OVERCOME RIGHT."

This line rang in Dublin that day : and, a
century after, rang round the world; for the
Wizard of the North wove stout John Purcell's
very line, and one more out of this marvellous
trial, into his immortal Romance.

Andrew Conner, proprietor of the ship *James*, of
Dublin, proved by the ship's books that James
Annesley sailed in her for Pennsylvania at a
certain date.

James Reilly and *Mark Byrne*, two rakehelly
fellows, swore they were bribed by Anglesey to
kidnap him at that date. They added to my
account some particulars of the boy's cries and
tears, and the impotent curses of the crowd as they
hurried him on board the ship *James*, of Dublin.

Being now the sixth day of the trial, they closed

this vein of evidence, and the claimant's case, by calling the defendant's own English attorney, Giffard. He deposed that he had been, for a long time, Lord Anglesey's man of business in England, and knew his affairs. Having suits with Lord Haversham, and the Annesleys, and being now menaced by the claimant, defendant said to Giffard, he would be glad to compound for two or three thousand a year, and surrender titles and estates to James Annesley; for it was his right, and, for his part, he would rather his brother's son should have all, than Frank and Charles Annesley: and, in that case, he would live in France. Accordingly, he sent for Mr. Stephen Hayes, to teach him the French tongue.

Q.—"And pray what altered his resolution?"

Giffard, in reply, told the truth, as you see it in my narrative, about the homicide at Staines, with this addition: "He said he did not care if it cost him ten thousand pounds, if he could get James Annesley hanged." He also described the clandestine way in which it was managed, the money wanted in the prosecution coming to him through Jans, Lord Anglesey's factotum.

The plaintiff's case closed, leaving Lord Anglesey an object of immense horror and disgust, and James Annesley the darling of the public.

Said Philippa, "After this, why do they not give him his rights, and have done with it? That miserable old man might have spared himself this exposure, by merely giving his title and estates to the rightful owner."

Says Chester, "It *is* odd, how people cling to these trifles, when they have held them undisturbed for a few years." Then, more gravely, "Niece, do not deceive yourself. We know nothing of the other party's case, as yet, and our own is prejudiced by this conduct of McKercher; he has done a monstrous thing, he has published a libel of the defendant."

"A libel of the defendant! Who can libel that old villain? Who can paint him half as black as nature has made him?"

"The blacker he is, the less need to write a novel about him. Why, in England, the defendant would have attached him for contempt of court. A pretty attorney!"

"He is a lawyer with a heart; that is all his fault. My James had been kidnapped by the old villain, and all but hanged, and he tried to assassinate him here in Ireland, and you cry out because poor, good, kind McKercher replies to bullets, halters, and ten years' slavery—with a book, a few words that break no bones, a few home

truths, that the villain himself hath made to be
so. This is your justice! this is how you cold-
blooded lawyers hold the balance. Oh! if my
eyes could kill the caitiffs, body and soul, I'd give
you something more to cry for. Prithee, speak to
me no more. Men with hearts are a sealed book
to you. There—I would not forget the respect I
owe you. I have done it once. For pity's sake,
uncle—that prince of villains hath fifteen counsel
to gloze his crimes for him; why need you make
the sixteenth, and drive me mad?" She trembled,
and her hands worked, and her eyes flashed fire.

The old man looked at her, thought of her
father, and said, softly, "That is true, and I am
silenced, completely silenced."

"Better so, than for us to quarrel. Forgive
me, uncle, but I do not love my James by halves,
and indeed I am but a woman, and so strung up
by this terrible trial, as I should quarrel with my
own father, if he said one word against my James."

"Nay," said the old man; "I never said a word
against thy James; and never will. He is an
honest man, and hath been cruelly used : and he
is not to blame that his attorney writes novels
pendente lite."

The defendant now opened his case, and called
a cloud of witnesses.

Aaron Lambert, Esq.—Lived near Dunmaine: never heard of nor saw a child of Lord and Lady Altham's. He impeached *Joan Laffan's* credit, unshaken by her cross-examination. He said, "Nobody would believe her, in my opinion, if she swore all the oaths in the universe."

Thomas Palliser, Esq., a squireen.—Lived but three miles from Dunmaine, and visited there. Never heard of a son and heir: but had understood there was a boy about, whose mother was one *Joan Landy.*

William Napper swore that Lord Altham was not succeeded in his estates by the present defendant, but by Arthur, the then Lord Anglesey: that he, the witness, acted for Earl Arthur, and took possession of the Ross estate, on which were near a hundred tenants, and not one made any scruple, nor mentioned a child of Lord Altham's.

Thomas Palliser, junior, delivered a romance illustrative of the time. He was young, and intimate with Lord and Lady Altham. Lord Altham told him one day he was determined to part with her, because he had no child by her: subsequently, by a "principle of selection" that looks rather odd to us English, my lord made his confidant the handle. He asked him to breakfast on mulled claret in a little room of Dunmaine House, called

"Sot's Hole" (a name that would have been more correctly applied to the mansion in general), and, after breakfast, made what the French dramatists call a "fausse sortie;" pretended to go to church, of all places. Palliser, having no other company, went to my lady's room, and sat on a stool. Presently there was a whistle, my lord and his servants burst in, cudgelled him, and, while he was insensible, "CUT OFF THIS EAR; AND THEY MIGHT AS WELL HAVE KILLED ME AS DONE THAT." He then swore there was no child in the house at that time—contradicting *Laffan*.

William Elms confirmed *Palliser, junior*, that the child came into the house after Lady Altham's departure. He swore *Joan Landy* had a child that lived with her, and was miserably dressed till Lady Altham left. Then it was taken into the house, and clothed. After that he came to Dunmaine one day, and saw the child playing at Lord Altham's feet, and Joan Landy came to the gate, and peeped in; and my lord swore, and told the man to let the hounds out and set them at her. He then said he would not for £500 the child should know that jade was his mother.

Thomas Rolph swore he was butler at Dunmaine until Michaelmas, 1715. Between Michaelmas and Christmas, 1715, was discharged, by letter from

Dublin, for *beating the gardener very heartily*. Now
this covered the period of the birth; and all the
plaintiff's witnesses but one had sworn Charles
Magher was the butler at this period. Rolph could
name more servants than any of the claimant's
witnesses could. There was no *Joan Laffy* there
in all his time. *Juggy Lundy*, as he called her,
was discharged, and her child was born soon after:
and he went to her hut to see her. "She lay upon
straw covered with a caddow, and a hurdle at her
head, to' keep the air of the door from her. There
was a place at the feet of the bed, where her brother
lay, and on the other side her father and mother;
and there were stakes drove into the ground and
wattled to keep the straw together." When he
first visited her, her child was but a few days old,
and he asked her whom she called the father, and
she told him. He deposed that he had often seen
the child after that, and given the mother broken
victuals at the stables, and, before he left in
Michaelmas, 1715, the child could go alone, and
ran about with a sort of blanket on its shoulders,
and nothing else. This child was christened, at
Nash, by *Father Michael Downes*. Lady Altham
never visited Joan's cabin, that he knew of. She
was as proud a woman as any in Ireland. She had
heard a scandal, and forbade the woman the house.

This closed that day's proceedings, and poor Philippa's throat was very dry, and her heart sick, and her mind amazed, to hear people swear such contrary things. "Ah, my child," said Thomas Chester, "why would you come here?"

Mrs. Anne Giffard lived near Dunmaine. Was familiar with Lady Altham. Never knew her to have a child. Undertook to prove an *alibi* for her at the time assigned for her birth. She went in a coach with Lady Altham to the Spring assizes at Wexford, 1715. Lord Altham and *Mrs. Heath* rode with them on horseback. Jack Walsh, of Moniseed, Masterton, his nephew, and one Doyle, an English clergyman, all Pretender's men, were tried. She and Lady Altham were in court, and *Cæsar Colclough, Esq.*, sat by them all day.

This *alibi* was sworn to by *Rolph* also, and *Mrs. Heath.*

Now came a pictorial figure of another class: for if all the costumes in this single trial could be faithfully produced, the miserable meagreness of our authorities on that head would be very striking. It was a priest, with his cassock, his huge shoes with iron buckles, and his cockle hat, *Father Michael Downes.* Had now lived forty-two years one mile from Dunmaine House. Dunmaine is in his parish. "No one could have a child in that parish, and I

not know it. Lady Altham never had one : and
Joan Landy had : it was in the year 1714. I was
asked to christen it, but *was rather shy of doing that
until I got a father.* Finally I bethought myself
*there could be no harm done to me for making a
Christian : so I christened him.*"

He deposed, further, that Lord Altham afterwards asked him, had he christened Joan Landy's
child. "I said, 'I have : *but I have got no retribu-
tion,*' meaning christening money. 'Well, well,'
says he, 'I'll requite you hereafter.'"

He deposed, further, that, some years after, he
saw the boy at Dunmaine House, and Lord Altham
swore at the child, and said, "Why don't you get
up and make a bow to him that made you a
Christian ? "

He kept a registry, and, by his own account,
kept it vilely. *Thought* he would have registered
a legitimate child by Lord Altham, *if my lord had
desired him.* Was not used to register illegitimate
children, and gave his "exquisite reasons," as
Shakespeare hath it.

There now stepped upon the table one of the
main pillars of the defence. A tall, elderly
Englishwoman, a glance at whom showed her condition. There was an air of decency about her ;
her clothes were well made, though they were not

rich, her full apron from waist to ancle, her snowy
cap, puckered, and some lawn about her bosom,
were very fine, and beautifully clean, and showed
she had lived with gentlefolks.   This was *Mrs. Mary
Heath*, referred to by so many of the plaintiff's and
defendant's witnesses. She swore that she was
Lady Altham's woman, and came over from
England with her in October, 1713, and lived with
her till the day of her death. Remembered going
down to Dunmaine. Remembered some of the
servants; Setwright the housekeeper, Rolph the
butler, Antony Dyer; Michael the cook, and his
scullery girl, Juggy Landy, who left soon after, and
had a child. Hearing some scandal, she was
curious to see who this child was like; so asked
the coachman's wife to have it brought to the gate,
for her to see. She did see it: it was about six
weeks old then, and had nothing but a clean
blanket. She gave it several things, amongst the
rest a fine cambric neckcloth she had brought from
England amongst her own things.

Her mistress never had a child, nor any expectation of one. She often confided to the witness her
regret, and once, in particular, she came upstairs,
after dinner, crying, and said that brute below
(meaning the defendant) had said he wished she
might never have a child: and my lady said she

wished she might but have a child, to inherit, and she did not care if she was to die the next hour. Was at Ross, with her lady, after the separation, and had no knowledge of *Lutwych, a shoemaker.* Her lady wore braided shoes, but white damask never, all the time she knew her. No child ever visited her at Ross.

Q.—" Was there any child brought to my lady as her child ? "

A.—" No, NEVER WAS. SHE HAD NO CHILD : I CAN SAY NO MORE, IF THEY RACK ME TO DEATH."

She swore that McKercher had called at her home in Holborn, and she had said to him, *inter alia,* " Think you if a child had been born to such an estate, they would not have had his birth registered ? "

This witness was violent, and argued the case too much : yet, under cross-examination, she gave, unconsciously, a picture of her fidelity and affection, that made it hard to believe she could be the woman to lie her unhappy lady's son out of his estate, if she believed he was her son. Counsel was cross-examining her, to prove that Lady Altham's memory was impaired long before she died in 1729, in fact when she came from Ross to Dublin.

" Was not she troubled with a dead palsy ? "

"I cannot call it a dead palsy, sir."

"Did not that disorder deprive her of the use of her limbs?"

"She lost her limbs by that disorder; but it came by degrees. WHEN SHE CAME FROM ROSS, SHE COULD GO ABOUT, WITH HOLDING BY ONE HAND. WHEN WE FIRST WENT TO LONDON, WITH ONE HAND I COULD LEAD HER ABOUT THE ROOM: AND THEN WITH BOTH HANDS; AND THEN NOT AT ALL. I WAS FORCED TO PUT HER IN A CHAIR, AND WHEEL HER ABOUT. BUT HER MIND WAS CLEAR. SHE KEPT HER OWN ACCOUNTS."

That touching, though incidental, picture of fidelity did not appear to strike the court, but it did Philippa Chester, and she felt sorely staggered, and sick at heart. She was silent this evening, while James and Chester and McKercher discussed the evidence.

Mr. Chester said her evidence was crushing, if true; but her manner was rather against her. "I think you may perhaps get over *her*," said he. "Are there many more?"

"Plenty," said McKercher: "but Heath is the only one I fear. She is an Englishwoman, and a Protestant: bad luck to her."

Martin Neif had seen Joan Landy with a child of her own at Dunmaine. Saw the same child afterwards at Dunmaine House. Saw him afterwards, with my lord, at Kinna. Has heard my lord say he would not, for any money, the boy should know Juggy Landy was his mother.

Arthur Herd was a barber's apprentice, and went out to shave Lord Altham at Carrickduffe. When he had shaved him, Lord Altham said, " Come and live with me ; you shall never want a piece of money in your pocket, a gun to shoot with, a horse to ride on, nor a lass to walk with." On this picture of domestic service, he ran away from his indentures without scruple. He found a boy in my lord's house, called Jemmy Annesley. He had a scarlet coat, and a laced hat. Knew my lord to correct him once, and say, " He had the thieving blood of the Landys in him : his grandfather used to steal the cauls out of his sheep, and half thresh his corn, and make the sheaves up."

Witness used to go sometimes and see his friends at Ross. On these occasions Master Annesley would send his duty to his mother; she was then in the service of a baker, at Ross. Since Mr. Annesley's return, had seen him and Mr. McKercher. McKercher asked him who was James Annesley's mother, and he told him it was Joan, or Juggy, Landy. He then reminded Mr. Annesley he had taken several duties from him to his mother, and brought several blessings from his

mother to him, and reminded him of a pair of
stockings he brought him of his mother's knitting,
and Mr. Annesley trembled, and turned pale, at
this discourse.

The claimant's case was now considered des-
perate. He himself seemed like a man awakening
from a dream.

Philippa was sick at heart. "Oh!" she moaned,
" will these dreadful witnesses never leave off ? "

As for McKercher, he disappeared that night.

Philippa went to the court next morning, pale
and disturbed; all her alacrity gone. She went
like one to execution : yet no entreaties could keep
her away : no, she would know the worst.

This day came a new costume, *Alderman King*
in his robes, out of respect for the court. He
deposed that Lady Altham lived in his house nine
months, as his guest, a little before she left Ireland.
She used to converse freely of her affairs, but never
mentioned to him that she had a son.

This closed the defendant's evidence.

What now remained but the speeches of counsel,
and a verdict for the defendant ? Not much, only
to conquer the Napoleon of all attorneys living or
dead. McKercher reappeared, and claimed, through
his counsel, to prove PERJURY on the part of certain witnesses for the defence. The court allowed

this, with the usual limitation—he must state his points first, and keep strictly within them.

Claimant's counsel stated four points, and then called, to defeat the *alibi* aforesaid—

Cæsar Colclough, Esq.—He swore that he was at Wexford Spring Assizes, 1715. Was in court all day at Masterson's trial; did not sit by Lady Altham and Mrs. Giffard; did not believe they were in court; and Parson Doyle was not tried that day, but just one twelvemonth after, and he, Colclough, was a juryman.

On the same line *Thomas Higginson*, collector of rents, swore Lord Altham went to those very assizes alone, and he called at Dunmaine with money due; and Lady Altham gave to him two glasses of white wine, and at the second he wished her a happy delivery.

Against Mrs. Heath they called an acquaintance of hers, one *John Hussy*, who swore that when the news of Mr. Annesley coming to claim his rights first reached London from Jamaica, and before the defendant's agents could get to her, she spoke of him to deponent as Lady Altham's son, and a much wronged man. *William Stephens* and *William Houghton*, persons intimate with *Arthur Herd*, swore that this formidable witness for the defendant had told quite a different tale to them before the trial.

R

Houghton gave some particulars of gossip. One
Mrs. Symons had come into his place, and told
him *Herd had turned tail to Mr. Annesley*, and the
trial was going against him. "Why, madam,"
said I, "I heard Arthur Herd express himself that
Mr. Annesley was the heir." Pressed for the exact
words of Herd, he said, "Upon my oath, and upon
my salvation, and upon everything, he said he did
believe him to be the true heir of the estate the
Earl of Anglesey now possesses." Both deponents
swore that a remarkable saying, which was now
ringing through every street in Dublin, came first
out of Herd's mouth, viz., "Annesley is the right
heir if right might take place."

Father John Ryan swore that Father Michael
Downes had told him he was to get £200 for his
evidence, and if he made a mistake he must get
absolution.

This closed the plaintiff's evidence in reply.

Then came an incident without a parallel. The
judges had now before them the greatest mass of
perjury ever delivered in Great Britain; and, not
being clear on which side the perjury predominated,
they took unusual means to test the witnesses.
They confronted them on the same table, and took
the examination into their own hands. Thus,
whereas in an ordinary case there are two battles

of evidence, in this immortal trial there were four:
and the last deserves a distinct heading.

The Duels on a Table.

William Elms, who had said Joan Laffan was a
person not to be believed on her oath, was put on
the table, and then *Joan Laffan* was ordered up.
When she came on the table, she curtsied, and
said, "Your servant, Mr. Elms."

The Court.—"Woman, do you know that gentleman?"

Joan.—"Yes, since I know anybody."

Court.—"Did you tell him at Dunmaine you
were nursing Lady Altham's child?"

A.—"I don't know, my lord; I never saw him
to speak to at Dunmaine but once."

Elms.—"I was high constable, and I spoke to
her several times at Dunmaine, when I went to
collect the public money. Don't you remember
that? Can you deny it?"

Joan.—"I protest I know nothing of it."

The Court.—"What was the nature of your
service?"

Joan.—"I was chamber-maid."

Elms.—"She was laundry-maid."

Joan (ironically).—"Very well, Mr. Elms."

The Court, having brought them to this issue,

looked into the matter, and found, by the evidence
of Heath and others, she was chamber-maid, and
not laundry-maid.

About Joan Landy's cabin, Joan said she only
knew it while the child was there. It was then a
handsome house, with handsome things in it.

The Court (to Elms).—"Pray was there any such
fine room as she describes?"

Elms.—"I never saw it, WITHOUT IT WAS UNDER-
GROUND. I saw no furniture at all: there was a
wall made up of sods and stones."

Joan Laffan.—"Oh, fie, Mr. Elms: I wonder
you'll say so." Then she clasped her hands. "BY
THE HOLY EVANGELISTS, THERE NEVER WAS A SOD IN
THE HOUSE."

They continued again about the coach-road; and
this much-abused witness, Laffan, distinctly proved
that the respectable Mr. Elms and Rolph had pre-
varicated about the coach-road; and that it did
not go where they said it did, but only to Joan
Landy's cabin.

The Court (to Joan Laffan).—"Was it known by
the neighbours that my lady had a son, and that
the child you nursed was that son?"

Joan (composedly).—"MY LORD, IT IS KNOWN BY
TWO THOUSAND PEOPLE; AND EVERYBODY KNOWS IT
IF THEY WILL PLEASE TO SPEAK TRUTH."

Elms.—" I NEVER HEARD OF IT, FOR ONE."

The two priests were now put on the table cheek by jowl.

Father Downes denied that he ever rode and conversed with Father Ryan on any Sunday morning; but, on Ryan reminding him of a circumstance, he conceded the riding : but denied that he had ever conversed about this trial on a Sunday morning.

Then the Court made Ryan repeat to his face about the £200, etc.

Downes.—" Does this man swear this?"

Court.—" He does."

Downes.—" Well, then, I'll tell you, by virtue of my oath—I never was promised a farthing, and IF YOU BELIEVE THIS GENTLEMAN, YOU MAY HANG ME: FOR HE IS A VILE, DRUNKEN, LICENTIOUS DOG IN THE COUNTRY."

The next duel was between *John Hussy* and *Mary Heath.* They were put on the table together, and the Court asked Mrs. Heath if Hussy had drank tea with her since the account came from abroad about Mr. Annesley.

Mrs. Heath.—" Several times."

Court.—" Had you any conversation with him thereupon ?"

Mrs. Heath.—" I have often said to him what a vile thing it was to take away the earl's right—my

lady never had a child. And I can't say no more
if you rack me to death."

Court.—" What is Mr. Hussy's character ?"

Mrs. Heath.—"I can say no more than that
some said he was a gentleman's servant, and some
said he lived by gaming."

The Court.—" Repeat the words you say she
said before you."

Hussy.—" She told me the Duchess of Buck-
ingham sent for her : and then she said, ' Poor
gentleman, I'm sorry for him, from my heart,
for no one has reason to know his affairs better
than I do, for I lived long with Lady Altham, his
mother.' "

Mrs. Heath.—" BY ALL THAT'S GOOD AND GREAT,
I NEVER SAID ANY SUCH WORD." Then, turning on
Hussy, "I never thought you were such a man.
I've heard people say you were a gamester, and
lived in an odd way; but I would never believe it
till now. I took your part, and always said you
behaved like a gentleman."

Hussy.—" I am a gentleman, and a man of
family. Indeed I heard you say it, and with all
the regret and concern imaginable."

Thus ended the greatest conflict of direct and
heterogeneous evidence ever known in this country
before or since ; and, if it does not interest my

readers more than the rest of this story, let us have no more of the miserable cant about Truth being superior to Fiction; for Truth has very few pearls to offer comparable to this great trial.

The Court adjourned, and Philippa and James Annesley both thanked God it was over, and agreed they would never have gone through it, had they known what they were to endure.

" Sweetheart," said she to him, " I have much need to see you gain your estates ; for I have lost my youth. I was so young before this dreadful trial, and now they have made me old. They have shown me mankind too near. What ! is it really so, that Christian men and women can stand up side by side, and take the gospels of their Redeemer in hand, and one swear black, and t'other white, of things they both do know ? and all we, looking on amazed, can see nought in either face but truth and honesty ? Land and titles, quotha ! What are they that men and women should fling away their souls ? Why, if each of these false witnesses were to be Ireland's richest landowner, and England's highest earl, still 'tis the devil that hath the best of the bargain. Oh ! I am sick, sick. Shall England ever come to this ? Then methinks 'twere time for honest men and women to run into the sea, and so to another world for Truth."

Having relieved her swelling soul, the noble girl laid her hand on James's shoulder, and said, pathetically, " I have but one comfort in this wicked world : that he I love is an honest man."

" Yes, I am an honest man : too honest to trouble you any more, if the jury shall say I am that woman's son."

" Oh, James, what words are these ? Think you I care whose son men say you are ? "

She made light of it, not knowing at the time the gloomy resolution James had come to.

Yet, after all, now I think of it, she may have had some vague misgiving : for she said to Thomas Chester, almost crying, " Uncle, dear, if it goes against him, you will be very kind to him—for my sake ? "

" I will : why should I not ? But, if you mean give him my niece and her fortune all the same— why no : not till he resigns litigation, that is a curse, and takes to some honest trade."

Next day Philippa had a terrible headache : but nothing would keep her out of court.

Four counsel for the defendant spoke in turn : of these Malone was one, and he spoke four hours, with all the zeal and cogency of a great forensic reasoner : often, during his speech, poor Philippa said, " Oh, will he never leave off ? " and, when he did leave off, the claimant's case seemed prostrate.

Nevertheless, next day, Counsellor Marshall, for the plaintiff, spoke one hour only, but with such lucid order, such neatness, cogency, and power of condensation, that he set the claimant's case on its legs again. He was followed by three more.

I shall give one point of the many on which they countered; but I give it only because the judges, by some strange delusion, unaccountable in men so able, actually omitted to say one word upon the point; though, to my mind, the case lay there.

PRIME SERJEANT MALONE.—"It is a rule well known, that every case ought to be proved by the best testimony the nature of the thing will admit: and surely this Joan Landy was the very best witness that could have been produced on the side of the plaintiff. It is sworn for her, by others, that she took this child from its mother, and nursed it for fifteen months. Why, then, is she not produced? She is named on their list of witnesses; and the gentlemen on the other side did, very early in the case, promise we should see her. But, by-and-by, they told us she was a weak woman, and might be put off the thread of her story. But this was plainly not the real reason: the weakest man or woman can speak truth, and

will probably, on their oath, say no other. It is
a hardship for a weak mind, that knows a fact not
to be true, to colour it, or make it appear true.
Their consciousness that Joan Landy was un-
willing, or unable to do this, must have been their
only reason for not producing her. Good-will to
the plaintiff she could not lack; she is, by their
account, his wet nurse; and an Irish nurse, as
Mr. McKercher told those who suspected this
woman of being something more to the claimant,
has a maternal affection, and is willing, *by all
honest means*, to promote her nursling's welfare.
Joan Landy knows better than any one whether she
has had a son by Lord Altham, or not. Yet she
is not called: and so, because Joan Landy knew
too much about the sham to stand an examination,
Joan Laffan, the pretended dry nurse, is put
forward to give Joan Landy's evidence."

SERJEANT MARSHALL, in reply to the above:
"What we said to the gentlemen was 'that Joan
Landy had been *tampered with*,' and we repeat it.
On that account we did not examine her; but we
offered her to the gentlemen on the other side, if
they pleased to examine her: and they declined.
Yet she is their witness. She plays, in their case,
the part Lady Altham plays in ours. Their re-
fusing to examine her is as if we should refuse to

examine Lady Altham, were she alive ; yet we had Joan Landy in court for them, and they declined her."

The last conflict was over : the three judges summed up. Baron Dawson flimsily : the Chief Baron and Baron Mountney with great pains, closeness, method, and impartiality, on every point, but the conduct of the counsel in not calling Joan Landy. This, by some strange crook of the Celtic intellect, they all ignored.

The jury retired.

James Annesley waited a few minutes, and then, unable to bear it any longer, cast a look of agony at Philippa, and left the court. McKercher followed him.

Philippa sat in all the tortures of suspense.

While she sat twisting her hands, a line from McKercher was brought her. " My dear young lady, keep your eye on him. He has bespoke a passage to Pennsylvania."

She handed it to her uncle, and clasped her hands.

" No," said Thomas Chester, " there is no need for that. We must think of something. What ! the jury come back so soon ? Well, they are agreed then. I was afraid they never would.

Better so, my child, than to go through this all
again."

" SILENCE ! "

Then the usual question was put to the jury,
and their foreman delivered

A VERDICT FOR THE PLAINTIFF.

There was a loud " huzza " from the crowded
court. Ladies waved their handkerchiefs, and
Philippa gave a cry, and was carried almost fainting from the court.

She had not been at home many minutes when
in rushed her lover, exalted in proportion to his
recent despondence, and demanded her hand in
marriage that very minute.

What woman, however much in love, could put
up with such conduct? She coquetted with her
happiness that moment, like any other daughter
of Eve. " Marriage ! time enough for that." At
present she preferred to revel in her lover's
triumph, and " not talk nonsense "—so she said,
however. Her lover then informed her that the
Irish estates and the title in perspective would
not compensate him for what he had endured.
McKercher had been fighting for land and honours ;
but he for her.

Mr. Chester put in his word. " Come, niece, a
bargain is a bargain. Prithee, make me not a

"She preferred to revel in her lover's triumph."—*Page* 252.

liar. I ne'er broke faith when I was young; and shall I begin in my old age?"

"I would do much to oblige *you*, uncle," says the young lady, smiling, and colouring high at what she saw coming.

In ran McKercher, boiling over, to say he had arranged bonfires, bells, and torchlight procession.

"The marriage first," said Annesley: "or none of your public shows for me."

Finding him as obstinate as a mule, the pliable McKercher shifted his helm; got a parson, and distinguished witnesses, all in an hour, and the deed of settlement was produced by Chester, and signed, sealed, and witnessed, and the marriage solemnized in private, as usual among the great, and Matthews rode home, to prepare his house to receive the bride and bridegroom.

At night, McKercher, all in his glory, arranged the torchlight procession, with all the bells a-ringing, and bonfires blazing on the neighbouring heights. It was a splendid cavalcade, both of men and women: for the young lord, as they called him now, was the darling of the hour; and all the quality clustered round him. Then James must show his darling Philippa all the places where he had suffered privation and misery. They made a progress. They went in triumph to Frapper Lane, and other of the places; to Smithfield, where he had held horses, and to Ormond Quay.

One incident occurred worth mentioning. They passed John Purcell's door, and the old man stood in his doorway, to see the show, as all the neighbours did. Annesley caught sight of him, instantly dismounted, and fairly flung his arms round the old man's neck, and kissed him on both cheeks. The old man kissed him, in turn, and sobbed a word or two: but, when James looked for his Mammy, he shook his head. She was gone from the joys and troubles of the world: and this is the sorest wound to gentle hearts, that those who have been kindest to us in adversity cannot stay below to share our prosperity.

The crowd huzzaed louder than ever when the young lord kissed the humble, sturdy benefactor of his youth; and then the bright cavalcade resumed its march. They took that sore-tried, but now triumphant, pair, a mile out of Dublin: then they broke into two companies: the larger rode back to drink their healths in Dublin, the smaller rode with them to Captain Matthews, waving torches, and hurrahing lustily at times. He kept them all, and their horses, that night, with Irish hospitality.

How sweet is pleasure after pain! Such a day

as this comes to few, and to the happiest but once in a life: and all the past trouble, mortification, doubt, and suspense, made it sweeter still; indeed scarcely credible, it was such rapture.

I could tell more about the " Wandering Heir ; " but Fiction is not History, and I claim my rights: even the " Iliad " is but a slice out of Troy's siege; so surely I may take these marvellous passages of an eventful life, then drop the curtain on the doubtful future.

Whether or not he holds his estates, and gets his title from the Peers, he has been poor, and now is well to do; a slave, and now is free; alone in the world, and now blessed with Philippa; there lies his best chance of enduring happiness, when all is done: for few things in this world keep their high flavour; custom blunts them so: wealth palls by habit; titles cease to ring in sated ears; French dishes pall the appetite in time; power and reputation have no spells against satiety: only pure conjugal love seems never old, nor stale, but ever sweet: if it declines in passion, it gains in affection; it multiplieth joy, it divideth sorrow, and here, in this sorry world, is the thing likest Heaven.

APPENDIX.

"THE Wandering Heir" was first published and registered as a drama, 18th December, 1872, to hinder dramatic pirates from stealing the subject in the theatres.

A few days later it appeared, as a story, occupying the whole Christmas number of the *Graphic*.

The sale in Europe was 200,000 copies—the price one shilling.

In the United States, Messrs. Harper & Co. sold 150,000 copies in their *Weekly*, and 80,000 in book form.

Messrs. Rose & Hunter (Toronto), 10,000 in journal, and 5000 in book.

The pirates in America and the Colonies sold about 90,000 more, as I am informed.

A writer in a leading London journal once told his little public and me, that his circulation was *public*, and mine was *private*.

That journal sells about 80,000 copies—at one-third of the price at which the World took 500,000 copies of "The Wandering Heir."

Were criticism ever to be studied scientifically, and were you to ask such a critic, how a world-wide success

8

can be achieved by an islander, that scientific person would tell you that it is not a matter of spelling; it does not matter one straw, whether the author writes his name S-c-o-t-t, or C-o-l-l-i-n-s, or D-e-f-o-e, or J-o-n-e-s, or C-o-o-p-e-r, or P-o-e, the feat is only to be accomplished by happy choice of a subject, coupled with a good method, and a rare union of different qualities of imagination, judgment, observation, research, excited brain, self-control, imitation, invention, love of the production, and yet the stern self-denial to prune it, ay, lop it, though it is the author's child.

But certain criticasters, or unscientific critics, have another theory; that no rare gift, nor unwonted labour is required; any insular dunce can fire the globe, provided he is dishonest on a large scale.

Now this is a comfortable theory; because, you see, dishonesty is within the reach of all.

Mighty Fiction—when its immediate spell has waned, and men close the blessed book, that has given them the only keen yet cheap excitement, and the only cheap ravishing delight this earth affords—oppresses the unimaginative reader with too great a sense of the writer's superiority. The comfortable theory aforesaid relieves him of this oppression, and his elastic vanity springs back with a bound to its throne in his heart.

This foible in mankind smooths the Detractor's path to the public conscience. To pander to the vanity, and —sure concomitant of vanity—the ingratitude, of an author's readers is as easy as it is hard to write a big, short story: and this is why some public detractor always barks after a master-piece, and curs innumerable echo the ululation.

But it may be worth while to show the more enlightened part of the public by what shallow arts they are duped into undervaluing the great and difficult art of swift and fiery Fiction, and who are the people that play this game under cover of the Anonymous, that unhappy system, which is the curse and the degradation of letters in England, and yet is thoroughly un-English, being opposed, as any lawyer will tell you, to the spirit of all our wise institutions.

Upon the same day, viz., the 4th January, 1872, there appeared two Pseudonymous letters, one in a weekly called the *Press and the St. James's Chronicle* — this letter was signed " Cœcilius : " — the other in the *Athenæum*, signed " C. F."

Both these Pseudonymuncula described " The Wandering Heir " as a mere plagiarism from Swift : both advanced, by way of proof, a single passage of the story, and certain well-known lines of Swift. Both writers, to make the reader think I had borrowed very servilely from Swift, had recourse to the same artifice ; they both suppressed all Swift's lines, that had no counterpart in my narrative ; and suppressed all the lines in my narrative, that took nothing from Swift. This, of course, disturbed the true proportions of the alleged plagiarism.

But one swallow does not make summer, nor one parallel passage, adroitly tampered with, make an entire story a plagiarism from Swift ; so both these Pseudony-

muncula told one stale, but alas! always successful,
falsehood. They both gave the public to understand
that the selected passage was *not an exception but a
sample; the whole work being borrowed from* Swift. This
fraud is called the "Sham-Sample Swindle."

Moreover, each of these correspondents showed singular malice; "Cœcilius," not content with libelling a
single work of mine, went into excessive personalities;
he deliberately wrote, and printed, that I was a person
"who might write novels if I had but imagination, and
could write English." He also described me as "an
illiterate scribbler." Now this was the language of extraordinary malice, not of ordinary veracity. There
was an unusual and unprecedented stroke of malice in
"C. F.'s" letter. He accused me of a fraud in
business.

PROSE AND VERSE.

MR. CHARLES READE has written a novel in the *Graphic* newspaper. It was accidentally brought to my house at Christmas,
and, looking at a page of it, I was reminded of Dean Swift's
"Journal of a Modern Lady." Mr. Charles Reade writes :—

"Down, they sat, and soon their eyes were gleaming, and
their flesh trembling with excitement. Mistress Anne Gregory
held bad cards; she had to pawn ring after ring—for these
ladies, being well acquainted with each other, never played on
parole—and she kept bemoaning her bad luck—' Betty, I knew
how 'twould be. The parson called to-day. This odious chair,
why will you stick me in it? Stand further, girl. I always
lose when you look on.' Mrs. Betty tossed her head, and went
behind another lady. Miss Gregory still lost, and had to pawn
her snuff-box to Lady Dace. She consoled herself by an insinuation, ' My lady, you touched your wedding-ring. That
was a sign to your partner here.'—' Nay, madam, 'twas but a
sign my finger itched. But if you go to that, you spoke a word

began with H. Then she knew you had the king of hearts.'—
'That is like miss here,' said another matron. 'She rubs her
chair when she hath matadore in hand.'—'Set a thief to catch
a thief, madam,' was miss's ingenious and polished reply.—
'Hey-dey,' cries one.—'Here's spadillo got a mark on the back:
a child might know it in the dark. Mistress Pigot, I wish
you'd be pleased to pare your nails.'   It was four o'clock
before they broke up, huddled on their cloaks and hoods, and
their chairs took them home, with cold feet and aching heads."

The Dean writes :—

> " With panting heart and earnest eyes,
> In hope to see *Spadillo* rise ;
> In vain, alas ! her hope is fled ;
> She draws an ace, and sees it red.
> In ready counters never pays,
> But pawns her snuff-box, rings, and keys ;
> Ever with some new fancy struck,
> Tries twenty charms to mend her luck.
> ' This morning when the parson came
> I said I should not win a game.
> This odious chair, how came I stuck in't ?
> I think I never had good luck in't.
>
> * * * * *
>
> Stand further girl, or get you gone ;
> I always lose when you look on.
>
> * * * * *
>
> I saw you touch your wedding ring
> Before my lady called a king :
> You spoke a word began with H,
> And I know whom you meant to teach,
> Because you held the king of hearts ;
> Fie, madam, leave these little arts.'
> ' That's not so bad as one that rubs
> Her chair to call the king of clubs,
> And makes her partner understand
> A matadore is in her hand.
>
> * * * * *

> Spadillo here has got a mark ;
> A child may know it in the dark ;
>
> I guess the hand ; it seldom fails ;
> I wish some folks would pare their nails.'
>   *   *   *   *   *
> At last they hear the watchman knock
> ' A frosty morn—past four o'clock.'
> The chairmen are not to be found.
> ' Come, let us play the other round.'
> Now, all in haste they huddle on
> Their hoods and cloaks and get them gone."

Again Mr. Reade :—

" At twelve next day Miss Gregory was prematurely disturbed by her lap-dog, barking like a demon for his breakfast. She stretched, gaped, unglued her eyes, and rang for Betty. ' Here child. Let in some light. Nay not so much : would'st blind me ? I'm dead of the vapours. Get me a dram of citron-water. So. Now bring me a looking-glass. I will lie a-bed. Alack ! I look frightfully to-day. If ever I touch a card again. Did'st ever see such luck as mine ? Four matadores, and lose codille ! "

Again the Dean :—

> " The modern dame is wak'd by noon.
>   *   *   *   *   *
> She stretches, gapes, unglues her eyes,
> And asks if it be time to rise ;
> Of head-ache and the spleen complains ;
> And then to cool her brains,
> Her night-gown and her slippers brought her,
> Takes a large dram of citron-water.
> Then to her glass ; and, ' Betty, pray
> Don't I look frightfully to-day ?
> But was it not confounded hard ?
> Well, if I ever touch a card !
> Four matadores and lose codille ! ' "

Again Mr. Reade :—

"Miss Gregory was at her glass when Betty returned with the tea. 'Madam,' said she, with a sly sneer, 'the goldsmith waits below, to know if you'll redeem the silver cup.'—'There, give him that for interest.'—'And my Lady Dace has sent her maid.'—'That is for her winnings. Never was such a dun. Here, take these ten pistoles my lord left for the wine-merchant. They are all light, thank heaven ! "

Again the Dean :—

> "Madam, the goldsmith waits below ;
> He says, his business is to know
> If you'll redeem the silver cup
> He keeps in pawn ?—'Why, show him up.'
> Your dressing-plate he'll be content
> To take, for interest, *cent. per cent.*
> And, madam, there's my Lady Spade
> Hath sent this letter by her maid.
> 'Well, I remember what she won ;'
> And hath she sent so soon to dun ?
> Here, carry down those ten pistoles
> My husband left to pay for coals :
> I thank my stars they all are light. "

Again Mr. Reade :—

"   A mercer with silks, patterns and laces from Paris : so the toilette was not complete at four, when a footman knocked at the door with, 'Madam, dinner stays.'—'Then the cook must keep it back, I never can have time to dress; and I am sure no living woman takes less.' "

Again the Dean: —

> "Now to another scene give place,
> Enter the folks with silks and lace ;
> Fresh matter for a world of chat,
> Right Indian this, right Mechlin that :
> 'Observe this pattern ; there's a stuff ;'
>   *   *   *   *   *

This business of importance o'er,
And madam almost dressed by four,
The footman, in his usual phrase,
Comes up with 'Madam, dinner stays.'
She answers in her usual style,
'The cook must keep it back a while:
I never can have time to dress;
No woman breathing takes up less.'"

I have read little of Mr. Reade's story beyond what I have quoted. There may be more stuff of the same sort in it, as Mr. Reade makes a slight reference to "Swift's Polite Conversation." If this is how novels are made, surely novel-writing must be an easy art! Vulgar rumour says that Mr. Reade was paid for this at the rate of a penny a word! Who is to receive the pence for that part of the work which clearly belongs to Dean Swift. Was the great writer ever paid so well?   C. F.

I saw one hand in the two letters, and thought them an abuse of the Anonymous. I think so still. If they are not, why then the Anonymous is a worse thing than even I consider it.

I addressed a letter of remonstrance to Sir Charles Dilke, because he is the proprietor of the *Athenæum*, and proposed to him, as a matter of fair play, to give my letter the same circulation he had given to the letter of "C. F."

Sir Charles Dilke objected, privately, to this course, on the ground that he was not the Editor of the *Athenæum*. He said he had been much amused by my letter, but had erased his name from it, and returned it to the Editor, as it was evidently meant not for an individual, but for the journal. He expressed no regret.

To this I replied, in effect, that if he was an individual so was I, and it was not my Shadow his servants had attacked, but me. His weekly was sold for his benefit, as much as my story for mine. Slander of a meritorious author was a spicy and saleable article, and he was responsible to those he injured unfairly by the sale of spice. He had no excuse for evading that responsibility in my case, since I had treated him, in my letter, with proper courtesy.—" P.S. I am sorry my letter has amused you ; sorry for your sake. Young gentlemen should endeavour not to be amused, when their lackeys have thrown dirt upon their seniors."

However, the question between Sir Charles Dilke and me is very debatable. No blame attaches to him for the course he took, nor yet to me for mine. But I think the matter may be fairly disposed of by inquiring what says the law of the land to a man unfairly bitten by an anonymous, or pseudonymous, polecat ?

Why it says "Don't you be so simple as to go fighting with shadows, or marching, with manly breast, up to masked batteries manned by anonymuncula, pseudonymuncula, and skuncula ; collar some *man*. Sue him, or indict him by his Christian name and his surname. As to the Anonymuncula, or Pseudonymuncula, or Skuncula, who wrote the libel, the *law will lend you no assistance to discover them*—as it would to detect other offenders—because you have a remedy against the vendor of the libel."

Very well; I took the Law for my guide ; only I did not sue the vendor. I thought an earnest, but temperate, remonstrance quite enough in a case where the vendor was above suspicion of personal malice or trade malice.

My letter was refused admission to the *Athenæum*, upon these terms. Yet, would you believe it, Mr. McColl, the *soi-disant* Editor of the *Athenæum*, commented upon it, and told his readers this letter which he suppressed "was about my plagiar*isms* from Swift."

I published my letter to Sir Charles Dilke in *Once a Week*.

THE SHAM-SAMPLE SWINDLE.

To The Editor of "ONCE A WEEK."

SIR—The above literary fraud was first exposed and named in your pages—No. 34, New Series, August 22nd, 1868. I shall feel obliged if you will strike it another blow, by inserting a letter that has been suppressed, yet misrepresented, in the *Athenæum*, Jan. 18 :—

THE SHAM-SAMPLE SWINDLE.

SIR CHARLES DILKE—The above fraud is worked as follows : —The Detractor takes an exceptional passage from a meritorious work, cites it in full, and then slily suggests that the whole work is of that character. This fraud can never fail to deceive, because the little bit of truth is presented to the senses, the enormous lie is hidden from them. Having exposed, dissected, branded, and, above all, named this fraud, I hoped I had done with it; but I find I had only scotched the reptile : it is at me again in the *Athenæum*, Jan. 4, and this time with defamatory suggestions, which compel me either to sue you for libel, or to test your character as a gentleman, by an appeal to your honour and humanity. I take the latter course.

A Pseudonymuncule, said to be in the pay of your weekly, pretends that he is an outside correspondent, and his initials

are " C. F."; and he alleges that he has got a house, and that
the "Wandering Heir" was brought to it—by the wind, or
by some one who said, "Slander me now this tale?"—and
that he opened this tale at random, and, being familiar with
Swift, fell at once on a passage he recognized as adapted from
verses by Swift; and—being not familiar with Swift—is convinced the whole story, or the bulk of it, is adapted from the
same source, and any fool could write it, which implies he
could write it himself, and so places me at the bottom of the
human intellect.

One would think that this was enough. Yet he proceeds to
indelicacy, and from that to libel. He undertakes to say,
without giving his authority—some printer's devil probably—
that I am paid for this tale by the line, or by the word, or in
some form that makes every word I have taken from Swift a
commercial injustice to my publishers.

Now, sir, I am an old gentleman, honourably connected with
Letters; you are a young gentleman, honourably connected
with Letters. A Pseudonymuncule has not a character to
lose, nor a name that can be lowered; but you and I have
both. It is to you, therefore, I must appeal to re-consider this
insult. In all my long experience, nothing so utterly snobbish,
as the above insinuation, has ever been published about an
author and a gentleman in a respectable weekly. What! is a
writer, who would not be admitted to my kitchen, far less to
my confidence, to be allowed to tell the public, in your
columns, that he knows, or thinks he knows, how I treat with
my publishers, and to found on that indelicate conjecture a lie,
which is a libel?

I feel sure that on reflection you will be sorry anything so
unworthy of you has crept—perhaps in your absence—into the
weekly of which you are the proprietor, vendor, and editor;
and, as I shall expect some expressions of gentleman-like regret
from you, I hereby give you the material. Writers of my
stamp are not paid, like Pseudonymuncula, by the line: my
contract with the proprietors of the *Graphic* was for a fixed
sum; but the bulk was not determined. Of course there was a
minimum fixed; but they were liberal on their side, and I, who

am an artist, and not a mere trader, gave them *nine columns over the minimum.*

My literal use of Swift, honestly examined, is about twenty lines. What becomes of the charge that I take money for every word, and sell Swift's words for Reade's?

You will, I am sure, withdraw this insinuation. The writer has little personal claim on you; for observe, if he is "C. F." in the *Athenæum*, January 4, he is "Cœcilius" in the *Press* January 4, and a scurrilous trickster in both. I send you his article in the *Press*, that you may see from how unscrupulous a mind comes that libel in your own columns, which I hope you will now disapprove; and, in that hope, I proceed to correct the mere intellectual detraction with good temper. It is founded on two things—1. The sham-sample swindle, which I have defined. 2. On a pardonable blunder.

The blunder is one into which many criticasters of my day have fallen; but a critic is more scientific, more discriminating. The scientific critic knows there is a vital distinction between taking ideas from a homogeneous source, and from a heterogeneous source; and that only the first mentioned of these two acts is plagiarism : the latter is more like jewel-setting. Call it what you like, it is not plagiarism.

I will take the fraud and the blunder in order, and illustrate them by a few examples, out of thousands.

By the identical process Pseudonymuncule has used to entrap your readers into believing "The Wandering Heir" a mere plagiarism from Swift, one could juggle those who read quotations, not books, into believing :

1. That the Old Testament is *full* of indelicacy.

2. That the miracles of Jesus Christ are none of them the miracles of a God, nor even of a benevolent man—Giving water intoxicating qualities, when the guests had drunk enough, goodness knows ; cursing a fig tree ; driving pigs to a watery grave. This is how Voltaire works the sham-sample swindle, and gulls Frenchmen that let him read the Bible for them.

3. That Virgil never wrote a line he did not take from Lucretius, or somebody.

4. That Milton the poet, is *all* Homer, Euripides, and an Italian play called " Adam in Paradise."

5. That Molière is all Plautus and Cyran de Bergerac, " en prend *tout* son bien où il le trouve."

6. That the same Molière never writes grammatical French.

7. That Shakspeare is *all* Plautus, Horace, Hollingshed, Belleforest, and others.

8. That Corneille had not an idea he did not steal from Spain.

9. That Scott has not an original incident in all his works.

10. That five Italian operas are all English and Irish music.

11. That the overture to " Guillaume Tell " is all composed by Swiss shepherds.

12. That " Robinson Crusoe " is a mere theft from Woodes Rogers and Dampier.

Not one of these is a greater lie, and few of them are as great lies, as to call the " Wandering Heir " a plagiarism from Swift.

Now for the blunder. That will be best corrected by putting examples of jewel-setting, and examples of plagiarism, cheek by jowl.

Corneille's " Horaces," a tragedy founded on a heterogeneous work—viz., an historical narrative by Livy—is not plagiarism. His " Cid," taken from a Spanish play, is plagiarism. Shakspeare's " Comedy of Errors," and Molière's " Avare," are plagiarisms, both from Plautus. Shakspeare's " Macbeth," taken from a heterogeneous work, a chronicle, is no plagiarism, though he uses a much larger slice of Hollingshed's dialogue than I have taken from Swift, and follows his original more closely. The same applies to his " Coriolanus." This tragedy is not a plagiarism; for Plutarch's life of Coriolanus is a heterogeneous work ; and the art with which the great master uses and versifies Volumnia's speech, as he got it from North's translation of Plutarch, is jewel-setting, not plagiarism. By the same rule, " Robinson Crusoe," though Defoe sticks close to Woodes Rogers and Dampier, in many particulars of incident and reflection, is not a plagiarism, being romance founded on books of fact. The distinction holds good as to single incidents, or short and telling speeches. Scott's works are literally

crammed with diamonds of incident and rubies of dialogue,
culled from heterogeneous works, histories, chronicles, ballads,
and oral traditions.   But this is not plagiarism—it is jewel-
setting.   Byron's famous line—

> " The graves of those who cannot die,"

is a plagiarism from another poet, Crabbe; but Wolsey's famous
distich, in Shakspeare's " Henry the Eighth," is not a plagiarism from Wolsey: it is an historical jewel set in a heterogeneous work, and set as none but a great inventor ever yet set
a fact-jewel.

And, to compare small things with great—since Science is
never so great, so just, so scientific, as when she applies her
equal laws to things identical in kind, though differing in
degree—Swift's verses are not fictitious narrative, but a photograph, painting the inner life of many Dublin ladies at an epoch
long gone by ; and I—desirous, as an artist, to give touches of
true colour to my invention—did well to set that jewel in my
heterogeneous work, and therein was not a plagiarist, but followed the highest and noblest masters of fiction in a distinct
branch of their art.

Fiction is not lying; or Pseudonymuncula would really find
it as easy as they pretend.   Let any man look into fiction
scientifically, for a change, and he will find all fiction worth
a button is founded on fact; and it matters less, than the unscientific suppose, whether those facts are gathered by personal
experience, or by hearsay, or from the experiences of others, as
recorded in manuscripts or printed records of fact.   I have used
one of Swift's experiences of real life ; but please observe under
what circumstances; the inner life of Irish people in 1726–40
is a matter so inaccessible and recondite, that Macaulay was
in open despair over it; and, unfortunately for me, Froude's
researches were not yet public.   When I write of my own day,
I have three great resources—experience, memory, and print;
but, in writing " The Wandering Heir," I had but one source.
Then, either I must do as the sham novelists do, drift into
recklesss blundering, and present for the eighteenth century the
nineteenth century daubed with " Foregad ! " and " Pshaw ! " or

I must take the scholar's way, and labour hard, grope as only scholars can, and put my labour to some profit. I took the scholar's way—I ransacked Dublin for old records; I raked out things even Macaulay missed; I gemmed my tale with many a recondite jewel of fact, aud I used *one solitary passage* from so common a writer as Swift; but then that passage was a gem. I used it without disguise. I positively invited my readers to read Swift. The invitation was noticed in the *Athenæum* of December 27; and, shuffling apart, it was that very invitation sent the Pseudonymuncule to Swift. December 27, I was accused in the *Athenæum* of showing off my learning; and January 4, of disguising it.

Some things, sir, can never be judged without their alternatives. Suppose I had not used that photograph of an Irish lady's life, what trash should I have written out of the depths of my inner consciousness? It was Swift, or lies; for that phase of Irish life he photographs has left no other trace. No, sir, to set this unique jewel of truth in my heterogeneous work was no crime, intellectual or moral. My only crime is this: I have written too well. Invention, labour, research, and, above all, a close condensation, to be found in few other living English novelists, all these qualities combined have produced a strong, yet finite, story, which has fallen like a little thunderbolt among the "contes à dormir debout" of garrulous mediocrity. This is the crime that has made Pseudonymuncule writhe with envy, and so boil with rage, that your weekly did not suffice to his hot hate; he must insult me, *on the same day*, in a weakly (*sic*) that is dying for a kick from me, and will have to die without that honour. My real crime, I say, is indicated in certain lines from the *Times* newspaper, which deserve immortality. Please rescue them from unjust oblivion:—

"There is no vice of which a man can be guilty, no shabbiness, no wickedness, which excites so much indignation amongst his contemporaries, as his success. This is the unpardonable crime, which reason cannot defend, nor humility mitigate.

'When Heaven with such parts has blest him,
Have I not reason to detest him?'

is a genuine and natural expression of the vulgar mind. The man who labours as we cannot labour, speaks as we cannot speak, writes as we cannot write, and thrives as we cannot thrive, has accumulated in his own person all the offences of which a man can be guilty. Down with him! why cumbereth he the ground?"—*The Times.*

I am, sir—with thanks for your courtesy and politeness in inserting so long a letter—your faithful servant,

CHARLES READE.

Next week the howls of the *Athenæum* showed me I had hit the Bull's-eye, and the Law was wise in telling us to leave the Shadows of skunks alone, and collar substantial men.

" C. F." replied to this letter and rather smartly.

MR. READE'S PLAGIARI*SMS.* (*sic.*)

January 25, 1873.

I MUST beg you to give me a little space to defend myself from an attack made upon me by Mr. Charles Reade, in a contemporary periodical. My letter to you of January 4th, on Mr. Reade's plagiarism of Dean Swift, has drawn from Mr. Reade some rather curious language; and to show how inappropriate that language is, I must give some description of myself. I am a quiet woman living in a country village, which I scarcely ever leave. I have never written for the press, nor done any literary work whatsoever, therefore I need hardly add, I have never received money for anything written. I am quite unknown to the world. I seldom look at a newspaper, or read modern literature. I did not even know, until yesterday, of the present existence of that periodical in which Mr. Reade reviles me.

Mr. Reade calls me "a trickster, a scurrilous skunk, a pseu-donymuncule;" and, moreover, says he would not admit me to his kitchen; and that I have told "a lie, which is a libel;" also that I am in the pay of the *Athenæum;* also that what I wrote concerning his plagiarism was "snobbish," whereas, he says his own crime is that he has "written too well." I, a woman, entirely unknown, find myself becoming famous when a great (?) novelist takes the trouble to answer my letter and call me a *scurrilous skunk.* As to the hybrid word *pseudonymuncule,* I suppose it means a little writer under a false name: I can only say that I am not a writer, as the word is understood, and that C. F. are really the initial letters of my name. You are at liberty to give Mr. Reade my name and address, if he requires them, and if you think that his great anger will not bring him down to our quiet village to frighten a poor lady.

Mr. Reade defends himself by saying that Virgil, Milton, Molière, Shakespeare, Corneille, Scott, Defoe, all plagiarised, but he forgets that they improved what they used, whereas Mr. Reade merely converts good poetry of Swift's into very commonplace prose. There is in the *Anti-Jacobin,* page 86, January 22nd, 1798, a note (probably by Canning) on the expression "kidnapp'd rhimes," kidnapp'd implies something more than *stolen.* It is, according to an expression of Mr. Sheridan's (in the *Critic*), '*using other people's thoughts as Gipsies do stolen children—disfiguring them to make them pass for their own.*' This is a serious charge against an author, and ought to be well supported." The italics are in the original. In my letter of January 4th I did thoroughly support the charge I made.

Mr. Reade styles himself, "*an old gentleman, honourably connected with Letters.*" I am a young woman, not connected with letters, beyond the enjoyment and entertainment afforded me by books; but I think I may modestly say to Mr. Reade, in the words of the title of one of his novels, "It is never too late to mend." C. F.

THE SHAM-SAMPLE SWINDLE.

To the Editor of "ONCE A WEEK."

SIR—"C. F." writes at me in the *Athenæum:* says she is a woman, and I have attacked her. Not exactly. It was she who attacked me: played off the sham-sample swindle— to which, by-the-by, she still clings—by asserting that a

T

solitary and exceptional passage was the rule of my story; and had the vulgarity to tell the public I was paid by the word, and so had done an unfair thing to my publishers.

Now, if to all this she had added that she was a woman, I should only have said, "You had better in future consult with some man, worthy of the name, before you write about authors and gentlemen."

I now withdraw every opprobrious epithet I heaped in error on this soft, gentle, modest, kindly, womanly creature; and she will understand my letter thus. If a man had written her first letter, he would have been a snob, and a calumniator. If a man had written her second letter after reading mine, he would be an incurable liar, and shuffler. But, as it is only a woman who has written both,—why, it is only a woman.

I observe the sub-editor of the *Athenæum* writes at me in his weekly, though he suppressed the letter he comments on.

He played the same game when I defended Mr. Tom Taylor against unfair detraction in his columns.

Is this gentleman a woman, too? To cut all this shuffling short, Sir Charles Dilke displaced Mr. Hepworth Dixon as the editor of the *Athenæum*, in order to control it himself. This is notorious. It is equally so that he does exercise a certain control at this time. He is also the proprietor and vendor; he is the person responsible to the law, and is therefore fairly open to such a letter as mine, which treated him with courtesy, and appealed to his better feelings—and, I think, not in vain. Time will show.—Your truly,

Feb. 1.   CHARLES READE.

I beg to add here that, in point of fact, I did not apply those opprobrious terms to "C. F.," but to some individual unknown, whom I accused of writing not only the letter of "C. F.," but also the letter of "Cœcilius," in another weekly. See my letter in proof of this.

When you have admired "C. F.'s" wit at my ex-

pense, please observe that she makes the public believe
" C. F." is a clue to her whole name; so she is not
a Pseudonymuncule—that she is out of the reach of
literary envy, is a quiet outsider, reading old authors,
and not *troubling her head with modern productions, and
has no other reason for concealing her address from me*
than the fear that I should go and play the ruffian in
her village.

Mr. McColl co-operated with his correspondent by
declaring that the letter in the *Press* was not written by
the person who had written the letter in the *Athenæum;*
and concealing *that both letters came out of the same
house and the same mind.*

Thus this veracious, candid pair conveyed to their
readers that two pure-minded, independent critics had
condemned me fairly on the same day: a coincidence,
which, if true, was discreditable to me, and to nobody else.

There the correspondence ceased, leaving " C. F."
and McColl masters of the field, and Reade a hot-
headed, wrong-headed, writer, who suspects collusion
and trade-malice in fair, impartial, disconnected critics.

So much for the veracity of Pseudonymuncula and
the candour of a McColl. Now for the truth.

" Cœcilius," and " C. F." live together in the country.
They planned the two letters together, and issued them
under different signatures, and made the public believe
that I had been guilty of wholesale fraud, and that two
patterns of honesty had detected it, each without assistance from the other.

Now if this lady and gentleman had done the right

thing, and signed their names to their letters, I should
have treated them with due respect, and should never
have applied those bitter terms of invective to them,
which figured in my letter to Sir Charles Dilke; and
since I do know them now, I lay aside vituperative
terms, and confine myself to hard facts.

Who and what is " Cœcilius ? " He is my rival in
business and in nothing else. He is a novelist. He is
prolific, but not popular. His surname has a great and
merited reputation; but it has never been able to drag
his Christian name after it up the steps of "the Temple
of Fame."

Now my Christian name keeps up with my surname.
Disgusting!

But that is not all. " Cœcilius " used to write for
the *Graphic;* but towards the end of 1872 that market
was closed to his prolific, but not popular, pen.

The novelist, fertile in failures, to whom the *Graphic*
was closed for a time, sees another novelist write a
story in the said *Graphic*, and learns the *Graphic* has
sold a vast number of copies. Thereupon he and his
wife sit down, and multiply Malice. Under cover of
the Pseudonymous they write and publish not one, but
two spiteful, scurrilous, letters, denouncing their successful rival as a dunce and a cheat, which letters they
were ashamed to sign their names to; yet they attack
their brother novelist by name, and pretend *their only*
reason for withholding their own name is—that the injured person is a ruffian; a man likely to come and
make a brawl in their village.

Now neither " Cœcilius " nor his wife can have any personal malice against me. It is an example of Trade-malice on the lower level; and that deep degrader of the literary character, which makes men down into women, and women into adders, that constant Temptation, that steady corrupter of the conscience, and curse of the soul, Anonymous criticism of rival by rival, is even more to blame than the unsuccessful novelist, and his wife, whom that Anonymous system tempted to palm themselves off as critics, and, in that disguise, pull down their intellectual and moral superior—because he was their rival in trade.

Another example—Mr. Trollope wrote an admirable novel called " Ralph the Heir." Everybody praised it, more or less; and nobody found a moral flaw in it; for there was none to be found. I saw gems in it that ought not be lost to the British Stage, so barren of English life, English characters, and English idioms. I dramatized, and produced it. Trollope, condensed by Reade, succeeded with the public by a law of art, which is as inevitable as the law of gravity. The independent critics, being gentlemen who are steeped to the throat in French Mediocrity, and newspaper dialogue with sentences a mile long, such as man never yet *spake*, did not relish it as the public did; but they were civil, and honest in their strictures, and the most adverse found no moral flaw in the production.

Yet four or five newspapers published a wicked and criminal calumny, which, if I had been as vindictive as my foes, would have ended in several indictments at the Old Bailey. They said the play was indecent. The writers of these libels all flattered the actors, and even praised, *at my expense*, a couple of promising novices.

In their criminal mendacity, and hatred of the author, coupled with their lickspittle adulation of inexperienced actors, my experienced eye saw at once a little clique of well known public traitors, bad playwrights, disguised as critics, and conspiring in trade-malice. I said so in a letter to the *Daily Telegraph.* The then Editor of that paper, though a good friend of mine, did not believe me. Indeed, he corrected me severely; and so, as usual, poor Mr. Reade was hot-headed, wrong-headed, etc., until the thing came to be *sifted* in a court of law (Reade *v.* the Licensed Victuallers); and then it came out that what I had stated was the exact truth; the play was so pure that Mr. Justice Brett, who read every line, declared he could not find a sentence with any flavour of indecency in it; and the libels originated with a clique of playwrights, disguised as critics, whose habits are notorious; they consort in low clubs and sometimes in public-houses, where the conversation teaches the art of naughty interpretation and distortion of honest words. They publicly demand of the Licenser the most immoral French plays; they praise "*Nos Intimes*," which is a singularly indecent play. They truckle to the actors, and praise each other's farces, stolen from the French, and fly like hornets at every outsider who writes a good play.—TRADE-MALICE.

In Reade *v.* Licensed Victuallers, Mr. Richard Lee, a

vile playwright, who, in the disguise of a critic, wrote
the malicious calumny for which a jury gave me £200
damages, swore in the witness-box that he had no personal malice against me, and hardly knew me by sight.
He swore the honest truth: he had no personal malice
whatever. I also swore the truth, viz., that he and his
fellows acted from trade-malice: and, what I swore then
upon the gospels of my Redeemer, I now repeat upon
my honour as a gentleman. These calumnies all arise
out of Trade-malice.

And therefore I earnestly implore the Proprietors and
Editors of respectable journals to profit by these two
flagrant exposures of a public abuse, which we all know
is being perpetrated on a gigantic scale; and not to
allow any playwright to criticise his pals and his rivals
without signing his name, nor any novelist to criticise his
rivals, *without signing his name.* There will be nothing
new in this; on other subjects, all respectable Editors
take due precautions to keep their columns incorrupt.
But why cleanse four columns in a page, and let the
fifth be a sink of venality and spite? At present, in
some respectable and leading journals, the dramatic
column is quite behind the Press and its habits: it is a
secret instrument of Black-mail, and an openly smoking
dunghill of venality, trade-malice, and trade-collusion;
all which the Editors can stop for ever in a single day,
if they care to confer a benefit on their country, and
rescue one of the noblest branches of literature,
Criticism, from the deep degradation into which it is
descending.

By the same rule, if a bad novelist wants to write an anonymous letter, and blacken a good novelist, let him send it by post to the author's house, as so many cowards do. But no respectable Editor should print what comes from so suspicious a quarter, with a request that the writer's name may be concealed from the rival he vilifies.

You have heard calumny call itself criticism; now hear criticism. It is a great rarity, and worth hearing.

"The Wandering Heir" owes nothing to any preceding figment, and so there is no plagiarism in it. But it is written upon the method I have never disowned, and never shall. On that method—viz., the interweaving of imaginary circumstances with facts gathered impartially from experience, hearsay, and printed records—my most approved works, "It is Never too Late to Mend," "Hard Cash," "The Cloister and the Hearth," etc., have been written, and that openly. My preface to "Hard Cash" contains these words :—

"Hard Cash," like "The Cloister and the Hearth," is a matter-of-fact Romance; that is, a fiction built on truths; and these truths have been gathered by long, severe, systematic labour from a multitude of volumes, pamphlets, journals, reports, blue-books, manuscript narratives, letters, and living people, whom I have sought out, examined, and cross-examined, to get at the truth on each main topic I have striven to handle.

The mad-house scenes have been picked out by certain disinterested gentlemen who keep private asylums, and periodicals to puff them ; and have been met with bold denials of public facts and with timid personalities, and a little easy cant about Sensation* Novelists; but in reality those passages have been

---

* This slang term is not quite accurate as applied to me.

written on the same system as the nautical, legal, and other
scenes : the best evidence has been ransacked; and a large
portion of this evidence I shall be happy to show at my house
to any brother writer who is disinterested, and really cares
enough for truth and humanity to walk or ride a mile in pursuit
of them.

In the present case I will go a little farther, and enable
the curious reader to trace my footsteps in many places
of this story if he likes; and I not only invite, but even
presume to advise, young writers to look closely into my
work, and into that method to which I owe so much. It
is a method, by adopting which, and labouring hard in
it, as I do, many a young novelist might double his
value.

The first strata of facts I had to build my figment on
were two reported trials; in one James Annesley was
defendant, on a charge of murder; in the other (Craig *v.*
Anglesey), he was virtually the plaintiff in a trial at bar,
for great estates and titles. You will find the first case
in " Howell's Collection of State Trials." The second,
Craig *v.* Anglesey, is badly reported in Howell. I used
the folio report, published by Smith & Bradley, Dublin,
1744. This book shall be deposited with my publishers,
that any novelist, or critic, who likes, may see the use
I have made of it.

The next source of fact was the "Memoirs of an
Unfortunate Nobleman," written by James Annesley's
attorney. Upon the whole it is a tissue of falsehoods;

Without sensation there can be no interest : but my plan is to
mix a little character and a little philosophy with the sensational
element.

but there are a few invaluable truths in it. The lies
declare themselves trumpet-tongued; the truths are
confined to James Annesley's adventures whilst he was
a slave in the colonies, and his return home with
Admiral Vernon. I used a few of the truths, and
shunned all the falsehoods. "The Memoirs," being rather
a rare book, shall be deposited with my publishers, for
inspection.

In the three books I have now named lies half a plot.
But only *invention, of equal power with the facts,* could
make it a whole plot. Therefore I invented Philippa,
and all her business, and the whole sexual interest of
the story.

I tell you this union of fact and imagination is a kind
of intellectual copulation, and has procreated the best
fiction in every age, by a law of Nature.

To go into smaller details, the Irish schoolmaster and
his "tall talk" are from facts supplied in print by
Carleton.

The Irish curses I have used are culled, with great
study, from three authors, Carleton, Banim, and Griffin,
and selected from an incredible number.

The decayed Irish gentlemen, "the scornful dog who
eats dirty puddings," is fact, taken from "A Tour in
Ireland," published 1740, to be found in the British
Museum.

The country costumes, the price of salmon, and other
particulars, are taken from the "Post-chaise Companion
in Ireland," and "Twiss's Tour in Ireland." The great
salmon leap from "Twiss's Tour in Ireland." The turf

backgammon board, with a boy for dice, from oral tradition—it was told me, forty years ago, by an Irish gentleman, who had it from his father.

The incomparable speech, "Arrah people, people," etc., I had entire from the mouth of an Irishman, who heard it actually delivered in a fair.

The abductions, and sham abductions, of Irish girls, from "Ireland, Sixty Years Ago," and Sir J. Lubbock's "Origin of Civilization," etc., etc.

In the other Hiberniana of the story I have used the various histories of Dublin, and Cork, by Gilbert and others, the *European Magazine*, the "Post-chaise Companion in Ireland," "Letters from a Gentleman in Ireland to a Gentleman in Bath," rather an uncommon book ; and a very rare collection of old Irish journals I obtained by groping that city for them.

The charming series of incidents, in which John Purcell figures, are from his sworn evidence, and almost verbatim. The abduction of the heir in open daylight is also sworn evidence. See Craig *v.* Anglesey.

The uncle beating his niece, her flight to foreign parts, and his apprehension on a charge of murder, is a recorded fact. I got it out of a chap-book; but it has been referred to by jurists in my own day, and I also possess in a ballad called the "New West Country Garland." James Annesley's adventure with Christina McCarthy, her sham penitence, her cajolery, and attempt to poison him, were told by James Annesley to his attorney, and printed by him in "The Memoirs;" and I have set that gem of female nature in my story. The discovery of James, on board Admiral Vernon's ship, by his old schoolfellow Matthews, rests on the same basis of recorded fact. The curious advertisement by Jeweller Drummond is an actual advertisement of the day, taken verbatim from the *Gentlemen's Magazine.* Banker Drummond's ancestor inserted it.

Elizabeth Shipley's character and her remarkable dream about Wilmington—this and other Wilmingtonia are condensed from Ferris's "History of the Original Settlements on the Delaware," and from Barker's "History of the Primitive Settlements."

But whatever, in that part of the story, bears upon the flagellation and other punishments of men and women, and the legal relation of the planters to their white servants, has been taken direct, with careful study and precision, from the various "Charters and Acts of Assembly" of each separate State, at, or near, the date of my story. And here my method has kept me clear of the errors of James Annesley's attorney, who says, in "The Memoirs," that two of James's companions were executed in the *State of Delaware* for elopement and suspicion of adultery. Now the law in that State inflicted no such punishment. It imprisoned, whipped, and lettered. It did not kill. These colonies were hard upon religious offences, but, on the whole, they did not take life half so recklessly as the mother country did at that time, and, with regard to sexual criminality, they exacted such difficult *proofs*, that their laws on that head were much thunder and little lightning.

The Anglicana generalia have been culled with care from periodicals and Books of Fact too numerous to specify. The masculine costume the women wore in the morning rests on Addison, *Mist's Journal*, the *London Journal*, *Gentleman's Magazine* for 1730, *Daily Courant*, and other contemporaneous authorities which are full of detail. The entire reversal of female costume in the evening rests also on contemporary books, periodicals and pictures.

Lord Anglesey's levée and toilet are put together from *Mist's Journal* and various passages in the "Pictorial History of England."

In my novel of "A Simpleton" there is a dressmaker's bill, 1872.

In "The Wandering Heir" there is a dressmaker's bill.

I got the modern dressmaker's bill by asking three or four ladies of my acquaintance to oblige me with the original accounts. They did so.

I was about to pursue the same plan in "The Wandering Heir," when I found, to my disgust, I could not raise the dead. So I had to ransack libraries,—"The graves of those who cannot die."—*Crabbe.* I found the truth I wanted in "The Book of Costume, or Annals of Fashion," by a Lady of Rank.

The parson of Colebrook charges the best bred ladies of his day with gross ignorance. I found that in numerous authorities, Lady Mary Wortley Montague's letters, Mrs. Stone's "Chronicles of Fashion," and, alas, in my own family letters before and after that date. As

for their bad spelling, that continued long after the
date of the parson's observations; other ladies spelled
phonetically, besides Miss Tabitha Bramble. That
ladies of fashion, at the date of my story, had vermin
in their heads I knew by oral tradition from two pro-
vincial hairdressers living in different parts of England;
they were both old men when I was nine, and their
grandfathers had been hairdressers. From these artists
I learned that every hairdresser of that ancient period,
and, indeed, much later, kept white precipitate by him
in large quantities, and dusted the lady's colony freely
before he dressed her hair.

That in England and Ireland the men drank hardest,
but the women gambled most, I gained from essays and
plays of the time.

How Dublin gentlemen lived, I got from "Barring-
ton's Memoirs," "Ireland Sixty Years Ago," etc.; and
how a Dublin lady passed her time, I got from Swift's
photographic verses, which carry truth as plainly written
on them as Livy and Tacitus carry falsehood.

If I could have raised three ladies of Dublin from
the dead, I would not have troubled Swift. But I
can't raise the dead any more than Mr. Home can, and
I have no personal experience of the year 1730, so I
took the only remaining source of truth, and interwove
printed, but reliable, fact, with my figment.

Now let us conduct that comparison loyally which
"Cœcilius" and "C.F." have dealt with more ingeniously than becomes a man's rivals in trade when they
are indicting a scholar, and a man of fair reputation in
his business.

Dean Swift begins with a few preliminary lines, which warn the reader that he is not going into fiction, but fact.

> " I but transcribe ; for not a line
> Of all the satire shall be mine."

He then describes, not a strict sequence of events, but the actual habits of the ladies.

I, on the contrary, am telling a story. " The Wandering Heir" reaches his father's house. Then, to show the sort of men and women whose door he had come to, I describe, in strict sequence, what the males and the females had been actually doing during the twenty hours that preceded his arrival. In this narrative what *facts* are borrowed from Swift are italicised, and so are the corresponding passages in Swift.

"Oh Madam, an' if it please you, where does my father live?"

"'Tis in Frapper Lane, the corner house. What, will you be going, and no supper? Nay, then, God speed you. Give me a kiss, sweetheart. So. Your breath is honey. Sir," said she, curtseying to him, all of a sudden, "I do wish you well. When you come into your estate, sir, prithee remember Martha Knatchbull, that took your part when fortune frowned."

"Ay, that I will, good, kind lady," said James, still overpowered by her glorious costume; and so he shuffled off, limping fast, and, in the hunger of his longing heart, forgot his hungry belly for a time

To give the reader some idea of the house he was going to, I will sketch the domestic performances from nine a.m. on the previous evening. Lord Altham and friends had a drinking bout, at the end of which he was assisted to bed, and his friends sent home in chairs. But the ladies did not drink; they gamed their lives away. Mistress Anne Gregory received Lady Dace and Mistress Carmichael, and other ladies gloriously dressed, and, at first starting, most polite and ceremonious; they drank tea, and soon warmed into scandal—*each accusing some other lady of her own especial vice*—till at last they got upon politics. Inflamed by this topic, they soon

By nature turn'd to play the rake well,
As we shall show you in the sequel,
The Dublin Dame is wak'd by Noon,
Some authors say not quite so soon ;
Because, though sore against her will,
She sate all night up at Quadrille.
She stretches, gapes, unglues her eyes,
And asks if it be time to rise ;
Of Headache and the spleen complains,
And then to cool her heated Brains—
Her night-gown and her slippers brought her,—
Take a large dram of citron-water :
Then to her glass; and "Betty, pray
Don't I look frightfully to-day ?
But, was it not confounded hard ?
Well, if I ever touch a card,
Four Mattadores and lose Codill ;
Depend upon 't I never will.
But, run to Tom and bid him fix
The ladies here to night by six."
" *Madam, the goldsmith waits below,*
He says his business is to know
If you'll redeem the silver cup
You pawned him first;" " Well, show him up."
" Your dressing-plate he'll be content
To take for interest cent. per cent.
And, Madam, there's my Lady Spade
Hath sent this letter by her maid."
" Well; I remember what she won ;
And hath she sent so soon to dun ?
Here, carry down these ten pistoles
My husband left to pay for coals.
I thank my stars they all are light !
And I may have revenge to-night."
Now loytring o'er her tea and cream
She enters on her usual theme ;
Her last night's ill-success repeats ;
Calls Lady Spade a hundred cheats ;

U

boiled over : *voices rose over voices ; not a single tongue was mute a moment ; and such was the Babel,* that at last the fat lazy *lap-dog* wriggled himself erect, and *barked furiously* at the disturbers of his peace. Then a Neptune arose to still the raging voices : in other words, Mrs. Betty set out the card-tables. Down they sat, and soon their eyes were gleaming, and their flesh trembling with excitement. Mistress Anne Gregory held bad cards; *she had to pawn ring after ring—for these ladies, being well acquainted with each other, never played on parole*—and she kept bemoaning her bad luck. "Betty, I knew how twould be. *The parson called to-day. This odious chair, why you will stick me in it ? Stand further, girl. I always lose when you look on.*" Mrs. Betty tossed her head, and went behind another lady. Miss Gregory still lost, and *had to pawn her snuff-box* to Lady Dace." She consoled herself by an insinuation. " *My lady, you touched your wedding-ring. That was a sign to your partner here.*"

" Nay, Madam, 'twas but a sign my finger itched. *But, if you go to that, you spoke a word began with H.* Then she *knew you had the king of hearts.*"

"That is like miss here," said another matron : "*she rubs her chair when she hath matadore in hand.*"

" Set a thief to catch a thief, madam," was miss's ingenious and polished reply.

She slipt Spadillo in her breast
Then thought to turn it to a jest,
There's Mrs. Cut and she combine
And to each other give the sign.
Through ev'ry game pursues her tale
Like hunters o'er their evening ale.
    Now to another scene give place :
Enter the folks with silks and lace ;
Fresh matter for a world of chat,
" Right Indian this ; right Mecklin that ;
Observe this pattern ; there's a stuff ;
I can have customers enough.
Dear Madam, you have grown so hard,
This lace is worth twelve pounds a yard.
Madam, if there be Truth in Man,
I never sold so cheap a fan."
    This business of importance o'er,
And Madam almost drest by four,
The footman, in his usual phrase,
Comes up with " Madam, dinner stays."
She answers in her usual style,
" The cook must keep it back a while ;
I never can have time to dress,
No woman breathing takes up less ;
I'm hurried so, it makes me sick,
I wish the dinner at *Old Nick.*"
At table now she acts her part,
Has all the dinner cant by heart.
" I thought we were to dine alone,
My dear, for sure, if I had known
This company would come to day,
But really 'tis my spouse's way,
He's so unkind he never sends
To tell when he invites his friends ;
I wish we may but have enough ; "
And while with all this paltry stuff
She sit's tormenting every guest,
Nor gives her tongue one moment's rest

"Hey-dey!" cries one.   "*Here's spadillo got a
mark on the back: a child might know it in the dark.
Mistress Pigot, I wish you'd be pleased to pare your
nails.*"

In short, they said things to each other all night,
the slightest of which, among men, would have filled
the Phœnix Park next morning with drawn swords :
but it went for little here : they *were all cheats, and
knew it, and knew the others knew it ;* and didn't care.
It was four o'clock before they broke up, *huddled on
their cloaks and hoods, and their chairs took* them
home with cold feet and aching heads.

At twelve next day Miss Gregory was prematurely
disturbed by her lap-dog, barking like a demon for
his breakfast. *She stretched, gaped, unglued her eyes,
and rang for Betty.* No answer. She rang again, and
beat the wall viciously with her slipper. Betty came
in yawning.

"Here, child. Let in some light. Nay, not so
much : wouldst blind me ? I'm dead of the vapours
Give me a dram of citron-water. So. Now bring me
a looking-glass. I will lie abed. *Alack! I look
frightfully to-day. If ever I touch a card again.
Didst ever see such luck as mine? Four matadores,
and lose codille!* "

"Nay, madam," said Mrs. Betty, who was infected

In phrases batter'd, stale, and trite,
Which Dublin ladies call polite,
You see the Booby Husband sit
In admiration at her wit.

    But let me now a while survey
Our Madam o'er her evening tea,
Surrounded with her noisy clans
Of Prudes, Coquettes, and Harridans;
When frighted at the clamorous crew,
Away the god of silence flew,
And Fair Discretion left the Place,
And Modesty with blushing face.
Now enters overweening Pride,
And Scandal ever gaping wide,
Hyprocrisy with frown severe,
Scurrility with gibing air,
Rude Laughter seeming like to burst,
And Malice always judging worst,
And Vanity with pocket-glass,
And Impudence with front of brass;
And studied Affectation came,
Each limb and feature out of frame;
While Ignorance with brain of lead
Flew hov'ring o'er each female head.

    Why should I ask of these my Muse
A hundred tongues, as Poets use,
When, to give ev'ry Dame her due,
A hundred thousand were too few,
Or how should I, alas! relate
The sum of all their senseless prate,
Their inneundoes, hints, and slanders,
Their meanings lewd, and double entendres?
Now comes the general Scandal charge,
What some invent, the rest enlarge,
"And, Madam, if it be a lie,
You have the tale as cheap as I.
I must conceal my Author's Name,
But now 'tis known by common Fame."

with the tastes of her betters, "with submission, you played bad cards."

"Hoity toity, wench," cried the lady, "was ever such assurance? What is the world coming to?" And she packed her off contemptuously, to get her tea and cream.

Betty turned pale with wrath, but retired. Once outside the door, she said, "Ill be even with the jade. I'm as good as she."

Miss Gregory was at her glass when Betty returned with the tea. *"Madam,"* said she, *with a sly sneer, "the goldsmith waits below, to know if you will redeem the silver cup."*

"There, give him that for interest."

"And my Lady Dace has sent her maid."

"That is for her winnings. Never was such a dun. Here, take these ten pistoles my lord left for the wine merchant. They are all light, thank Heaven!"

At two, being half dressed, and the room tidied, but not a window opened, she received the visit of a fop. He paid her hyperbolical compliments, at which you should have seen Mrs. Betty's lip curl, and was consulted as to where she should put her patches; but was driven out, like chaff before the wind, by a

Say, foolish females, cold, and blind,
Say by what fatal turn of mind
Are you on Vices most severe
Wherein yourselves have greatest share.
Thus every fool herself deludes ;
The Prude condemns the absent Prudes ;
Mopsa, who stinks her spouse to death,
Hercina, rank with sweat presumes
To censure Phillis for perfumes ;
While crooked Cynthia swearing says
That Florimel wears iron stays :
Chloris, of ev'ry Coxcomb jealous,
Admires how girls can talk with Fellows,
And full of indignation frets
That Women should be such Coquettes :
Iris, for Scandal most notorious,
Cries " Lord, the World is so censorious ; "
And Rufa, with her combs of lead,
Whispers that Sappho's hair is red ;
Aura, whose Tongue you hear a mile hence,
Talks half a day in praise of silence ;
And Silvia, full of inward guilt,
Calls Amoret an arrant jilt.
　　　Now voices over voices rise ;
While each to be the loudest vies,
They contradict, affirm, dispute,
No single tongue one moment mute,
All mad to speak, and none to hearken,
They set the very lap-dog barking.
Their chattering makes a louder din
Than Fish-wives o'er a cup of gin :
Not schoolboys at a barring-out
Rais'd ever such incessant shout :
The Jumbling particles of Matter
In Chaos make not such a clatter ;
Far less the Rabble roar and rail
When drunk with sour election ale.
　　　Nor do they trust their tongues alone—

creature more attractive, to wit, *a mercer, with silks, patterns, and laces, from Paris; so the toilette was not complete at four, when a footman knocked at the door with* "*Madam, dinner stays.*"

"*Then the cook must keep it back. I never can have time to dress; and I am sure no living woman takes less.*"

However, she soon came down, distended with an enormous hoop, glorious with brocaded skirt and quilted petticoat, and cocked up on red high-heeled shoes; bedizened, belaced, powdered, pomatumed, pulvilioed, patched, perfumed, and everything else —except washed: yet less savage than the men in one respect: the commode and all the pyramidal scaffolded heads had gone out; her hair was her own, and, though long, was compressed into a small compass, whereas the gentlemen had full-bottomed wigs that smothered their heads, contracted their cheeks, flowed over their shoulders, and befloured their backs.

My Lord Altham and two to three other gentlemen were there and three ladies. Lord Altham, a little dark man with a loud voice, received her with great respect, and told her they waited only for his brother, Captain Richard Annesley.

"Nay, he will not come methinks," said she. "He and I had words t'other day."

They speak a language of their own ;
Can read a nod, a shrug, a look,
Far better than a printed book ;
Convey a Libel in a Frown ;
And Wink a Reputation down ;
Or by a tossing of a fan,
Describe the lady and the man.

But see, the female club disbands,
Each, twenty visits on her hands.
Now all alone poor Madam sits
In vapours and hysteric fits.
" And was not Tom this morning sent ?
I'd lay my life he never went.
Past six, and not a living soul ;
I might by this have won a vole."
A dreadful interval of spleen !
How shall she pass the time between !
" Here, Betty, let me take my drops,
And feel my pulse, I know it stops ;
This head of mine, Lord, how it swims !
And such a pain in all my limbs."
" Dear Madam, try to take a nap."
But now they hear a footman's rap.
" Go, run and light the ladies up ;
It must be one before we sup."

The table, cards, and counters set,
And all the gamester ladies met,
Her spleen and fits recover'd quite,
Our madam can sit up all night.
" Whoever comes, I'm not within,
Quadrille the word, and so begin."

How can the Muse her aid impart,
Unskilled in all the terms of art ?
Or in harmonious numbers put
The deal, the shuffle, and the cut ?
The superstitious whims relate
That fill a female gamester's pate ;
What agony of soul she feels

Nay, then, let the churl hang.   Who waits?"

A flaring footman appeared as if his string had been pulled.

" Bid them serve the dinner."

" I will, my lord."

For the conversation during dinner, see Swift's " Polite Conversation."   You will be a gainer by the exchange ; for the discourse at Lord Altham's board was half as coarse, and not half so witty.

Soon after dinner the host proposed " Church and State."

From that moment the ladies were evidently on their guard and ready for flight.

" Parson," says my lord, " I'll tell you a merry story."

The ladies rose like one, and retired.   My lord having achieved his end, for at this time of night the bottle was his mistress, until it became his master, substituted a toast for his song :

> " The finest sight beneath the moon
>   Is to see the ladies quit the room."

He then ordered the present bottles and glasses to

To see a knave's inverted heels;
She draws up card by card, to find
Good fortune peeping from behind,
With panting heart and earnest eyes
In hope to see Spadillo rise.
In vain, alas! her hope is fled;
She draws an ace, and sees it red.
In ready counters never pays,
But pawns her snuff-box, rings, and keys.
Ever with some new fancy struck
Tries twenty charms to mend her luck.
" *This morning, when the parson came,*
I said I should not win a game,
This odious chair, how came I stuck in't?
I think I never had good luck in't.
I'm so uneasy in my stays,
Your fan a moment, if you please.
Stand further girl, or get you gone,
I always lose when you look on."
" Lord, Madam, you have lost codille;
I never saw you play so ill."
" Nay, Madam, give me leave to say
'Twas you that threw the game away;
When Lady Tricksey play'd a four
You took it with a matadore,
I saw you touch your wedding-ring
Before my lady call'd a king:
You spoke a word began with H,
And I knew who you mean to teach,
Because you held the king of hearts;
Fye, Madam, leave these little arts."
" *That's not so bad as one that rubs*
Her chair to call the king of clubs,
And makes her partner understand
A matadore is in her hand."
" Madam, you have no cause to flounce,
I swear I saw you thrice renounce."
" And truly, Madam, I know when

be exchanged for others that would not stand upright, the stems of the glasses having been knocked
off, and the decanters being made like a soda-water
bottle. This insured so brisk a circulation that,
although they were gentlemen who had all "made
their heads" in early life, the claret began to tell,
as was proved by the swift alternations of super-
fluous ire, and hyperbolical affection, and peals of
idiotic laughter; when in the midst of the din, an
altercation was heard in the hall: the disputants
were three, and each voice had its own key; first
there was a sweet little quavering soprano, appealing to a flaring footman, then there was a flaring
footman, objurgating the cherubic voice an octave
lower, then came the commanding alto of Mrs.
Betty.

Instead of five you scor'd me ten."
" *Spadillo here has got a mark,*
A child may know it in the dark ;
I guess the hand, it seldom fails,
I wish some folks would pare their nails."
    While thus they rail, and scold and storm,
It passes but for common form,
All conscious that they all speak true
And give each other but their due ;
It never interrupts the game,
Or makes them sensible of shame.
    The time too precious now to waste,
The supper gobbled up in haste ;
Again afresh to cards they run
As if they had but just begun.
At last they hear the Watchman's knock,
" *A frosty morn—past four o'clock."*
The Chairmen are not to be found—
"Come let us play the t'other round."
Now all in haste they huddle on
Their hoods and cloaks, and get them gone.
But first the winner must invite
The company to-morrow night.
Unlucky Madam, left in tears,
Who now again Quadrille forswears,
With empty purse and *aching head,*
Steals to her sleeping spouse to bed.

You have now the true proportions in which the two heterogeneous works resemble each other. But there is another thing to be considered ; the form and construction of the two compositions.

The order of the topics in Swift's verses is—

1. Time twelve to four p.m. The lady's morning scene, and her ill success at cards over-night not presented, but referred to by herself.

2. Dinner-time. The lady's affectation and ill manners.

3. Evening tea. Scandal.

4. Separation of the ladies, ennui.

5. Another meeting for cards. Gaming till four a.m.

My order and construction is—

1. Time, nine in the evening till four a.m. Gentlemen drinking apart from the ladies, till carried home, or to bed.   Ladies — Tea — Scandal — Cards — Bed — in an unbroken sequence.

2. Twelve o'clock till seven. Bed-room scene. — Mercer—Dinner—The gentlemen's way of getting rid of the ladies—The gentlemen's habits—Precautions to secure intoxication—all in one unbroken series.

Thus I treat the gentlemen's lives, and the ladies, in far less compass than Swift gives to the ladies. This duplication of topics, and entire change of form, and improved sequence of facts are not the method of the servile plagiarist, but of the inventive scholar who has the skill to select, and interweave another writer's valuable facts into his own figment.

"C. F." says in her second letter that the great

writers whose method I profess to follow, always improved what they took; but I have merely turned good
poetry into very commonplace prose. This is a double
error.

1. Great writers have not always improved the ideas
they borrowed. To take two examples out of a hundred,
Virgil watered Lucretius vilely with his "Duo fulmina
belli Scipiades;" and Shakspeare, in "All's Well that
Ends Well," has in places vulgarized Boccaccio.

2. Swift's lines are not good poetry. They are not
poetry at all; they are slipshod doggerel. It is the
matter that redeems them; the form is worse than
prose. Often the thought is complete in one line, yet a
superfluous line is added to effect the rhyme. Now
follow the particles of Swift into my prose, and see if
you can cut out a line of that prose without diminishing
the sense in proportion. The few golden particles of
Swift I have taken are therefore not disfigured by being
set in the closest prose of the day, and in the improved
sequence of a narrative.

To sum up—Fiction is the art of weaving fact with
invention. If it were mere arrangement of fact, thousands could write it; if it were pure invention, the
young would beat the elderly at it. Instead of that, the
young, with all the advantage of their ardent imagina-
tions and generous blood and elastic energy, write flimsy
stuff for want of Fact. If Dickens appears an exception,
that is only because Dickens ripened early, and was
initiated into that sort of Fact which is good material
for fiction ten years sooner than other writers.

Of Fact there are three sources—experience, hearsay, printed records.

An individual's personal experience is so narrow, that it can carry him but a little way in fiction. We none of us know much except from print.

In writing an historical tale, experience and hearsay dwindle, and the printed facts we have gathered, many of them unconsciously, become the main material.

To interweave these in fiction is the same intellectual operation as to interweave the facts we have seen and heard. Whoever denies this is a fool; whoever admits it, yet cannot realize it, and apply it to the question of plagiarism, is weak of mental digestion, and, though he may criticise all his life, will never be a critic. To borrow scenes and dialogues from a novel of Swift, and put them in a novel, would be plagiarism. But to transplant a few facts out of many in a heap collected by Swift, and then, by change of form and sequence, wield them with another topic into a heterogeneous work, this is not plagiarism; it is one of every true inventor's processes, and only an inventor can do it well. It is precisely the same intellectual crime I was guilty of, when I took the fact of the turf backgammon board, and the dice boy, from the lips of a friend, and wove it into my tale; or when in "A Simpleton" I interwove the numerous facts I had gathered at first-hand in auction-rooms.

Spawn and millet—millet and spawn—without the pair, nature cannot produce a single herring, nor art a single fiction worth its weight in sawdust.

And when Fiction adds to its difficulties, when it aspires to deal with the past, to raise the dead from their graves, and make them live, and move, and dress, and act, and speak, and feel again in a strong domestic story, then must ripe learning and keen invention meet, or gross failure ensue. Then must the spawn be more copious than ever, and the millet more strong and vivifying. To this occasion the words of Horace apply particularly—

> " Nec studium sine divite venâ
> Nec rude quid possit video ingenium ; alterius sic
> Altera poscit opem res, et conjurat amice."

An artist is seldom a critic, and you may think it presumptuous of me to lay down the law. Permit me to explain. I studied the great art of Fiction closely for fifteen years before I presumed to write a line of it. I was a ripe critic long before I became an artist. My critical knowledge has directed my art, but the practice of that art has not diminished my studies.

Forty years examination of masterpieces, and their true history, have qualified me to speak with some little authority.

Nevertheless, the lawyers say—

> " Aliquis non debet esse judex in propriâ causâ."

That is such very bad Latin, I am sure it must be good law; so this discussion shall be closed for the present by the judgment of public writers, who are, I apprehend, above all suspicion of prejudice in the matter.

X

Extract from a letter by a Queen's Collegian, Cork, to the Editor of *Once a Week.*

Having read Mr. Charles Reade's able vindication of his literary fame, I hope you will kindly permit me to offer a remark on the subject. The manners and drawing-room life of the Irish aristocracy in the early part of the last century cannot be reliably ascertained from the "History of Ireland," or from political pamphlets. The only writer of eminence who ventured to describe, with anything like minuteness, the style of living among the upper classes in this country at that period is Swift; and his description, certainly, though not elaborate, is life-like and powerful. I do not hesitate to say that, had Mr. Reade neglected to make use of the passage in Swift's poem referred to, his portraiture of Irish upper-class society would be necessarily imperfect, as, in a tale like "The Wandering Heir," in which the manners of bygone times are reproduced, authentic accounts must be referred to. Otherwise, would not the attempt to paint the state of society at a period when it was totally different from that of the present day—in the absence of good authorities—be a mere fancy picture, without a tittle of connection with reality? How, in the name of goodness, could any writer reproduce the spirit of the past in his works without some description by an experienced critic of the period to guide him? It is the shallowest pedantry, in my opinion, on the part of the Pseudonymuncule, to charge Mr. Reade with plagiarism for laudably seeking and using the information he obtained from a work so well known, and so valuable for its picture of contemporary high life, that it may well be called a book of reference. Nor is this proceeding of Mr. Reade's by any means without precedent. Sir Walter Scott freely acknowledges the benefit he derived from forgotten MSS. and ancient poems, as well as from more modern sources. Indeed, he is rather ostentatious in his prefaces as regards his authorities. He made use largely of various documents in writing "The Heart of Midlothian," the foundation of which, as is well known, is a famous Scotch trial. Then, again, in those historical novels depicting earlier periods, such as "Ivanhoe," "Kenilworth," etc., he has embodied a

large amount of antiquarian description borrowed from various
records. In "The Fair Maid of Perth," he has made use of
Wintoun's old poem on the battle of the clans Quhale and
Chattan; and he has ingeniously given part of the verses in the
introduction. And surely we cannot call Scott a plagiarist for
this? No more can we apply the term to Reade. I have no
doubt the literary world, recognizing as it does the worth of
one of the greatest—if not, indeed, the greatest—of living
English novelists, will laugh to scorn the puny snarler who has
attempted to injure a noble reputation. Charles Reade is admired in Ireland and America as much as he is in England.
He has stamped himself indelibly on the age as a moral reformer
by "It is Never too Late to Mend," a deep student of human
nature by "Hard Cash" and "Put Yourself in His Place," and
as an enchanting story-teller by his other novels.

MR. CHARLES READE AND HIS LAST CRITIC.

MR. CHARLES READE—as all the world knows, because all
the world has read it—has just written for the *Graphic* one of
the most charming stories possible, almost as charming as "Peg
Woffington." Mr. Somebody Else, whom probably the world
does not know, has just found a tremendous mare's-nest about
it, and has been spreading his wings and cackling over it
through two long columns of the *Athenæum*. This is his wonderful discovery:—Mr. Reade proposed to himself, in writing
"The Wandering Heir," a different plan to that followed by
most historical novelists. He actually tries to represent his
characters not only dressed in the eighteenth century costume,
but talking, thinking, and acting with eighteenth century ideas.
It may be surprising to the *Athenæum* correspondent, but that
is what Mr. Reade proposed to do. And in order to do it, he
turned to account his reading of the literature of the period;
and when he has to describe a party of fashionable ladies at
cards, he takes Swift's "Journal of a Modern Lady," which
every schoolboy knows, and pictures just such another said
party as that of Swift's. Moreover, in the conversations of the
ladies, Mr. Reade, as the mare's-nest critic discovers, has
actually reproduced at least a dozen lines of the great Dean's

own words. Here is a precious to-do! We look at each other in amazement. None of our immortal works are safe, then. Here is a man who is actually capable of putting into the mouths of his characters some of the best-known lines in the English language, without acknowledging them. Next he will be taking the Church Catechism, or some other equally familiar work, and making Celia, or Philip, or Jack try to pass it off as his own. Seriously, it seems to me that the editor of the *Athenæum* has made a great mistake in allowing this most ridiculous letter to appear in his highly respectable paper. If you are to throw your time back two hundred years, you have no other way possible but *to use the literature of the period.* Mr. Reade has gone to the best, and best-known writers of the time. He takes a poem with which every student in English literature, even the most superficial, is perfectly familiar—one about which the word plagiarism could not possibly be employed—and transmutes it, by the power of his genius, to serve the purposes of his prose. But the scene is Reade's, not Swift's; and it is the merest captiousness to object to the use of a few lines which everybody knows are Swift's, but which fit perfectly with the context. Of course, the question involved is a large one—no other than the right of using the literature of the past. To me it is evident that in no other way can an historical novel, or a novel of bygone times, be written at all; unless—as in * * * —you are content to give your characters nineteenth century ideas and fifteenth century dresses. The *Athenæum* writer remarks at the close—it is exactly what one would expect him to remark—that "if this is how novels are made, surely novel-writing must be an easy art." Very easy indeed. You want nothing but a few years of hard and patient labour, and then—like a spoonful of salt in your soup—just a pinch of genius. But I have got a proposition to make to the finder of mares'-nests. If he has not read "The Cloister and the Hearth," I will sketch the plot—*i.e.,* the life of Gerard—for him. I will give him the works of Erasmus and Rabelais, with the whole corpus of early French novelettes, the table-talk of Luther, the poems of Clement Marot, and any other books of the period he may wish to read. I will then furnish him with a bundle of quill pens, and a ream of paper, and invite him to write, from these materials—the same as those used by Charles Reade—a rival novel to "The Cloister and the Hearth." Or, if that would take too long, let him, with Pope, Swift, Addison, and Steele at his elbow, be good enough to give the world a nove-lette. He will find it "very easy," I have not the least doubt, to equal Mr. Charles Reade; and when it is done, I have also not the least doubt that the editor of the *Graphic* will give him, too, a chance of pleasing the quarter of a million people who have bought "The Wandering Heir." Other portions of the works of Swift might be read by the *Athenæum* critic to good purpose, particularly a few lines—he will easily find them—such as the following—

> " We all behold with envious eyes,
>   Our equals raised above our size.
>   Who would not at a crowded show
>   Stand high himself, keep others low ?
>   What poet would not grieve to see
>   His brother write as well as he ?
>   But rather than they should excel,
>   Would wish his rivals all in h—ll ?
>   Her end when Emulation misses,
>   She turns to envy, stings, and hisses.
>   I have no title to aspire—
>   Yet, when you sink I seem the higher."

[The foregoing note was in type before we received Mr. Charles Reade's communication. After having received it, we see no reason to omit our own remarks from our present issue.]

PRINTED BY WILLIAM CLOWES AND SONS, LIMITED, LONDON AND BECCLES.